"I'VE NEVER SAID I DIDN'T LIKE YOU, PIERRE."

"But you would deliberately block me in my attempts—"

Margot had been going to say, "to find my father." But Pierre broke in harshly, "I'll be quite frank in my opposition to that."

She said desolately, "Well, if you take that attitude, I can do nothing about it."

Margot wished there wasn't so much to admire in Pierre Laveroux, so much that was, above all, kindred in spirit. He loved all the things she herself loved so passionately.

Pierre must be very sure it would be undesirable for her to reveal herself to her father, certain that her appearance would cause discord. But she still wanted to find out who he was—to just see him. Would Pierre deny her even that?

HARLEQUIN CELEBRATES

Thirty-five Years of Excellence

1 **General Duty Nurse**
2 **Hospital Corridors**
3 **Court of the Veils**
4 **The Bay of the Nightingales**
5 **Leopard in the Snow**
6 **Dakota Dreamin'**

Essie Summers

The Bay of the Nightingales

Harlequin Books

TORONTO • NEW YORK • LONDON
AMSTERDAM • PARIS • SYDNEY • HAMBURG
STOCKHOLM • ATHENS • TOKYO • MILAN

Original hardcover edition published in 1970
by Mills & Boon Limited

ISBN 0-373-15104-7

Harlequin edition published November 1970
Second printing September 1971
Third printing (as part of Harlequin Omnibus 31) April 1976
Fourth printing February 1977

Harlequin Celebrates Thirty-Five Years of Excellence
edition published November 1984

CHAPTER ONE

MARGOT CHESTERTON packed the Chinese armorial mug with all her usual care, her fingers lovingly fitting the tissue paper into the curves of the handle with a touch that was a caress in itself, but her mind, naturally, was busy with her coming dinner-hour interview.

She'd thought all the testamentary business attendant upon her uncle's death was over and done with, but this must be important because Mr. Silverton had rung personally to ask her to call. Silly to feel so apprehensive. But so much had happened in so short a time, after twenty-five years of a very uneventful existence, that she felt tense waiting for another blow to fall.

She took herself to task. Wondered if her state of mind was due not so much to this time of bereavement as to her uncertainty of mind over Jonathan, who had told her quite firmly last night that she must make up her mind very soon.

Not that she didn't love him. She loved him far too much for her peace of mind. She loved him the way every girl hoped she might love some day, but she was not at all sure he loved her with equal fervour. Oh, he wanted to marry her and settle down but ... well, every time she thought about it she came up against that unanswerable 'but'. Yet the thought of saying no to Jonathan gave her the taste of ashes in her mouth.

Margot applied her make-up with extreme care, slipped out of her coral nylon smock embroidered in black, and picked up the loose jacket of the suit that was the same bright shade. She undid the gauzy bow that tied her hair back, shook it free, then decided after all to tie it back. She walked out of the antique shop with all the care that was part of the training, till she was out in the freedom of the London street.

To passers-by she must have looked like any other carefree girl, tall, with an elegant walk, with shining golden-brown hair turned up at the ends, eyes like dark purplish-brown pansies, the otherwise perfect oval of her face cleft by a decided dimple in the chin. No one could have guessed at her tenseness.

Mr. Silverton was kindness itself. But he was just a little too careful in his efforts to take it as a matter-of-fact affair.

'Margot, this need not disturb you unduly. Just something your uncle thought you had a right to know. He learned it himself only just before your aunt died. He thought it would be kindest to explain it by letter, but asked me not to hand it on to you till you had time to recover from his death. He said that by the time you read it you'd probably be engaged, if not married, and it ought not to upset you. I think it would be a good idea if you went into my little inner office and read this letter. And I'll be here, on my own, if you want to discuss it in any way, though after twenty-five years I don't think it ought to affect you much.'

Margot stood up. She said quietly, 'Mr. Silverton, I know that when my mother died when I was three weeks old, Aunt Ruth adopted me—and changed my name later to hers, when she married. You—you aren't trying to tell me I was an illegitimate baby—that Aunt Ruth was my mother, are you?' Then before he could answer her she said, 'Oh, how stupid of me ... my father's name is on my birth certificate: Francis Nightingale.'

Mr. Silverton said, 'Your uncle has expressed it all in his own words, rather better than I could tell you, I think. I'd rather you read it.' He waved her to his sanctum.

Margot took in the first paragraph of Uncle Noel's letter almost at a glance. 'Margot, my darling, at the time of your aunt's death I came into possession of a piece of knowledge that really surprised me. I think you ought to have known long ago, but evidently Ruth thought it in your best interests that you should not. It is simply that your father is—probably—still alive. But he does not know he has a daughter.'

Margot stared incredulously at the one paragraph, unable to read on till she could make herself accept this. Then she read on: 'I am going to ask you not to harbour any hard feelings against Ruth. She did this, evidently, for your welfare, thinking you would perhaps be bumped about from pillar to post and never have the advantage of a settled home. It is very hard indeed, she said, for a footloose man to bring up a child, and Ruth said she could not bear to think what sort of life you might have had with him.

'This is what she probably told herself when she first determined on her course of action, Margot, but at the end she faced up to things and felt she must get off her conscience what she had done. She was quite definitely wrong never to let Francis know he had a daughter. I will not blame you if you resent what she did, but I would ask you to put in the other side of the scales her years of devotion to you. She loved you as her own child.

'She told me quite frankly that when her much younger sister married Francis Nightingale, she was lost and lonely. She was always possessive in nature, but I loved her in spite of it, and when she had both me and you, she lost a lot of that. She cried as she told me, the day before she died, that she had made mischief between your father and your mother. Francis didn't have much money and Ruth prevailed on them to set up married life in part of her house. The first mistake. Your mother, I strongly suspect, had been a little spoiled, though very sweet. Spoiled at first by her rather elderly parents, then by her sister. Ruth just wouldn't let them stand on their own feet and Francis wanted his independence. I think every time Laura wanted something he could not afford, Ruth bought it for her. I suspect he felt Laura would never grow up, and men prefer women to child-brides.

'It came to a showdown and they left and lived in a flat. Ruth, I'm sure, was never off the doorstep, always sympathising with Laura about having to scrimp and scrape. Francis couldn't take it. He and Laura quarrelled more and more about this. Every time they had a tiff, Laura would run back to Ruth. Francis was an engineer and in sheer desperation he put in for a job in Canada. He thought that on their own, he and his wife would become a family unit. But Laura was desperately homesick and wouldn't settle. One day she ran away from Francis. Ruth, most unwisely, had sent her some money telling her that if ever she couldn't bear it, she'd have money for her fare home.

'Francis came home to find a note, telling him that if he really loved her he would come back to England. He blew up. He had a letter awaiting her at Liverpool when the ship docked, telling her to take the first ship back, that he would never return, that a wife's place was with her husband and she was to choose, once for all, between him and her sister.

'Laura thought he would capitulate when he missed her enough, and realised she was not going back. So time went on with neither yielding an inch. Then Laura found out you were arriving. Margot, you are not to think she did not want you. Ruth said she was thrilled, and was ready to return to your father on the very next ship. This is the part where Ruth admitted she had been very wrong. The rest she glossed over, but I guessed how it had been.

'In a letter Francis had said, "I want you to return to me for one reason and one alone ... that you can't live without me. That's the only basis for a happy marriage."

'Ruth told Laura Francis would think she had only returned to him for the child's sake. It preyed on Laura's mind and she became the victim of indecision. Ruth told her that if Francis really loved her, when she'd been away long enough, he was bound to come back to England for her sake. Unfortunately Laura became ill—some form of blood-poisoning. She was in and out of hospital. Ruth admitted she told Laura the doctor had said any travelling or emotional strain might damage her baby. Laura decided to wait till you were born, then send for Francis to come to take you both home.

'All this was upsetting to me, Margot. Ruth, at the last, was in great agony of mind over it. I think she had seen clearly, for the first time, what a monstrous thing she had done. Before that, I think she must have kidded herself into believing she was acting in Laura's best interests, sheltering her from care. As soon as you were born, Laura seemed to come right again. She knew her life was to be with her husband and daughter, and that she had been very foolish. But she was only twenty-one then, Margot. She wrote Francis, asking him to come as soon as he could, and that when ever she was strong enough to travel, they could all three go back to Canada.

'I hate to tell you this about your aunt, but she did not post the letter. Laura had told her what she was going to do, had been bravely defiant about it. Then, quite suddenly, Laura developed the blood-poisoning again and succumbed to it. Even though Ruth was confessing this to me, in the hope of getting it off her conscience, she still tried to justify her subsequent actions. She said she felt Francis Nightingale was better left in ignorance. That he had no settled home, that he might not have had the money for a housekeeper, that you might be neglected, even ill-treated. So she kept silent. He was simply told his wife had died.

'I tried to find out from Ruth if there was any chance of

finding him now. She said she couldn't remember his last address in Toronto and that many years later she had heard he'd married a French-Canadian and emigrated to New Zealand. She said he had connections there—French people, she thought. Francis had a bit of French blood in him. That's all I know, Margot. I think Ruth was relieved when he went so far away. She had always dreaded his finding out about you and claiming you. That was why she changed your name to Chesterton when she married me, though I had no idea at the time. I expect, seeing New Zealand is so far away, she felt much safer.

'I felt the secret must not die with me, Margot. I'm sorry, darling, that you had to know this, but it seemed wrong not to tell you. Please don't think too hardly of your aunt. I don't think you ought to try to find your father. Too much water will have flowed beneath the bridge since and he will have another family now. Besides, you will be marrying Jonathan and settling down. I like to think you two will be living on in our home.

'I'm too weary to write any more now, Margot. Just God bless you. I've always loved you as a daughter of my own. And you have been a great comfort to me since Ruth died.

>   'All my love, now and always,
>   'Uncle Noel.'

It was not for herself Margot felt sad. It was for Uncle Noel, who hadn't been capable of an unkind or mean action and who had had to reveal his wife's duplicity. But most of all she knew an immeasurable pity for her young father, who had acted like a man, who had taken a stand for independence, for happiness, for freedom from interference and who had lost everything; who might have suffered deeply from regret, blaming himself for not having gone to his wife. Pity, too, for her mother, just a girl, younger than herself, who had hoped to retrieve a mistake and who hadn't had time to do it. Oh, the wrongs one could not right, the things one couldn't undo. Margot stood up, put the letter in the shoulder-bag she'd taken off, and went out to Mr. Silverton, ostensibly busy with some papers.

She managed a smile. What a life solicitors must have ... always dealing with other people's problems and emotions. Very wearing. She must spare him all she could.

Her smile, however, was a little crooked. 'Just imagine,' she said lightly, 'I thought I was an orphan, but find I have a

11

father. But he's at the other side of the world and married again, possibly with a family, so it need not bother me much, need it?'

Mr. Silverton looked immensely relieved. 'Sensible girl. That was the way Noel hoped you'd take it. After all, at your age, and on the brink of an engagement, you hardly need a father. You are about to enter on the first stages of a family life of your own.'

Well, she supposed she was, at that. But one question she must ask. 'I'm not thinking of making any enquiries, Mr. Silverton, but for curiosity's sake, would you have any idea at all of whereabouts in New Zealand my father lives? Oh, I know they have big cities too, and it wouldn't mean very much if I did know where he was, but I'd like to know. Only perhaps even my aunt didn't know, so how could you? How silly of me.'

The solicitor said slowly, 'I think I do know. I can't be sure—but it ties in. I found a receipt from a shipping company. I think your father must have decided to send for some possessions of his—perhaps stuff he left behind till they should get a home of their own in Canada. He mustn't have known she was married, because she had signed the consignment chit with her single name—though it was some time after she had married by the date. I gather from this that she did not want him to be able to contact her after that. Especially as she had changed your name. And I think he must have felt the same, because the address he had given her was simply the Post Office of the town.'

Despite the fact Margot had said she wouldn't be likely to want to trace her father, she knew an irrational despondency at the thought she would never know his address, but she said, quite easily, 'And what was the town?'

'Akaroa, a town on the east coast of the South Island. Know anything about New Zealand at all?'

She shook her head. 'Nothing to speak of. Just the little we learned at school. I don't remember Akaroa. It's a Maori name, isn't it? Is it a large town? I only remember the four main cities, Auckland, Wellington, Christchurch, Dunedin.'

Mr. Silverton grinned. 'I knew a bit more, but not much. And that only because I was in the Middle East during the war and finished up in a prisoner-of-war camp in Italy with a New Zealander who came from a sheep-station on the Canterbury Plains. We used to talk a lot, very nostalgically, about our boyhood days, all of us. This chap was always recalling the annual holidays they used to spend at Akaroa. It ties up all right with what we know of your father. I mean marrying a French-Canadian. She probably had connections in Akaroa too. It's a French settlement. Well, a mixture of both, according to this chap, with a bit of German too. Dating back to pioneer days.'

Margot looked surprised. 'I'd thought New Zealand purely British and Maori. I know there are a few colonies in the Pacific that are French ... New Caledonia and Tahiti and so on, but ...'

'Oh, this was a Company formed to settle on Banks' Peninsula after the Maoris there had sold a lot of land to the captain of a French whaling vessel. In the old days there were whales in plenty round that coast. But when the first French ship got there, they found British sovereignty had been proclaimed earlier over both islands. Later, some of them did go off to Tahiti, but most of them stayed and settled down very happily, from what Ewan said. That's about all I can tell you. It seemed to be a dairying district, combined with holiday homes.'

'And the stuff was consigned to——?' asked Margot.

'Merely to Mr. Francis Nightingale, Post Office, Akaroa, New Zealand. It appeared to be mainly books, by the details on the consignment note. Just one packing-case. You won't be trying to trace him, will you, Margot? I honestly feel you might meet up with trouble if you did. I mean a second wife might not like the thought of a child she didn't know about turning up.'

Margot said quietly, 'No, I wouldn't do that. I feel my father had—undeservedly—a very rough deal over his first marriage. I hope he's happy now. I wouldn't do anything to rake up the past for him.'

She knew Mr. Silverton thought she was taking it very sensibly, but as she walked away she found her mind was in a turmoil, milling over the implications of this, and that it was going to be hard to check the wistfulness she knew. She saw a Lyons and went in for a quick cup of tea and a sandwich.

It was a busy afternoon, which kept her mind off the situation a lot, but by closing time she had a thumping headache and wished she wasn't going to this lecture tonight. Normally Margot loved anything to do with her work, but she felt she already knew enough about Venetian glass, Bristol and Waterford.

But Roxanne loved company at these things and liked Margot to take notes, and anyway, Jonathan was on duty at London Airport, so perhaps it was better than sitting at home thinking about the father and mother she had never seen.

She met Roxanne in Chelsea, in the old house that was used for these lectures. It was exquisitely kept by the couple who acted as caretakers and the drawing-room was a magnificent size. Even so it was crowded tonight. As she and Roxanne Gillespie sat down, Margot noticed a screen was in position.

'Is he going to show slides of the glassmaking or something, Mrs. Gillespie?'

'Oh, we've had a switch, Margot. I heard just after dinner. Mr. Lemayne's wife has been taken off to hospital, so they had to get a substitute at very short notice. Promises to be rather different too. From New Zealand. I think he's been living here a year or two. Mr. Lemayne knows him and proposed they ask him. He's not in antiques but evidently did part-time work at a museum when at university and happens to live in a small coastal town where they run a cottage museum. What did you say, Margot? No, I'm sorry, but I can't remember the name of the town. Some Maori name. They all sound alike to me. But the man's name is Pierre Laveroux.'

Margot knew instinctively, she thought later. A French name. A New Zealander. Yes, he would be from Akaroa. Life was like that. You had only to hear an unfamiliar word and it appeared over and over again in your reading, in subsequent days. She felt her thumbs prick and, squashing down her excitement, told herself it was hardly likely this young man from the Antipodes would immediately mention one Francis Nightingale.

Pierre Laveroux said he was a fourth generation New Zealander, then vividly sketched in life in Akaroa today with British and French blended into harmonious living, each enriching the other.

'Our streets are Rues and the willows at Takamatua Bay are believed to have been brought from Napoleon's grave by Monsieur François le Lievre, and we have our vines and our mulberries, our walnuts and our mignonette ... even some

14

stunted olives. And a French influence is still to be seen in many of the exquisite cottages, gabled and small, in our existing pioneer homes.

'Years ago a Christchurch journalist, Mona Tracey, described its blended beauty in this way:

"At dusk in Akaroa town,
When embered sunset smoulders down
And softly wreathes the evening mist
In whorls of tender amethyst,
The air is charmed with old-world spell
Of chanting bird and chiming bell;
And garden plots are redolent
Of poignant, unforgotten scent,
Where gillyflower and fleur-de-lys
Bloom underneath the cabbage tree,
And crimson rata strives to choke
With amorous arms the hoary oak,
And jonquil mocks the kowhai's gold——
Ah, sweet it is ... so young, so old!

So young, so old! So old, so new!
I wonder, at the fall of dew,
When from the evening's grey cocoon
Comes glimmering forth the moth-like moon,
And winds, upon the brooding trees,
Strum soft, nocturnal symphonies,
If kindly ghosts move up and down
In tranquil Akaroa town;
If voyageurs from storied France
Bestride the streets of old romance,
If laughing lads and girls come yet
To dance a happy minuet;
If Grandpère muses still upon
The fortunes of Napoleon,
And Grand'mère by the walnut tree
Sits dreaming on her rosary?"

He caught them all with this. They were suddenly in this little French–English–Maori town thirteen thousand miles away. He showed them slides of houses clustered round bays of a deep volcanic harbour, bitten into hills that before it was cleared for dairying had boasted some of the richest timber

15

trees of New Zealand, *totara, kowhai, kahikatea.*

The town was a Sleepy Hollow type, where the pace was leisurely, where French gabled cottages dreamed among evergreen native trees and birdsong echoed from morning till night, with bell-birds calling in silver chimes and *tuis* chuckling and twangling; where in autumn poplars from Normandy lit the dark green bush with torches of living gold, and Bourbon roses ran riot over trellises and arbours.

During the winter there were five hundred residents ... in summer this swelled to two thousand. Many Christchurch people had lovely holiday homes here. Pierre said, 'Many of you here tonight will have spent holidays at Brunnen on Lake Lucerne in Switzerland, walked on the waterfront there. You could walk on the waterfront at Akaroa, under the Phoenix palms and the gnarled old *ngaio* trees, and imagine you were walking by Lucerne, especially as from there you cannot see the Heads or the open sea and it looks like a great inland lake.

'It is all part of Banks Peninsula, named for Captain Cook's great naturalist, Sir Joseph Banks.' He grinned. 'Some of you may even know a descendant of his, Captain Stephen Banks, who is a consultant to the trustees of the British Museum—well, this Peninsula is a ragged circle of a great volcanic upheaval, fretted with deep inlets that run bluely into hills that are sometimes grey, sometimes tawny, sometimes grape-blue. These inlets look like fiords, but as they are not glacial, can't be called that. Some are private, with no public access, or reached only by stiff tramping, and are almost completely pastoral.

'The fiord-like appearance belongs to the Eastern Bays. The Bays inside Akaroa Harbour itself are gently curving ones, easy of access, and in sheltered spots they grow many semi-tropical fruits and flowers. Akaroa occupies the corresponding southern latitude that Nice does in the northern hemisphere. Timaru, a hundred miles south, corresponds to Genoa.'

He had had a slide made from a map and showed it at that point. His ruler slid round the ragged fringe of the Eastern Bays, naming them. 'I have an especial affection for this one, as it was named for my family.'

Then he came to one, inside Akaroa Harbour but opposite the town. Rossignol Bay he called it. It lay like an iridescent pendant set in green enamel, below Mount Bossu, the

16

Hunchback. 'A kindly hunchback,' said Pierre. 'In fact my mother vows he has a real personality. There are other lovely peaks ... Mount Brazenose, Purple Peak, French Peak, but my mother goes outside every morning before breakfast and says: "Good morning, Bossu," and she always included him in our bedtime stories, telling us Bossu was our guardian angel and loved children. He does preside over Akaroa Harbour with a beneficent air.

'But back to this Bay. It was named after the Rossignols, who came out on the *Comte de Paris* in 1840. Their homestead is still called Maison Rossignol, and is charming, small at first, but added to as the need arose. On the estate still lives Madame Rossignol—she married a distant cousin from France and so retained the name and is very much a Frenchwoman. Most of us, of course, are by now a mixture of French and English, with a strong dash of Irish—and a bit of German and Maori here and there. That is as it should be.

'The younger generation farms the property now, but Madame retains the old house.'

Maison Rossignol was charming, with fields sweeping down to the road that girdled the Bay, and was set against the hillside in dazzling green, white and black. Pierre Laveroux had slides of the interior too. He grinned. 'I thought these would make up for the loss of Mr. Lemayne's slides of the glass. Most of our antiques are French or English. Many of them, in the days when people wanted modern stuff and were sweeping older things out of their homes, were lost, though occasionally some quite valuable stuff turns up in the former dump of some homestead.

'The settlers had a habit, especially in the far bays, of filling in a gully with household rubbish, so some suff has been retrieved. But Maison Rossignol suffered less than most homes and the original furnishings are still there.'

Roxanne Gillespie whispered to Margot, 'These are indeed treasures. My mouth waters! Did you see all those houses with the attics under their gables? I guarantee they're still jammed with what people call junk. I wish it wasn't so far away, I'd rescue some of it. Oh look, he's showing a slide of Madame Rossignol herself. Isn't she sweet? Like a living miniature.'

A little lady, with an imperious air, belonging to the setting of the house, yes, but also to the salons of France. Pierre Laveroux had warmth in his voice when he spoke of her and

17

he had taken her in period costume with a hand on the architrave of the door, when she had dressed for a re-enactment of early colonisation. Other slides showed Madame winding up a beautiful old French clock; Madame looking wistfully at a portrait of her husband, Louis Rossignol; Madame in her garden beneath a great mulberry tree.

Pierre said, 'It will seem strange to you people here in Europe where your history goes back centuries and centuries that our history—that is, the history of European colonisation—goes back only such a short time. Madame Rossignol is eighty and is the granddaughter of Monsieur Etienne Rossignol, and remembers him vividly. She heard her stories of the landing of the *Comte de Paris* at his knee. And everyone in Akaroa knows its history. Because in Akaroa, the past is only yesterday.'

He laughed. 'Do forgive me. I'm becoming almost maudlin. Put it down to *mal du pays*. It sweeps over me at times—this homesickness. And then I fly across to France—something that is easy, financially, when you work at an airport and get such wonderful concessions—and in the little French villages, I am back in Akaroa. Till I came here I'd no idea how French Akaroa is.

'What I would like to stress, to those of you who may find themselves touring New Zealand some day, is that you visit Akaroa. So many people go and when they come back have seen only the thermal area, the lakes and the mountains—the highlights. Akaroa is off the beaten track—its roads end in the cliffs at the Heads—so it is often ignored, but it is only fifty miles from Christchurch, with a perfect road, and to visit there is to realise a dream, to step back into yesterday.'

As he finished Margot heard a woman say, 'I've enjoyed this tremendously. Such a change from our usual lectures—antiques, antiques, antiques! Oh, how I would love to see Akaroa!'

Margot closed her eyes for a moment. How *she* would love to see Akaroa! Oh, why wasn't it as close as France or Holland? Why did it have to be thirteen thousand miles away ... and a very costly trip? Imagine had it been as near as Brunnen ... why, Switzerland was only an hour or two away by air! Oh, if only she could pace those Rues, wander round those Bays, perhaps in some magic moment find the name Nightingale painted on one of those mailboxes she had seen at every gate. In fact, it could be as simple as finding

Francis Nightingale in a telephone directory.

Not that she'd want to make herself known, but just to find out what sort of a house he lived in, what he looked like, if he was happy. And you never knew ... if you did, and his circumstances were such that he needed a daughter ... say he was widowed and lonely, then perhaps—Margot caught herself up on the wistful thought. This was crazy, crazy. She was going to marry Jonathan. Well, probably. That must be her life; perhaps it was a pity that Aunt Ruth's secret had not died with her. It was so unsettling to know you had a father on the other side of the world. She must be very sensible and not let it disturb her too much. No doubt in time this impact of longing to find her father would die down. Time always lessened the first pangs. Yes. Besides, Roxanne was looking at her curiously.

'Oh, I'm sorry, Mrs. Gillespie, I went into a day-dream. What did you say? Yes, it did look exactly like that French clock we sold Lady Begborough.'

At suppertime the gathering became informal, with people chatting to the speaker. Margot, as befitting an employee, helped serve, and found herself irresistibly drawn to Pierre Laveroux.

He talked to Margot in the most animated fashion about some of the treasures in the room, relating them to stuff seen in New Zealand in museums. 'I'm talking shop most unrestrainedly. Someone ought to stop me. Trouble is, after my experience at Christchurch in varsity days, I got so interested, then coming here and being at the Airport I've missed dealing with antiques. Did you know that back home, in Canterbury Museum, we have a reconstructed pioneer street section for all the world like the one at York?

'I'm very keen on small museums being set up all over New Zealand, run by locals on a roster, with here and there in larger places a paid curator, to preserve, in the very place of origin, the links with the past.

'We have a magnificent one in Akaroa itself. The Langlois–Eteveneaux Museum. Most delightful house, original, possibly the oldest in Canterbury, in the Rue Lavaud. A small French home, with many of the treasures that came out in the *Comte de Paris*.'

Margot felt herself getting caught up in his enthusiasm. 'What must be so wonderful is that the actual history of the

19

pieces you have there will be traceable. You'll know it must have come to New Zealand within a stated time—what date did you say the Nanto-Bordelaise settlers came? 1840? Then you must be able to follow the ownership of those pieces from the time they landed at Akaroa.'

That set him off. He drew her a little apart from the others, his cup and saucer in his hand. Around them was a buzz of animated conversation, shutting them off in a sort of synthetic privacy. They turned their backs on their immediate neighbours, and as they were on the dais, they were looking down the immense drawing-room over a screen of palms and pot-plants.

Margot said, 'I expect if you're working at Heathrow, you'll live nearby and possibly know Osterley House?'

He nodded. 'One of my favourite places. As a matter of fact, I've a flat in Church Road, Osterley. St. Mary's is on the corner. Do you know it?'

Margot nodded. 'I go to that church. I live in Jersey Road, near Osterley Park. I love Osterley House. I lived with an uncle and aunt. They—they both died fairly recently.'

'Do you live alone?'

'Not exactly. I have my own quarters. The house lends itself to being shared. I've a retired couple from the Argentine living in most of it till they decide where they would like to buy.'

In actual fact, it was only till she made up her mind about Jonathan. Jersey Road would be ideal for his work. Oh yes, much of the set-up was ideal. Much, but not all. Only that was probably her own fault, looking for something that was too idealistic.

She mustn't wool-gather. She went on talking of Osterley. They were looking down the drawing-room. She must ask this chap in a moment if he happened to know Jonathan, though with the thousands of employees at Heathrow, it wasn't likely.

All of a sudden Margot saw Jonathan come in from a side-door. As always, she knew that little leap of the heart. He must have got off early and come for her. The doubts in her heart fled. He was making his way through the crowd looking for her. Margot faltered in what she was saying ... Pierre Laveroux looked at her sharply ... that was twice she'd gone into a day-dream. Rather deflating. He followed her gaze.

20

At that moment, in a cleared circle of people, Jonathan stopped dead in his tracks as if someone had called 'Halt!' Why?

Margot completely forgot the man at her side.

Because a girl on the far side of that circle of people was the one on whom Jonathan's attention was riveted. Margot was looking at the girl at the very moment the girl saw Jonathan. To be more specific, as she *recognised* Jonathan. And what a recognition it was!

The girl was a plain little thing, but if ever a face was transformed as she caught sight of him, hers was. Margot glanced swiftly at Jonathan, and saw, with hideous emotional impact, the same look mirrored on his face. Incredible delight. A wonder. Almost a fulfilment. This was how Margot analysed it later that night. At the time the blow numbed her.

Then the two figures in the drama, for drama it certainly was, diminished the space between them, and their hands went out to each other. Margot's lips were parted, but she drew no breath. Everything in her seemed stilled. What now?

Just then Jonathan and the girl seemed to become aware of the crowd about them and looked embarrassed. Then he drew her to one side and indicated the door he'd come through. Their heads bobbed through the crowd till they reached it, opened it, went through.

Pierre Laveroux's voice said in her ear, 'You saw that? Of course you did. What a delightful thing to witness! And here of all places. It looked as if it were a case of journeys ending in lovers meeting, don't you think, Miss Chesterton? Quiet idyllic. And the nicest thing of all was that she was such a plain little girl, not glamorous at all, but all starry-eyed the moment she caught sight of that fellow. A real-life romance, I'd say.'

Margot was surprised to find her voice sounded ordinary. She even managed a laugh. 'Yes, all that and more. Like one of those dramatic short-shorts you read.'

He nodded. 'Yes, we would call it a *vignette*. I wonder what it meant ... let's guess. I thought it looked as if they had been parted and had never expected to see each other again. Or am I being fanciful?'

'Well, if you are, I'm being fanciful too. It looked exactly like that. Oddly enough, I think we could be the only two to witness it. Because we were up here.'

'Yes, it happened under everyone's noses down there, but they were too busy talking. How sad that we shall never know the end of it. Ships that pass in the night, eh? Heavens, I'm getting sentimental ... but somehow that was very lovely. Miss Chesterton, the people who arranged this laid on a car for me. Since we live so near each other, may I drop you home? No need for you to take the tube.'

Margot spoke swiftly, because now she'd come out of her trance, she must do something about this, find out what was going on. Oh, surely there'd be some explanation. She mustn't leap to the devastating conclusion that here was Jonathan's true love. It was plain stupid, fostered by this impressionable and romantic Frenchman.

'Thank you immensely, but I'm being taken home—which reminds me, I've people to see and my boss, Roxanne Gillespie, may need me. I work in her antique shop. Excuse me now. I've loved meeting you, and seeing the slides, and I just wish Akaroa wasn't so far away.' How true.

Somehow she managed to evade those acquaintances who would have delayed her. She must find Jonathan and the girl. She slipped out of the side-door into the garden of the Chelsea house. Would they have gone to the front? Probably not, too many cars there, too many people leaving ... too many lights. But the back garden, though small, offered privacy. There was even that little latticed summer-house and a tinkling fountain, to say nothing of massed hydrangea and lilac bushes for seclusion. Margot went noiselessly upon the flagged path.

She heard a murmur from the summer-house. Best be brave, Margot. Best go in and face it. Perhaps you'd better call out 'Are you there, Jonathan?' as you go. Even as she parted her lips, she heard him groan. Not a groan to indicate physical pain, but one that revealed emotional anguish.

'Oh, Betty, Betty,' his voice said, 'if only we hadn't had our lives snarled up like this.'

It stopped Margot dead in her tracks. *She was going to listen.* This might be her only way of getting at the truth. Never mind if it were not ethical, never mind if eavesdroppers were supposed to hear no good of themselves. She was going to do it.

Betty's voice had a note in it that hurt Margot. A sort of numbness. 'I know, Jonathan, I know. Listen, it is all right.

We can't do anything about it. I ought not to have come tonight. But—but I couldn't help myself. I heard you were not going to be here, that you were on duty till ten. I just wanted to see her. To find out what she looked like—oh, I don't mean her looks. But to see if she looked as if she would make you happy. And she does look that way. I was going to slip away and no one would ever know I had been there. Not her. Not you. But someone fastened on to me, insisted I have a cup of tea and something to eat and wouldn't stop talking.

'Then just as I turned to go you came towards me. I couldn't believe it, Jonathan. Oh, you don't think Margot saw, do you? I don't know where she was. I—she even brought me a sandwich. But it's too late, Jonathan. You've asked her to marry you. I can't imagine she'll refuse. Who could? Oh, perhaps it's silly to talk it over now, but Jonathan, Jonathan, why did we let Geraldine make mischief? But then you see I was—oh, how can I put it?—I just couldn't believe that anyone like you could love someone like me—a very poor background, not much education, unsure of myself. So I was ready for Geraldine's lies. But never mind, I've been a little happier since I found out they weren't true. Oh, I'm so glad Berenice thought I ought to be told the truth. At least now I'm not disillusioned about you—but oh, why couldn't it have come sooner? But I'll manage, Jonathan. Because we can't break another girl's heart.'

Jonathan's voice was heavy. 'No, I can't act like a cad. I was trying to patch up my life. Margot is—is a dear. She's been through a very bad time, she lost her aunt last year, then later her uncle. She's quite alone. At least you have your family. But oh, Betty, Betty, if only you'd come a month ago. Oh, I was keeping company with Margot before her uncle died, and everyone assumed we were serious, but only a day or so ago did I tell her she must make up her mind. I didn't fall in love headlong this time. I was wary. I felt disillusioned too. The way you laughed at me and taunted me ... it seemed so foreign to you. And of course it was—it was all pretence, to pay me back for what I was supposed to have done. I'd like to twist Geraldine's neck. But, Betty——'

'Yes, Jonathan?'

'I've no right to say this. Not yet. But—don't run away again, will you? Not—till Margot gives me her answer.'

'No, I won't run away. But I won't see you either. Here's an old envelope with my address on. But—I couldn't bear to

23

go on seeing you. It would only make it worse. You'll have to go. Margot may have got a glimpse of you. Just leave me here.'

Margot drew back with a start, glanced round to see if there was sufficient cover and melted into the shrubbery, but could still hear.

Jonathan's voice. 'In a moment. Roxanne always stays to the very end. But, Betty ... this may be the last time we'll ever see each other. Give me ... two or three minutes?'

Margot fled quietly down a path that was only leaf-covered and would not betray a careless sound. She found she was breathing hard, and didn't want Jonathan coming in search of her. As she went in she saw Pierre Laveroux just going. As he said goodbye to someone she said breathlessly, 'Mr. Laveroux, does that offer still stand? It will—will save the people who were taking me home going out of their way, if I come with you.'

'I'm delighted,' he said, and his eyes were glad, but that didn't mean a thing to Margot. The only thing was to get away swiftly now, before Jonathan finished saying goodbye to his Betty. *His?* Oh yes. He didn't know it yet, *but his.* She, Margot, would have no reluctant bridegroom. Beyond that, as yet, she could not think.

She found Roxanne and said she was having a lift. She managed to make all the correct replies to Pierre Laveroux as he chatted about the London he so loved. Then they were out of the fiercest traffic and bowling along the Great West Road, over the Grand Union Canal, and cutting in towards Osterley Park.

There was a light on. Margot said quickly, because it would postpone the post-mortem she would have to conduct in her mind on the overheard conversation, 'Would you care for another cup of coffee? It looks to me as if Mr. and Mrs. Roslyn are still up—an interesting couple from the Argentine. Or are you on early duty tomorrow?'

'No, I'm not on till ten and I'd like it very much. I can walk home after that.'

They said goodnight to the driver and went inside. Margot said, 'If they're just going off to bed, I'll make it for you in my sitting-room, but I think they won't have been in long. They were at a theatre tonight.'

They were delighted to meet Pierre Laveroux and he them. It was a charming home, nothing too blatantly new, or too dilapidated through age, and the Roslyns had distributed some of their South American mementoes throughout, very effectively.

Margot hoped the Roslyns wouldn't mention she might be getting married, but the talk stayed on the surface and kept to Akaroa and South America mostly.

Margot pushed the other thing to the back of her mind and listened hungrily. It would be quite possible, talking of a town of five hundred residents, for Pierre Laveroux to mention one Francis Nightingale. But his talk was mainly of French descendants and the cosmopolitan lot of whalers that had haunted that coast in pre-colonial days, when whales could be caught close to shore.

It was late when he took his leave. As Margot saw him to the door he said, 'I've visited Osterley House on my own twice. Care to bear me company there on Sunday? You know so much about antiques that it would greatly add to my enjoyment.'

Margot knew that by Sunday she would be filling in time, that she might need the soporific of someone's company, to numb the pain. Besides, she wanted to keep him talking of Akaroa.

CHAPTER TWO

WHEN Pierre Laveroux called for her on the Sunday, he couldn't conceal his excitement. 'The most marvellous news! My father and mother are coming here for a year. Dad's being overdoing and Doctor Dumayne persuaded him the homestead could get along without him for a year. They've always talked of coming Home. Dad's mother was an Englishwoman and always hoped he'd visit her old home some day. And of course he'll want to visit Normandy too, look up our forebears. He's got a first-rate chap looking after the farm. They'll be here in a month.'

'They'll be flying, then.'

'Partly. Doc recommended a sea-trip, so they're doing it quite adventurously—going on a cruise that takes in Noumea in New Caledonia—that's the nearest French-speaking settlement to New Zealand, then to Tahiti. Dad has some distant connections there. Then they fly to the United States and across the Atlantic, arriving at Heathrow, of course. I just can't believe it. They've always felt they couldn't leave the farm. First there was the family to educate—I've three sisters, all married and away from the Peninsula. How they'll love this sort of thing!'

His eyes travelled round the magnificent trees of Osterley Park, just starting to show amidst their greens, the golds and russets of autumn. 'By the time they come these paths will be deep in crunchy leaves ... is there anything more idyllic than shuffling your feet through rustling autumn leaves?'

They came by the lake where children were throwing crusts to water-fowl so plump they were ignoring the scraps, and they walked towards the great front entrance.

Margot found she couldn't keep the conversation centred on Akaroa. Pierre, his dark eyes keen, his chin jutting, wanted to talk of Osterley. 'Wasn't there some disturbance when Elizabeth the First stayed here?'

'Yes—it's still on the records—about fifteen-seventy-something, I believe. Two women. They tore up palings and made a terrific din. We still have such happenings, but they call them student demonstrations now! It was in Sir Thomas Gresham's day—he was the founder of the Royal Exchange —and so rich that when the Queen expressed the view that the court was too large and would be more handsome if a wall divided it down the middle, he sent to London and overnight workmen got busy, and lo and behold, when the Queen arose, she found there were two courts, where the day before had been one! Of course it's been altered greatly since then, but beautifully, mainly in the hands of Robert Adam. That's what makes these stately homes so vividly alive still ... they aren't just perfect examples of one particular period, they've been added to, altered, modernised, even if some of the modernisation is still centuries old. So the story of the house is continuous, not static.'

Pierre looked at her sharply ... a modern girl in a coral turtle-necked jersey under her belted grey tweed coat, but— perhaps because of the love she had for antiquity—a girl who, if suitably garbed, would fit into any period. A girl with a perfectly oval face with a cleft chin and pansy-dark eyes, with golden-brown hair tied carelessly back with a bright gauzy bow ... yes, she could fit into any period, yet perhaps most of alxl she belong to the eighteenth century.

He said, 'I wish I'd met you earlier. Just imagine, I've been here a whole year. What a waste!'

In turn Margot looked at him sharply. He interpreted the look, the dark eyes glinting with laughter. 'I know exactly what you're thinking. I've had it said to me before. These Frenchmen! They pay extravagant compliments. They make pretty speeches. They're—oh, too full, much too full of *amour*! And it makes the girls wary. The girls today have no soul for romance. They distrust compliments. The girls of yesterday knew how to receive compliments. It was their due and they accepted it.'

Margot broke in heatedly there. 'Not all girls are devoid of romance ... that's far too sweeping, Pierre Laveroux! It's just that we've just met and you——'

He held up his hand. 'Pax! Pax! Will I get back into your favour, mademoiselle, if I confess something?'

'Perhaps, but what?'

He grinned. 'It wasn't a compliment to your undoubted charm. It was one to your knowledge.' His voice was suave, mocking. 'I was merely referring to your familiarity with history. Some of the girls I work with know even less than I do of local history. I expect it does impinge upon my notice because I haven't always grown up with it, but it's such a waste of opportunity it gets under my skin. Now, have I not been brave, if ungallant, to explain my compliment?'

Margot burst out laughing. 'I deserve to be deflated! And perhaps we are—modern girls, I mean—sometimes cheated of romantic moments because we shy away and don't know how to handle compliments. And I know what you mean. A woman who lives near us has never been to Hogarth's House, Chiswick House, Syon House or Hampton Court, all on her doorstep. Though I expect I have a head start on other people because I work for Roxanne. She's an authority, and you just have to be interested in history, period and reigns, when you handle things in use centuries ago.'

'Do I get a mark for having visited all those? But will you come with me to visit them again?'

Margot hesitated. He looked at her swiftly. 'Is there anyone with the right to object?'

She shook her head decidedly. 'No.' (Well, there wasn't. Not any more. Not after she posted this letter in the big pocket of her coat.) 'No, it wasn't that. Just that I may be going away.'

The narrow dark eyes narrowed even more. 'That has a curious ring of finality. You don't mean leaving here? Because——'

'No, but I go away frequently on buying trips.'

'But you'll be back?'

'Yes, there'll be nothing to keep me away.' (True. Nothing and *nobody* to keep her away. Because even if she found what she looked for, she could not stay, could not make herself known, probably. But it would be enough just to know that somewhere in the world there was someone to whom she belonged. Oh, she must try to head the talk back to Akaroa.)

It was hard to do ... they talked of the subsequent owners of Osterley Park, the elopement of Sarah Anne Child from this house with the tenth Earl of Westmorland and her father's resultant will that left his fortune to the second of Sarah Anne's children to ensure that the elder branch of the Westmorland family did not benefit financially.

Margot said, 'And that second child married George Villiers who succeeded as fifth Earl of Jersey and took the name of Child before Villiers. Their descendant, the ninth Earl, gave Osterley to the nation. All very fascinating, but as I've shown umpteen people round Osterley House, I'm really more interested in the history of Akaroa. Tell me, do you get many incomers? Do many people come out from England to settle in Akaroa these days? Or do they come from other places, say the States, or Canada—perhaps French-Canadians?'

Pierre shook his head. 'Rarely do they emigrate straight to Akaroa. People from England, for instance, usually go direct to the cities, and often they choose the ones where they'll get the most sun. Nobody seems to mention what a wonderful climate Akaroa has, though I think that in years to come, tourism will be our chief source of income. Margot, I'll talk about Akaroa tonight. I'm back in Elizabethan days ... those stables are Tudor, surely?'

So they talked English history, all through the beautiful rooms, talking of the people who had visited here, feeling they walked in the footsteps of Horace Walpole.

Margot's love of beauty and design took hold on her in such kindred companionship, pushing away the pain of knowing that once she posted Jonathan's letter she would be out of his life for ever ... there were the lyre-back chairs, the

28

gloriously massive writing-tables, the ceilings decorated with ivy and vines and intricately exquisite designs, the magnificent paintings, the pair of Derbyshire spar and ormolu candelabra on the chimney-piece of the eating room, that had been made at the Soho factory of Matthew Boulton, an engineer of remarkable versatility who had also made steam engines in partnership with Watt ... the gallery with its series of pier-glasses between the windows, the satinwood and mahogany chairs and sofas, the doors with their carved mouldings and elegant gilt brass handles, all these things were part of her working life at Roxanne's.

This vague sense of the comfort of beauty went with her through it all, the almost overpowering richness of the Tapestry Room, the elaborate State Bedchamber, the elegance of its gilt armchairs. But they found a mutual dislike of the Etruscan Room. It was interesting, no doubt, but for some reason struck a chill to the heart.

By the time they came out the afternoon was growing dusky. 'Just the day for hot toast by the fire and a dish of curry,' said Margot, 'but for goodness' sake remind me to post a letter at Osterley ... we'll walk up Thornbury Road and back.' (As if she could forget!)

As they came up through the shopping centre, that red pillar box took on a menacing look, it gaped greedily, she thought. Once she popped that letter into that slot, she couldn't recall it. She found it hard to keep her mind on the conversation.

Pierre said, holding out his hand, 'Give it to me, Margot.'

She said lightly, 'Oh, no bother ... I'll just slip it in.' And did. Just like that. Because he might, he just might know Jonathan. Though Jonathan worked for BOAC and Pierre for BEA.

When it was done, she felt a curious lightening of heart, though she knew that later she would feel bereft and know loneliness. Just as well Pierre was here tonight.

When he had gone she sat on beside her fire, on a humpty, her hands clasped round her knees, and gazed into the glowing embers. Nothing had been mentioned of one Francis Nightingale. She had asked what callings other than farming, tourism and fishing were carried on in Akaroa, but engineering hadn't been mentioned. But what did it matter? Because at the moment all she could think of was that tomorrow morning, when Jonathan was off duty, he would receive her letter. What would his reaction be? He would not be able to guess from it that this was her last gift to him, his freedom. Freedom to go to Betty, his true love. She, Margot, had never been that, only a second-best. She closed her eyes against the remembrance of the look he had given Betty. He had never looked at Margot like that. There had always been a reserve.

If he had known she had seen that exchange, had over-heard their anguished talk in the summer-house, his future happiness with Betty would have been marred. And Betty had been sweet. She had not wanted to snatch her happiness over the ruins of Margot's. Not all girls would have behaved like that.

So Margot had set out to put all their misgivings at rest. In fact Jonathan would recall her as rather a strange girl, almost callous about ending their association, and who was a career girl rather than the mother-and-wife type.

She fancied she had done it rather well, had told him that he had probably guessed her hesitation had been because she did not want to give up her present life. 'I've faced up to it, Jonathan, and come to terms with myself. I realise I'm not the one for you. The thought of settling down to suburban bliss makes me feel I'm condemning myself to a life far too restricted. I've tasted enough travel on my buying trips to have exceedingly itchy feet, and you'd hate a wife who resented being tied down.

'Fact is, I've been offered the chance of another buying trip, an extended and exciting one, with an increase of salary and with the promise of many trips to come, *provided I was free to travel*. This is the chance of a lifetime. I can't turn it down, even if it is selfish. But that's the way I'm made and it's lucky for both of us that I've realised this. That's why I didn't give you an answer straight off. I wasn't sure whether or not this trip was in the bag.

'Please don't try to see me, Jonathan. Not all the persuading in the world would or could change my mind. It would only be painful to us both. I'll just wish you well. I'm sure some day you'll meet someone who'll ask nothing more than to share your life. That's all.

'Margot.'

Margot left her fire and crossed to the telephone. Now was the ideal time to ring Roxanne Gillespie and tell her. Roxanne was a fine woman, one who had known enough change

30

and tumult in her own life, though very happy and settled now, to understand this. But Margot would swear her to secrecy.

Roxanne understood, but was extremely sorry to be losing Margot, and most concerned for Margot's happiness. But she realised that no girl, overhearing what she had, could be expected to do anything else but make a break. But she would miss her.

'Don't book your passage immediately, Margot. I believe it's extremely difficult to get a berth, because of so much emigration, yet you'll have to go by ship if you want to take your car. I think you could go by Canada much more quickly, so how about doing a bit of business for me over there? You could then sail from Vancouver.' She did not say, but thought that if homesickness set in quickly, Margot could come home from there much more easily than from New Zealand. Because this search for a father was a wild-goose chase if ever there was one. If he was the foot-loose type, he might have left Akaroa long since. And what sort of welcome would she get, anyway? Even if he reacted the right way, how about his wife? It would take a very big-hearted woman to welcome a daughter out of her husband's past.

Things moved very quickly. Jonathan rang up and asked to see her, but Margot was adamant. 'I've cut loose, Jonathan, and I want to stay that way.' She knew it was nothing but a sense of duty that had prompted him to do this, but she dared not see him, even while she honoured him for making the gesture, in case she betrayed herself.

Roxanne pulled all sorts of strings. Time was so short that she saw Pierre Laveroux only once more before she left, and she did not tell him she was going. She would let him know by letter—a letter he would receive only when she was on her way.

They visited Hogarth's House together the next Sunday afternoon, but he had to be back on duty immediately after, filling in for a friend who needed time off. This suited Margot very well, as she had urgent things to do.

Hogarth's garden was a haven of peace, even as it had been to him, despite the fact that his 'little country box by the Thames' was now hedged in by industrial buildings, tall flats and a busy arterial road with speeding traffic. But here, inside that high wall, in that wedge of a garden, was an air of ineffable peace.

Wonderful to see the mulberry tree from which the pies were made with which Hogarth used to regale the foundlings he found homes for in Chiswick ... it was little short of a miracle that it had not only survived the lightning which struck it in Hogarth's day, but also damage by bombs in 1940. They called down a blessing on the expert from Kew who had coaxed it back to life.

For a little while, steeping herself in the charm of the eighteenth century, Margot forgot she had lost Jonathan, had lost Uncle Noel, and must soon leave all this.

They were alone on the top deck of the bus going home, both of them, for some reason, strangely silent. As they neared Thornbury Road Pierre roused himself. 'This is a terrific anticlimax to an idyllic afternoon ... and I've got the most maddening shift all next week—two till ten. I won't be off when you are. But the next week we'll do a theatre together. But I'll see you next Sunday. What about Hampton Court?'

Margot said, 'Let's not make a definite date now. We can decide when you come. I've an idea, anyway, that Roxanne may be sending me away somewhere. I'll let you know. And thank you, Pierre, for two lovely outings.'

He rose, helped her from her seat. 'I'll see you safely off.' He preceded her down the swaying stairs. There was nobody but the clippie on the platform. As his hand came under her elbow to assist her to alight, and she dropped to the road, he bent down to her upturned face and kissed her.

His eyes danced. 'Pretty good aim ... for a moving recipient ... dead on centre! See you next Sunday, Margot.'

But he wouldn't. Not ever again. Because when Pierre Laveroux returned to his native Akaroa, Margot would be gone.

Unless ... and it would take almost a miracle ... it was possible for her to make herself known to her father.

By Saturday she was ready to leave for Liverpool. On the Friday night she wrote to Pierre. She smiled wryly over it and said to herself, 'Nothing but farewell letters. Cut and run, that's my motto now.' But she wanted him to have no idea where she was going. Even the Roslyns didn't know she was going further than Canada. Because Pierre just might call to see them, and she wanted no hint to get to Jonathan and Betty, and it was always on the cards that they might get to know Pierre. Her mail was to be forwarded care of Roxanne who would be discretion itself.

She made her letter light. 'Just as well we'd made no firm date for Sunday, because by the time this reaches you, I'll be on my way to Canada. I'm off on a buying mission again. But this time it's to be of indefinite duration. I'll probably spend some time in Canada, then go to the States, and then it will be a case of wherever Mrs. Gillespie sends me next. This is a grand chance—once in a lifetime—and it was a case of go at a moment's notice, or someone else would willingly have stepped into my shoes. I enjoyed meeting you, Pierre, and hope you'll continue to have a wonderful time plane-hopping round Europe and Scandinavia.

'With all good wishes,
'Yours sincerely,
'Margot Chesterton.'

She told herself that her resulting depression that was almost a feeling of guilt and meanness was simply a hangover from the pain of having given up Jonathan.

The new scenes helped. Last time, with Roxanne, Canada had been emerging from the spell of pearly snow and violet shadows into a luxuriant spring with every bough aching down with a wealth of leaf and bloom. Now it was aflame with the fires of autumn.

She was frantically busy, since her booking by ship from Vancouver to New Zealand had come earlier than expected. She wanted to fix up as much business as she could for Roxanne, who had been so kind, so she packed a lot in, but once she sailed into the Pacific on her way to Auckland, only one thing possessed her mind ... her search in Akaroa; only the trail was twenty years old.

But now she was almost there, and one part of her was filled with glad anticipation, and one with the butterflies of apprehension. Never mind, if only she could find her father, and see him, at least she would have made some sort of contact, even if secretly, with her sole relation in the world.

She had loved the drive of hundreds of miles from Auckland, through great timber forests, thermal areas eerie and beautiful, past great lakes, and beneath mountains that rose up individually from the central part of the North Island,

33

one, mantled with snow, but with the plume of volcanic smoke rising from its blown-off top. She had crossed on the overnight steamer from Wellington to Lyttelton, and, coming into the Harbour in the early morning, had seen with a quickening of the heart the hills not towards Christchurch, where most folk were looking, but on the far side of the harbour ... hills beyond which, south, was an older harbour, where, she hoped, her father might live.

A fellow-passenger, a Christchurch man, was pointing out landmarks, rather intrigued to find an overseas visitor taking an interest in the over-harbour hills.

'Most folk want to know what's on the Christchurch side ... the answer being plains and mountain ranges.'

Margot laughed. 'I've a yen to see Akaroa, have ever since I saw some slides in London. I'll only be in Christchurch a day or two.'

He grinned. 'Well, it's quite refreshing to meet someone like you. So many only hit the high spots ... literally high ... Mount Cook and so on.' This reminded her of Pierre. 'I mean many North Islanders have never been to Akaroa, yet it's a dream of a place, it's just that it's tucked away on the far side of the Peninsula.'

Margot said, 'I can see roads, not many, but one goes twisting up from that Bay ... the big one past that sort of triangular headland with all the pines dotted on it. Is that the way to Akaroa?'

'I'd not advise you to take that one—that's the long, high, rough way round. Especially as you'll be used to English roads, though our main ones are good. No, you take the road from Christchurch to Tai Tapu and round by Motukarara and Little River—Little River is a township, by the way, and up to Hilltop, then down to Duvauchelle Bay and round the harbour to Akaroa. A tarseal—macadam—road all the way.'

'And people don't use that road over there much?' Her tone was oddly wistful. She'd been wondering if her father ever came that way.

Her fellow-traveller shook his head. 'Not a lot. Even the folk from the Eastern Bays find it better to take the Summit Road, unless they're visiting the bays this side of Lyttelton Harbour ... Purau ... where the road climbs from, or Diamond Harbour, with the piney headland. Look, I've a map in my car. You can have it. I know all Canterbury roads like the back of my hand.'

He brought it back and they studied it together. She would make an immense circle from here to get there. Her thumbs began to prick.

They came about and began to back in and he had to leave her. 'See you some more,' he said, and Margot couldn't help a smile. The Kiwi *au revoir*! Even when a second meeting was hardly likely. A sort of endearing reluctance to end a new acquaintanceship.

He caught on and grinned back. 'You might be surprised. I'm often in Akaroa. Our youngsters love it. Look, you're bound to be in Christchurch some time. Just give us a ring— I'll give you an envelope with the address. My wife's an English girl. She'd love to see you. We live in Merivale.'

The small encounter warmed Margot's heart.

She drove her car through the new road tunnel, immense and a great time-saver. Her companion had told her earlier that the railway tunnel had existed since early pioneer days. She came out on the plains, with the spires and buildings of Christchurch in the distance, suburbs reaching out to these hills, and there beyond, like a white, linked chain of frosted peaks, the Southern Alps.

The next day she was on her way. It had seemed so odd to step from a Canadian autumn into a New Zealand spring, but how beautifully spring came here.

How far apart the villages—no, townships—were. How much room there was; she loved the great stretches of farmland. She didn't like all she saw. English villages were much more compact, neater, some of these were a bit straggly, but she liked these untamed-looking hills on her left, the sort of zest and sparkle of the air and the sense of freedom.

Round about Tai Tapu were many of the trees of home ... poplars everywhere, both lombardy and aspen, willows and pines, beech and birch, and, of course, many of the native trees she couldn't as yet name. There seemed to be pockets of forest—but New Zealanders said bush—tucked into every gully where streams flowed down from the watersheds of the hills.

She wound the windows down and the nutty aroma of the gorse scented the air, bright gold on all the hedges. Here and there she saw a hawthorn hedge; there seemed to be oaks and rowans round every school, what a blending of the old and the new. And many of the birds were the same, brought out in the old days.

35

She went into a roadhouse called the Black Tulip, where the road from Gebbie's Pass joined this road. She had a cup of coffee and the waitress told her that Gebbie's Pass led into Lyttelton Harbour right opposite the Heads. 'In the old days they used to sledge produce right through Gebbie's Pass to this end of the harbour, and then to Lyttelton, or Port Cooper as it was called then.'

Yes, it was true, the past was only yesterday. At that moment she knew the oddest stab of nostalgia. Not for home, oh no, but a sudden irrational wish that Pierre Laveroux might be showing this to her. How ridiculous! When there could be only one real wish in her heart—that Jonathan might have been here to share this beauty.

Immediately another thought disturbed her ... what if he had been here? Hadn't she sometimes found, as far as scenery went, that Jonathan was a little less than kindred? Wasn't that one of the doubts that had plagued her, had held her back? Oh, stupid to be thinking of him at all!

Margot drained her coffee, counted out cents fumblingly, went on. Now there was Lake Ellesmere on the right, a shining, pewter-coloured stretch of water that reached almost to the sea. It was dotted with hundreds of black swans, reminding her of the Australian black swans she had seen at Chartwell, a gift to Winston Churchill.

Valleys reached back into every arm of the hills, rich, fertile valleys, with great homesteads nestled against the heights above. The farms looked prosperous, gleaming in white and pastel paints, with huge woolsheds and cowsheds. There were evidences of struggling pioneer days in tiny weatherboard cottages with glassless windows that looked like sightless eyes. Margot felt sorry for them as for anything that had outlived its true life, but was not yet accorded decent burial. However, most of them were filled with hay, so some usefulness remained.

Oh, she wished she knew the names of these native trees, the ones that looked like palms but were really giant lilies she had been told up North were cabbage trees. They added an exotic touch to the skyline, and she could recognise the Australian gums now, with their multi-coloured trunks and peeling bark and aromatic pungency, but there were dozens of others unknown—as yet. But she would get a book so she could identify them. Nothing made you so at home in a country as being able to put a name to its trees.

The road turned left into the hills, ran through the sleepy township of Little River and began to climb. The sun grew hotter now, it was so sheltered in the folds of the hills.

Five miles up she breasted the hill and came to the Hilltop Hotel, magnificently sited above the whole stretch of Akaroa Harbour. It was the sort of view for which you instinctively braked. Margot drew into the car park, got out and gazed her fill. Or would it ever be possible to have one's fill of such a scene? There, cradled in the arms of the old, old grey hills, lay a harbour so opalescent Margot was reminded instantly of the *paua* shell jewellery on sale all over New Zealand. The water sparkled back in all shades of living greens and blues and under the surface, in patches, were actually some streaks of deep wine, a burgundy shade. Was it shadows or vegetation?

The curves of the bays were gentle and gracious and a long peninsula stretched out into the water at this end. She thought, quite erroneously, that it looked as if it had seen a thousand years of peace.

A faint zephyr came up to fan her hot cheeks. She felt her pulses racing. How beautiful a place this journey's end was ... where the road stopped. A place to end all journeyings. Heavens, what was she thinking? Because her father would have built a new life for himself, have forged new ties.

The road ran down to the water, touched briefly at Barry's Bay, and went uphill again to drop to the shore at Duvauchelle, a dreamy bay with a triangle of flat land widening out from the inevitable valley and sweet with trees ... not many buildings, a Post Office and a County Council Office. She was soon past.

Suddenly her foot went on to the brake. County Council Office? Might that not mean a County Council Engineer? She would go in and ask for something. What?

Ask for a map of the Peninsula. Maps of Canterbury did not give it in detail.

Outwardly she was calm, matter-of-fact. She saw a pleasant-faced woman behind the counter and warmed to her immediately, as she smiled and said, 'Good afternoon, can I help you?'

Margot suppressed a wild desire to say, 'Oh yes, please, you could help me find my father,' and asked instead if she might be able to purchase a map of the Peninsula. 'I'm an English tourist and I've heard the Peninsula is very beautiful. I'd like to explore it.'

The woman smiled. 'Then you intend to stay a few days. It can't be done justice to in twenty-four hours. So many overseas visitors are brought here on one-day tours and get no more than a tantalising glimpse of the bays. They often wish they could stay a week.'

Margot sparkled, 'From that Hilltop glimpse, I'd like to stay a month. I'm here for an indefinite time—a working holiday. But I'm not looking for a job yet. I hate tours that skim the surface only. I like to live in a place for a while.'

She smiled. 'I so agree. When I went to England I stayed with relations, didn't keep on the move all the time, and loved it. I hope you'll love New Zealand—and particularly Akaroa—just as I loved England. There are only two places in the world I'd like to live, and since I can't live in England, I live in Akaroa.'

She added, 'I've just made a cup of tea. I'm having it on my own because the County Clerk is closeted with the County Engineer at the moment. Would you like to have one with me?'

What friendliness ... the hospitality of a small place where there was no hint of the rat-race. And she had spoken magic words ... the County Engineer! Francis Nightingale had been an engineer. She wasn't looking for a miracle ... she couldn't expect to find her father before she even reached Akaroa, but one engineer might know another and it could be handy to find out this man's name.

'That's extremely kind of you. I'd love one. The sea air has given me an appetite.'

The office windows were open to the sound of birdsong, to the far-off but shrilly-sweetness of children's voices and the lap-lap of waters against the shore, and through it all a wind went soughing through the tree-tops. A dreamy, halcyon day where anything might happen.

They had their cup of tea, talking of England and places they both knew. Apart from her quest, this was delightful. When they finished out came the maps—one of Akaroa streets, one of the Peninsula. By this time Margot had found that Prudence Sheraton was a descendant of one of the original English settlers.

The map fascinated Margot. The ridges of the great volcanic Peninsula spread like a fan pulled back to almost a circle ... no wonder Captain Cook had thought it an island at first. It was fretted with countless bays with the most fascinating names ... Port Levy, Le Bons Bay, Decanter Bay, Long Lookout, Paua Bay ... she supposed you picked up *paua* shells there ... Good heavens, here was Flea Bay ... Sleepy Cove, Waikerikikeri, called Hickory for short, no doubt a corruption of its general sound ... Squally Bay, Nine Fathom Point, Tumbledown, Murray's Mistake ... then, within Akaroa itself, French Farm Bay, Rossignol's Bay, Brough's Bay, Robinson's Bay, Tikao, Wainui, Takamatua.

'These more English names were given in honour of the first folk who settled there, I suppose?'

'Yes, Robinson, for instance, was the first magistrate here, one of the two sent down by Lieutenant Hobson from Russell, north of Auckland, to ensure it was made quite clear, when he knew the French were on their way, that British sovereignty was in force here. Mr. Robinson is well remembered, because he fought a duel here in Akaroa with Captain Muter over some land claims.'

Margot, her finger tracing them, was repeating the names ... 'Peraki, that was the early whaling station, wasn't it? Horseshoe Bay and Robin Hood ... what pretty names. And isn't there a Nightingale Bay?'

Miss Sheraton's voice was astonished. 'Oh, there aren't any nightingales in New Zealand. Are you perhaps thinking of Pigeon Bay?'

Margot appeared to consider that. 'No-o. I'm sure it wasn't Pigeon. Actually I did know there were no nightingales in New Zealand. There was a splendid book on birds in the ship's library. I thought I'd heard someone say Nightingale Bay and thought it might have been named after people called Nightingale.'

Miss Sheraton shook her head. 'No, we've no one of that name living here. I believe, though, there are people of that name in Christchurch. A firm, if I'm not mistaken.'

Margot dismissed it as of no account. She mustn't be too specific. 'I must have been mistaken. Perhaps it was some other part of New Zealand. Or even in Canada. I've just come from there.'

Then she said, genuinely puzzled this time, 'But I thought there was a Laveroux Bay.' She gave it the French pronunciation. 'I don't see it.'

'Well, there is and there isn't. We now call it Laverick's

Bay—an instance, I'm afraid, of a corruption. It was called after Captain Charlie Laveroux. It's a beautiful bay, narrow, and the flat land is like a delta, and it's probably rich in minerals. Natural gas bubbled up there in the early days, in one of the wells, but the owner, Mr. Knight, had the well filled up, as his men were always watching the water jetting up instead of working. And another thing ... they used to tap the rock a mile or so up the hillside leading to the Le Bons saddle and could hear it in the house distinctly. Probably a vein of copper.' She laughed. 'I suppose if you wished you could call it Partridge Bay ... the Captain Charlie Laveroux the Bay was named for was anglicised as Charlie Partridge. Though that puzzles me as *perdrix* is French for partridge.' She had forgotten about the Nightingales, which might be as well. Just then the County Clerk walked through with the Engineer. Miss Sheraton said gaily, 'This is something that will please you. Here's an English tourist who plans to spend a month here.'

She introduced them. Well, she'd known before she heard the name that the Engineer couldn't be called Nightingale or Miss Sheraton would have said immediately, but at least this was a start. She had met one engineer in Akaroa. Later she could contrive to meet him again and who knew?—he might be able to tell her if ever an engineer called Nightingale had come here. Then her hopes were dashed when he said, 'You might be like me ... come for a month's holiday and stay on. Just as I did three years ago.'

If only she had known her father's mother's maiden name, because his French descent must have been on that side. Nightingale was undoubtedly an English name.

Margot felt she had already made a friend in Miss Sheraton as she took the road again, dipping into a succession of bays, with a mixture of pioneer and ultra-modern homes tucked into old walnut plantations, and with wading birds, oystercatchers, stilts and gulls on the shore.

Robinson's Bay, Takamatua, then Akaroa itself, with the quaint shops and gabled cottages Pierre had spoken of, with the pastel tints of the timbered houses that looked so continental, the steep roofs, the attics, the blossom and the birdsong, the sound of harvesting bees....

She came along the Rue Lavaud and turned up the Rue Jolie ... it was so tiny, so tucked in, but she wanted to see the length and breadth of it. She saw a notice, 'Akaroa

Motels' and decided that was what she wanted. She liked the motels of New Zealand. They were not cheap, but you had that priceless advantage, privacy. No sitting round in hotel lounges. You did your own cooking, though you could have a Continental breakfast served if you desired it. But you had your own TV, fridge, your complete suite.

This one delighted her. A little brook went chattering outside her window, down to the Bay where the French landed, the proprietor said. Huge glass doors slid back to a patio with table and central sun-umbrella, and chairs, and it was screened by rioting geraniums in great splashes of pink and red and by twisting vines and creepers heavily perfumed.

She went down to a store to lay in some provisions. A little bird with a huge tail like a fan was flitting about the shop. It seemed so friendly and had a diving flight. 'A fantail,' said the shopkeeper, 'they're always in here.' She had the most curious feeling going along the streets as if she must look closely into the face of every man of her father's probable age.

Margot decided on fish for her dinner. It was beautifully fresh, caught outside the Heads the day before, and she took cutlets of groper. There was one thing that boded well for her quest ... everyone round here had time to talk, and seemed ready to do so.

The fishman showed her his collection of old bottles, stored on a high shelf. He found Margot a ready listener. He recommended her to visit the Langlois-Eteveneaux Museum and she spent the evening studying the booklets he gave her, trying to decide on a plan of action. From her hat-box she took the only clues she had; she had found them tucked right away at the back of her aunt's wardrobe under some old hats, when she was clearing out junk before leaving. They were in a mahogany box that had once had a lock, but now just a rubber band served to keep it shut. There was a snuff-box, French enamel, she knew, and quite old. Even valuable. Eighteenth-century. That could have come across with her father's forebears, at the time of the French Revolution. She supposed they had been émigrés. There was a fine chain with a pearl-shell cross attached to it. Because of the shop, Margot knew it probably came from Tahiti. Pierre had mentioned that some of the French settlers finally left Akaroa and went to Tahiti. Was there a link there? There was a very fine rosary and a birthday card. The latter was

41

slightly yellowed, but had been chosen with care. It had garlands of red roses on it, and across it was written, 'To Laura ... "my love is like a red, red rose"—Francis.' Margot prized it above all the rest, for this was dear, this knowledge that even though things had gone so sadly for Laura and Francis, yet they had known, at least, *some* idyllic moments.

She fingered the rosary dreamily. Her touch was a caress, wistful, as if from this link with her unknown past, she would draw the essence of all the prayers that had been uttered on it. Who knew in what deep need, or in what rich surge of thanksgiving, these might have been voiced? Perhaps prayers for deliverance at the time of the Revolution? And a paean of praise at reaching the safe, if alien, shores of England. She looked at it again, less dreamily. This in itself might be a symbol of a problem if she found her father and there was room in his life for her.

Margot had been brought up Protestant. Had that been because her aunt was Protestant, or because her father was? There had been no hint in Uncle Noel's letter that Ruth's objection to the marriage had been on the grounds of religion. And anyway, to do Aunt Ruth justice, she had never been bigoted on that score. Many of her friends, and Margot's, had been Catholic. Very stupid to make any difference there, whichever side you belonged to, and there were bigots on both sides. Anyway, like the recipe for jugged hare ... first catch your hare ... she had first to find her father.

She spent a day or two exploring the Eastern Bays. As they were sparsely populated, she would eliminate those first. And, as they were further out, there just might be Nightingales that Miss Sheraton had never heard of, living there.

Laverick's Bay was the next bay to Le Bons. A road, steep and narrow, ran up the cliff to the shoulder of the hill that hid it from view. She drove slowly and carefully, came to the top with leagues of ocean down below, stretching east and south, and suffered a check. There the public road ended. A notice stated this was a private road. She thought she'd like to look over and see how many homesteads it sheltered, slipped across the paddocks, but could not see down, it was so narrow. She knew a pang not to do with her quest. She'd have liked to have seen where Pierre lived. She didn't know how laws of trespass worked in New Zealand and she did not want to draw attention to her quest.

But one thing was sure, Laverick's Bay was a bay apart.

Pierre and his parents were in England and no one could possibly connect her with him. Something struck her. It didn't seem possible that Pierre's mother could have seen Mount Bossu, which was over-harbour even from Akaroa, from this deeply-recessed bay. How odd.

The third day she climbed the hill to the cemetery above the Domain, on the road to the Kaik. It had occurred to her that if Francis was a family name, it may have been anglicized to that from François, so it could be she might find a clue to him in tracing which French family had the name recurring most on the stones.

Oh, the peace of this quiet acre belonging to God, where *matipo* and cypress grew happily together, and where French, German, English, Irish and Scots people of long ago lay asleep. Even more nationalities than that ... here was an Edwin Kotlowski and a Hansen! And what differences in ages ... here lay little Bridget O'Reilly, only twelve, and François Etienne le Lievre, who had been ninety-three, so had been born before Waterloo. And here was Justine, his wife. She went from grave to grave, copying them down. Here was a name Pierre Laveroux had mentioned. Rossignol. Charlotte and François Rossignol, and a Louis. Some graves were newer. What a beautiful name this one bore ... Victorine Louisa Brocherie ... she might as well have them all, in case later, examining records, something she did not recognise now might give her a clue.

That night she compared her list with the list of the original French settlers copied out of a book at the library, and knew the name of François would not help her. Even in the first settlers, as well as in the cemetery, François had been the most recurring name. *Wouldn't* it! François le Lievre, François Rossignol, François Rousselot, François Malmanche, François Narbey, even a J. Adolphe François. So François could be a surname as well as a given name, just as in England Francis could be both!

So any enquiries she might dare to make would have to be for one Francis Nightingale, who, with a French-Canadian wife, had come here in the last twenty years or so to trace connections who had been French, then had moved on. What a task!

She would, however, not be discouraged, but would go about it quietly, exciting no comment, hoping to stumble across something. She could afford to stay a month without working, then could take a position in Christchurch. If she could bring it about in a seemingly natural way, she'd contact the people of the name of Nightingale there, because Francis might have called on them.

Margot suddenly thought of something. She had not noticed anyone called Margot on the headstones, even though Margot was the French form of Margaret. There had been only a Marguerite. So perhaps she had not been named for her father's family. Perhaps her mother had simply liked the name. But on the heels of that thought trod another ... her name was Margot Rose and there were several Roses on that fragrant hillside. There had been Françoise Rose le Lievre, Virginia Elizabeth Rose ... and others. Oh, it could mean nothing, but—Margot's heart lifted a little.

She went to bed very late, hoping her mind wouldn't be too active. How terrible to go through life without ever tracing her father!

But she fell asleep immediately, lulled by the murmur of the little creek as it went its way to the sea from its secret haunts of fern and gully, but she did nothing all night but fall from one frustrated dream to another.

She was questioning men in French berets, drawn up on the shore beside that landing-point, and as she pointed at each one, he answered with his Christian name, till all the ones she had perused were used up ... Philippe, Emery, Jean Baptiste, Georges, Adolphe, Pierre, Etienne, Jules, Auguste. Jacques, and, at the end, twenty men who replied mockingly, 'I'm François ... I'm François ... I'm François.'

In another she was standing on the top of Purple Peak, looking down on the deep blue waters of French Bay below the motel and her father was pushing her over the edge, shouting, 'Who asked you to come here? Not me! Over you go!' Oh, dreams were horrible, and she woke, trembling and hot but glad to have shaken off the chains of nightmare slumber. She felt so depressed she did not dare go to sleep again, so she got up, made herself a cup of tea, and went on reading the Centennial book. It was rather wonderful, reading of the vicissitudes faced and conquered, and her foolish dread, a hangover from her dream, began to dissipate.

It was such a harmonious story this, the blending of the English, the French and the six German settlers who had been on the *Comte de Paris*. This was not a hostile place. And her mission was not impossible. Her aunt *had* sent those

44

things to one Francis Nightingale here, so he had been here long enough to write, have them sent by sea, and receive them.

What if he had gone back to Canada? His French-Canadian wife might have been homesick. Her heart quailed at the thought of making a search in Canada. Or might they have something approaching Somerset House there? Why hadn't she thought of it before? Only she had been so taken up with the thought of coming to Akaroa where her father had last been heard of.

She pulled back the drapes and watched the sun rise, waking the over-harbour hills with tender light and gilding the top of Mount Bossu, Pierre's kindly Hunchback, and gradually the little town around the water's edge woke to the life of another day. She waved to Bossu and said good morning to him. She instantly knew a lightening of the heart, felt near Pierre. As she realised this, she angrily pushed the thought away. Pierre was nothing to her. He had been an instrument, that was all.

The Langlois-Eteveneaux House was fascinating. It could have been in any French town. It had a high roof, ventilated through the cornice members, shutters and unusual inward opening casement sashes. The weatherboards were not pit-sawn as so many early Colonial houses were and she learned from the booklet that there was some traditional evidence that the building had been prefabricated in France.

Aimable Langlois had lived here first but had not stayed. By 1845 he was living in Honolulu and died at Pueblo-san-José, near San Francisco, later. San Francisco? Would he have called at Tahiti? Heavens, she was certainly clutching at straws.

She lost sight of her quest in the beauty of the rooms. The draped bed was exquisite, French Imperial in Provincial style, but made in Akaroa by a French carpenter for the marriage of Monsieur and Madame François le Lievre in 1851 and beautifully curved. There was a boot-polishing stand, a washing pedestal, candlesticks, a figure of the Madonna on the wall, smelling salts in a ruby glass bottle, a large circular table in the French Provincial style of the early eighteenth century and an armchair that was earlier. Margot wondered if the tingling at her fingertips was caused by her love of antiques, or something deeper, something stirring in her because these were the things of her own people.

45

She left the cottage and went into the modern museum behind it, where the greater number of local relics was gathered. This would do credit to any town. She revelled in it. This was representative of all the settlers and even further back, of Maori occupation and the whaling days.

So not all of it was French. But there were French ornaments, china shoes with gilt trim and cherubs and garlands, a Sèvres porcelain vase decorated with a pattern of tropical fruits and leaves in overglaze enamel ... oh, that was recent, a gift to Akaroa from the President of France to commemorate, in 1940, the centenary of the landing of the first French settlers. A French jewel casket and some of the iron filigree jewellery worn by the women of France during the Revolution and—something that made Margot's heart beat a little faster—a patch-box extremely similar to the snuff-box in her possession.

There was a wedding-gown of mushroom taffeta, a dinner-gown in grey taffeta trimmed with purple, a ball-dress of finest tussore silk, brown velvet and yellow embroidered ninon, parasols, bonnets so beautiful that Margot envied those long-ago girls who wore them, printed silk shawls, and exquisitely dressed French dolls.

Margot came back to the box for contributions and slipped a two-dollar note into it. Her eye fell on the visitors' book. She moistened her lips. What if, turning its pages, she saw 'Francis Nightingale' scrawled there? The curator came out of her office and smiled at her. 'You've been extremely interested ... I don't think you've missed one item.'

(No ... she had examined every card that bore a donor's name, hoping, hoping!)

Margot smiled back. 'I've been fascinated. I used to work in an antique shop in London, and my particular interest, for some reason, was in French stuff.'

'Oh, what a help to me you could be, if you lived near. We have to depend upon going across to Christchurch Museum to identify periods and pieces. But you'll not be here long, I suppose?'

'Well, that depends. I'm staying at a motel just now, but I've fallen in love with this place and might even stay on here for a while if I could get a job. But I suppose that it's too early for seasonal jobs? Would I need to come back in the holiday season ... Christmas is high summer here, isn't it? And January your busiest month?'

'Yes, because the children are off school then, but our season lasts till Easter. You mean you'd like a position as a waitress or something?'

'Yes, it would help things along. I know there's no scope for my sort of work here—anyway, I'm reasonably domesticated and thought I'd like a change. I'm not looking for a high wage, not much more than my keep, really.'

The curator nodded. 'I've something in mind, but I'd have to make sure first. I'll come along to the motel and see you tonight if there's anything in what I'm thinking of. If so, you could start immediately and it would certainly carry you over the entire tourist season. It could even be permanent, but if you're on a travelling holiday, you'd not want it longer than that?'

Margot did not commit herself to any set time, said it would suit beautifully and asked no questions. She looked at the visitors' book. 'May I browse through that some time?— it fascinates me to find out where people come from.'

'You'd be welcome, my dear. I like doing it myself. This is sometimes called Sleepy Hollow, but we get people from the four corners of the earth. Not everybody signs the visitors' book, though, unfortunately. Even so, in the first three years this was open, we had seventeen thousand signatures.'

Seventeen thousand in three years! Well, she wouldn't find it easy, but if need be she'd wade through dozens of such books in search of her father's name. Then she looked about her—this was obviously so new.

'When was this opened?' she asked.

'In 1964.'

Then it would not, probably, contain her father's signature. But she said, 'I suppose only visitors sign it. Local people wouldn't?'

'Oh, they do. There was a great rush when it was first opened. I should think every man, woman and child in Akaroa signed it.'

Well, she would concentrate on those early pages, though it was scarcely likely, since Miss Sheraton did not remember him, that he was here as recently as that. But if he were still in New Zealand, he might have come back on holiday some time. So she would go through the lot. She might even find his wife's signature, or his children's. It gave her a queer feeling. How odd, having regarded yourself all your life as an orphan and an only child, to think you might have half-

47

brothers and sisters. But they would not want you. You would be a usurper, your father's eldest child.

Mrs. Ericsson arrived at the motel promptly, sank down in an easy chair and said, 'I'll get right to the point. We're trying to widen the scope of our tourist attractions, which will be a good thing. We have so many other bays that could take the overflow of our summer trade. It tends to get too concentrated right here in Akaroa.

'Some new motels have been built at Rossignol's Bay. Don't suppose you've ever heard of it. It's past French Farm Bay but not as far as Wainui. Only a short distance from here, really, about ten or eleven miles. We're also developing a cottage museum there.

'It's a gem of a cottage, still lived in. Two cottages really, as one was added as the family grew. The old lady who lives there ought to have someone living with her. She's a direct descendant of one of the first French. She's very conscious that our history ought to be preserved and will donate one cottage to the Historical Society if we can arrange to have it looked after by someone.

'It wouldn't be onerous—except in the height of the season —and we've been casting about to find someone willing to live with the old lady, do a certain amount of housework— she does most of the cooking herself and enjoys it—and show visitors through. The owner of the motels is very keen to get this open. A lot of work has been done on it already, classifying it and so on. This man has lived there, farming, all his life, but wants to stay on when he retires, running the motels and living in one himself. This wouldn't be a highly-paid job, but it would be very pleasant and you would be the ideal person.' She mentioned the salary.

Margot said, 'That would suit me very well. My uncle and aunt, who brought me up, left me their London house and I have it let to tenants, so that gives me anything extra I need. Do you think they would have me? Could they interview me soon?'

'Oh, they said go ahead and grab you. It's yours. Now are you quite sure, or would you like to see the place before deciding?'

'No, I'm scared they hear of someone else.'

Mrs. Ericsson rose. 'I'll ring the old lady's nephew now. He'll be thrilled. At present one of his children goes down to sleep in the cottage every night and Frank feels it disturbs the youngsters at their homework.' She crossed to the phone.

Margot's hands clasped and tightened. Frank! The short form of Francis. Oh, don't be daft, Margot Chesterton! It's a name you hear a lot. You aren't going to be led straight to your father, you idiot! And anyway, Miss Sheraton would have known. It won't be Frank Nightingale!

Mrs. Ericsson said, 'Is that you, Justine? Is Frank there? I've good news for him. Charlotte and Leonie will be able to stay home at nights from now on. Miss Chesterton can come till at least March. She'll come to see you tomorrow. Would you like to speak to her? Right.'

She beckoned Margot, who picked up the phone, then put her hand over the mouthpiece, saying, 'What's his name? I can scarcely call him Frank. Isn't it stupid, I never even asked their name.'

Mrs. Ericsson laughed back. 'What a pair! I should have said, It's François Rossignol of Rossignol's Bay.'

Margot looked quickly down. The Rossignols! Great friends of Pierre's. The old lady of the slides he had shown, no doubt. Oh, dear. But what could it matter? Pierre was on the other side of the world and his parents too. He wouldn't be likely, if he was like most men, to be sending more than the occasional picture postcard to friends in bays other than his own, much less mention a girl he had met so briefly.

Like all the voices of the Akaroa French descendants, there was no trace of an accent in his voice. Most of these people used the occasional French word, that was all. She had noticed, however, that in the main, a rather pure type of English was spoken here, with only a faint, underlying New Zealand accent. Small places were like that, of course.

His voice was warm with pleasure and relief. 'We're most awfully glad about this, Miss Chesterton. To have someone with specialised knowledge of antiques would be marvellous. My aunt is so reluctant to leave the home she has lived in all her life. You see she was a Rossignol before she married a distant connection from France, and though it would be no trouble to have her here, my wife knows she would fret, suddenly feel her usefulness was over.

'I suppose Mrs. Ericsson has explained the set-up to you—we're on the same property and are constantly with her, but she clings to Maison Rossignol. This idea of a cottage museum is giving her a new lease of life. She loves meeting people and she'll be an acquisition. The tourists often want to meet someone of direct French descent and someone who can actually remember a grandfather who landed here in 1840. It gives people a sense of quite recent history, if you get me?'

'Yes,' said Margot softly, 'because in Akaroa, the past is only yesterday.'

There was a small silence, then Frank Rossignol said, 'I can tell you're a kindred spirit. I think Tante Elise is going to be very fortunate. Now, I'd better give you instructions on how to get here. When you get to the Bay, come through to the third turnoff. On the right, of course; there's only the sea on your left. A tiny distance uphill you'll see three or four mailboxes in a group. The first one says Francis Beaudonais. Our property is the first on the left, on a little side-road above the boxes. You see, I want you to come up to our house, not the cottage, which is below our house and has access to the shore road. Come about eleven and have lunch with us. In fairness to yourself you must have a look at the position first. You could get your stuff from the motel later. Though, like all of us, you'll fall under the spell of Rossignol Bay. It's a sort of Lotos-land, nobody ever wants to leave it.'

Margot chatted on for a time, asking questions, then repeated his instructions, 'Third turn to the right, uphill, and it's just past Francis Beaudonais's mailbox, on the left.' She laughed and said lightly, 'What an extraordinary lot of people called Francis live in Akaroa.'

'Yes. Most of them started off as François. But Tante Elise thinks the French influence should be preserved, so my daughters bear French names, Charlotte and Leonie. My son is Jules and my wife Justine. Incidentally, you've a French name yourself, or is it short for Margaret?'

'No, I was baptised Margot. I expect it was just a favourite name of my mother's. She died soon after I was born, so I don't know. But many English girls are Yvonne or Annette or Melanie.' (She didn't want anyone to guess she might have come seeking French connections.)

'That's so. But the fact that you're Margot will please my aunt—and my wife. Well, we'll look for you about eleven. Goodbye for now.'

Margot had no nightmares that night, or any more fears.

CHAPTER THREE

MARGOT woke with a kind of buoyancy within her she recognised for hope, a sense of being led to a place, guided. Living at this quiet bay she would be able to keep her eyes and her ears open. Anyway, she wasn't going to get all tense about it, or expect miracles. This would be a glorious interlude, even if nothing came of it. And at least she would be comforted by the knowledge that her father had once looked upon these scenes.

She went into the Post Office, absurdly thrilled to remember her father had once called here to take possession of his mementos of his shared life with her mother. Margot bought her stamps, then headed towards Duvauchelle, en route for Rossignol Bay. Some day she'd call in on Prudence Sheraton and tell her she loved her Akaroa and was spending a few months here.

These bays were delightful, with an atmosphere dreamily remote, despite easy access. The whole setting was vividly familiar from Pierre's slides. Before she turned uphill to the homestead road she saw Maison Rossignol just as she had seen it on the screen ... dazzling white, with its black facings and steep green-tiled roof. The tiles, she knew from Pierre's lecture, had replaced the original shingles split from *totara* slabs.

She turned in over the cattle-grids, swept round the house on the edge of an old-world garden, and on up to a beautifully proportioned modern home that sat above haphazardly arranged rock terraces in a blaze of sunshine, and had a belt of trees about it, like protecting arms. She began climbing the steps between the terraces to a wide, lemon-coloured door that stood hospitably open.

From it emerged two teen-age girls, running, almost, to greet her. At the same moment a bull-terrier, tawny as a lion, rushed from the far corner of the house to join in the welcome, leapt diagonally across the two top terraces to catch the girls up, overshot himself and crashed bulkily on to the steps, taking the legs from under them.

Margot tried to check, but not soon enough; the shrieking girls landed at her feet, clutched wildly and brought her down on them. They subsided, dog and girls, in a whirling heap of arms and legs.

The golden-haired girl clutched Margot's arm as they struggled to disentangle themselves. 'Oh, Miss Chesterton, we're so sorry ... are you badly hurt? Oh, creepers, Dad will be furious! He was so delighted to get someone and said we must be extra-specially nice to you ... and now look what we've done!'

The red-haired one grabbed her other arm. She seemed younger. 'Please don't get the wrong impression, will you? We were just trying to welcome you. We thought if you saw right away there was some young life about the place, you'd be more likely to stay. But it's this thing's fault ... stop it, Auguste! *Don't* lick Miss Chesterton's face! That won't make her feel any kinder towards you. Auguste! Stop it!' She tried to push him away, but Auguste was like the Rock of Gibraltar.

'Gosh,' said Margot with awe, regarding him, 'I've never met a dog called Auguste before. How terrifically impressive! Tell me, what do you call your cats?'

'Hortense and Marmaduke!' they replied in duet, and they all burst out laughing.

The girls leaned back and regarded her with great respect. 'You'll do us. Most folk would have been furious. But you aren't. You—you've sort of gone off at a tangent, just like Mum does. We like people like that.' This was the golden one.

The red one said: 'It would take some people ages to recover from having the legs knocked from under them. You must have poise.'

Margot continued to giggle helplessly ... 'Is it possible to remain poised when you're scuttled? I'd have thought it a physical impossibility.'

The red one looked up, said quickly, 'Uh-uh ... here's Dad. We're for it. Poor Dad!' She added, more loudly, 'It's all right, Dad, don't panic. She doesn't mind a bit. She can take things in her stride. Look, she's giggling.'

Her father glared at her. 'She may be giggling, Leonie, but she's bound to have a bit of skin off. You can thank your lucky stars she *has* got a sense of humour. I may have told you to escort Miss Chesterton up, but I didn't say knock her down. Miss Chesterton, I'm most awfully sorry. I——'

Margot said, trying to control her mirth, 'Don't worry ... I'm not hurt. I'm sure the girls got the worst of it. That dog really brought them down with a wallop, I only got the tail-end of it. Oh dear ... I didn't mean that to be a pun,' and off they all three went again.

He helped her to her feet, brushing her soft pink woollen suit down. He was absurdly like the golden girl, who must be Charlotte. How unalike the two sisters were. He was going a little grey and his hair was brown rather than gold, but he had been a very fair man and a handsome one. Leonie was striking, and her scattering of freckles only added to her charm. Margot spoke the thought in her mind, 'How lovely to have two daughters so absolutely different.'

Charlotte laughed. 'We say it's because of our mixed heritage. I'm like Dad, French. Leo is like Mother, redheaded, and, as Dad says, as Irish as the pigs o' Dublin. And Jules is dark and very like Mum's brother, who always vowed he was a throwback to a Spanish sailor wrecked off the coast of Ireland during the Armada.'

Mr. Rossignol said helplessly, 'This conversation is getting away from me. I feel we ought to be madly apologising to you, not embarking on the family tree. But by now, after twenty years and more of living with the maddest family in Christendom, I ought not to try to impress people. Miss Chesterton, you've seen us at our madcap worst the moment you arrived. Would you try to believe we're not always like this? And fortunately Tante Elise is completely different. She has everything we have not—poise, elegance, a sort of dignity.'

Margot sparkled, 'Please, Mr. Rossignol, don't apologise. I was shaking with nervousness at the thought of meeting you, but now I'm all relaxed. You just can't stay stiff after giggling. I think you've got a lovely family—so friendly, so interesting. And what fun. I was an only.'

The golden girl said, 'Are you related to Gilbert Chesterton the poet? It's an unusual name. I love his poem about the donkey, don't you?'

'No—at least I'm not related to him, but yes, I love his poem about the donkey.'

François Rossignol said firmly, 'Charlotte! That's quite enough. If we aren't careful we'll find ourselves involved in a discussion on favourite poems, or our pet donkeys, and Tante is waiting with great eagerness to meet Miss Chesterton. And I think Justine is putting the last touches to the lunch. Come on.'

Margot smiled, 'Don't you think, after all this, it could be just Margot?'

He nodded, 'It will fit so well into our family. It will sound like an all-French set-up.'

Margot said, 'Did you say pet donkeys? I love pet donkeys ... tell me, do they have French names too?'

Mr. Rossignol groaned. 'They do ... Celeste, Antoinette and Jacques. But the goats, at least, are Irish. My wife, Justine, is mostly Irish. So the goats are Patrick and Deirdre, heaven help them. Leonie, *will* you grab that animal by the collar and shut him in the shed!'

He led the way through a square hall with a deep burgundy carpet in a Persian pattern, and through into a room that jutted out at an angle from the house and had windows on three sides so that it got the sun all day. Every inch of wall space round chimney alcoves and beneath windows held bookshelves crammed with books.

A table with chessmen on it stood in a corner, an unfinished jigsaw lay on the west window-seat, a scrapbook of pictures of the English Royal Family beside it, and, sitting in a high-backed wing chair, was a lady with an imperious, yet kindly air.

She rose and came across to Margot, walking with a grace that reminded one of a bygone day. She looked taller than she was because her silvery hair was dressed high, and she had a little lace front to her frock and a high ruffled neckline to it.

The frock was grey, with a satin-embossed design on it, and longer than was fashionable, which was wise, because it suited her so. A knot of purple velvet was at her throat, with a pearl pin, and her hands, crepey with age and very white, flashed diamonds and opals.

Her nephew said ruefully, 'Tante, you probably heard— the girls and Auguste between them knocked Miss Chesterton clean down the steps. But she's unperturbed, so it hasn't put her off us.'

The finely marked and still black eyebrows rose, then the dark bright eyes beneath them laughed. 'I have long since given up being surprised at anything that happens to guests within our bounds. I'm only glad this is one who appears able to cope. Miss Chesterton, we give you welcome. Are you at all shaken, my dear?'

Margot laughed. 'Not in the slightest. After all, *I* fell

54

softly ... on the girls. Madame, I'm so very glad to meet you. I hope we have a very happy time together.'

The alert eyes regarded her shrewdly. 'You said that very naturally—perhaps someone has told you that I, alone of all the French descendants, am still called Madame? But if you find it easier to say Mrs. Rossignol, I do not mind. I am used to both. It was just that I married someone who came directly here from France, so he preferred me to be known as that. It has now become a custom.'

'I like it,' said Margot. 'I've always thought it a most pleasant form of address—easier to say, too, than Mrs. Rossignol all the time. Mrs. Ericsson told me you were a Rossignol before you were married to a distant connection.'

'That is so. I have never known another name. My husband came here with the French Ambassador from Wellington. He was an attaché. They came to see the Le Lièvres, and when they heard the name, they sent him across here. Our branch of the family had lost touch with our people in France, mainly because my grandfather was an orphan and had no close relations left in Normandy.'

Margot's eyes took on a sparkle. 'How romantic! I thought perhaps he'd come here to trace relatives. I suppose sometimes people do?'

No one could have guessed this was other than small talk.

'Yes, sometimes the French Ambassador in Wellington sends people to us. I mean to any of the French descendants. In fact, I—oh, François is coming with Justine at last.'

Justine was an older edition, as had been said, of Leonie, and her voice had a faint trace still of an Irish brogue.

She held out her hands. 'I ought to have been greeting you myself instead of fussing over the lunch, then the girls wouldn't have been pushing you over, but I had the mushroom sauce at the right stage for thickening. Now we're ready, if you'll all sit up. Margot—Francis says it's to be Margot—will you sit here, on Tante's right hand? Children, take your places. Jules is bringing in the chicken. Margot, I hope you'll excuse his not changing, but he's been riding round the sheep and must go out again directly, so I told him not to bother.'

Jules was so exactly as the girls had said, Spanish-looking, that Margot's mouth twitched. He had dark hair, with a hint of crisp curl in it, and wide dark eyes and aquiline features. Margot had an impish vision of how he would look in six-

teenth-century costume, with a pointed stiletto beard ...
Charlotte, her own eyes impish said, 'He *is*, isn't he, Margot,
like a Castilian nobleman?'

Jules, placing the casserole of chicken in front of his
father, grinned. 'As long as you don't call me Don Juan, I
can take it. And it's a lot of nonsense, Miss Chesterton.
There's no Spanish whatever in our family. It's just the
stupidly romantic notion of my silly sisters. If ever there's a
plain, down-to-earth Kiwi it's me! And don't, Leonie, don't
tell me I should have said: "It is I!"'

Madame, passing her plate to her nephew, said, 'Indeed, it
is stupid, Jules; before you know where you are this Spanish
nonsense will become a legend. Charlotte, if you must let
your imagination run away with you, put it into one of your
short stories. That is the place for fiction. I do not like fact
being embroidered, it can be very dangerous. Some people
get so into the habit, they do not know when to stop. Jules is
no more Spanish-looking than Pierre Laveroux, yet *he* has
no Spanish blood. He is only French, English and Irish.'

Margot was suddenly aware her colour had risen and
hoped nobody noticed. She took the mushroom sauce and
busied herself with it.

When lunch was over the girls were told the dishwashing
was over to them and that their parents and Madame were
taking Margot to Maison Rossignol. 'And,' added their
father in a tone that brooked no argument, 'until we've
finished showing Margot round, you're not to come down.
Margot is here primarily to look after the museum, not to
provide you two with companionship, though you will be
very fortunate if she suffers you now and then.'

Behind his back Charlotte closed one eye in a saucy wink.
'Yes, *mon père*. Leonie, we go. Showing how dutiful we
are.'

This time they went down the steps circumspectly,
François with a hand under his aunt's elbow, and took a
little path through a garden that was obviously Justine's
pride and delight. Then they opened a white wicket gate into
an older garden where tiny paths meandered at will. Primroses and violets bloomed here. Daffodils, too, were not quite
over, but the snowdrops had finished. Lilac showed purple
plumes, tassels of laburnum drooped goldenly, a great red
hawthorn overhung a garden seat, a row of Lombardy
poplars stood tall and green where the smiling paddocks met

56

the garden.

They emerged from the shrubbery into all the beauty of a formal garden, loved, old, treasured. This was yesterday's garden. Here were the Bourbon roses, in bud, bougainvillea rioting wherever it could gain a hold, alyssum frothing in the corners; there were beds of tulips, interspersed with forget-me-nots, pansies, lavender, rosemary, balsam. The whole air was spicy.

Margot stood enchanted, looking about her. She caught sight of a round bed that positively wafted fragrance towards them. It was completely circled with clove pinks, then with a row of mignonette, then the centre was full of spicy stocks clustered round a little stone cherub with a blob of green moss on his nose.

She said unthinkingly, 'Oh, how enchanting, it reminds me of that poem on Akaroa ...

> "... And garden plots are redolent
> Of poignant, unforgotten scent,
> Where gillyflower and fleur-de-lys
> Bloom underneath the cabbage tree."'

Madame blinked. 'Oh, my dear, how charming. How very sweet of you to be already familiar enough with our poetry to be able to quote it. But where did you find it? It was written so long ago.'

Margot was confused and blushed a little. She had asked Pierre to write it out for her the day they had gone to Osterley House.

She said, 'Oh, I read up all I could on Akaroa in Christchurch before I came here, in the Public Library. That poem I copied out.'

François Rossignol said, 'I like a tourist who reads up local history before seeing a place, one who comes armed with knowledge. I think you and Tante will be very happy together, Margot. You'll see our kindly ghosts. And they will like you.'

Yes, she thought, the kindly ghosts would like her. Because already she felt she belonged to Akaroa. That somewhere here, under a name very different from Nightingale, she would find connections of her father's living.

They took her into the original cottage first, stepping back more than a century as soon as they entered straight from the

57

front step into the sitting-room. This was a room still lived in, still loved, with the veneer of hand-polishing on the French walnut bureau, the rosewood writing-table, the curved sofa, beautifully restored with a modern brocade that followed an old design.

Small, elegant bookcases were fitted into the chimney recesses. Margot crossed to inspect them. They were so right ... Molière, De Maupassant, Mauriac, Voltaire. There was an exquisite embroidery frame—in use too. Those small stitches could be only Madame's.

Not all was French. 'Which is as it should be,' said Margot, happily, inspecting some Chelsea ware, some Bristol glass, some Waterford glass and some old Wedgwood. 'Not just the record of a migration from France, but of a family through nearly a century and a half, bringing in other treasures. Oh, how I shall love looking after this. I feel honoured to be entrusted with it.'

Madame saïd, 'Of course some of these things did not come in 1840. The first settlers were not wealthy people. Though age has enhanced the value of what they brought. But a lot of this my husband sent for, from his old home in France. His branch of the family had prospered. That table, for instance.'

This was indeed a treasure. It had cabriole legs and was mounted in ormolu with Sèvres panels, one of which was marked with the artist's initials. Margot guessed it would be Louis XVI.

There was a snuff-box of satinwood with the inside of the lid grooved to form a grater on which coarser grades of snuff could be reduced to a useable powder; and a vinaigrette in silver, the inner pierced grille containing a sponge soaked in aromatic vinegar. Margot sniffed it appreciatively. The very thing to restore one after a swoon.

The family portraits and photographs traced the fortunes and births of the family. Two reproductions of etchings caught her eye, and a name she knew—Charles Meryon. Her eyes lit up.

'Oh, now I realise I've heard of Akaroa before. Of course, Charles Meryon came here—my employer had a book about him. And I've seen some of his etchings and sketches.'

François nodded. 'We got those reproductions fairly recently—thought it would add interest for the tourists to see exactly what Akaroa looked like in—oh, when was it?—

about 1845.'

Madame said, 'He was an *Enseigne de vaisseau* on board the *Le Rhin*—an ensign, a junior officer—and later went in for an artistic career.'

Margot said, 'Yes, of course. In fact one of his admirers called him "the greatest etcher after Rembrandt".' She stepped up closer to read the inscriptions. The first had been done of Miners' Point, showing the hills and the sea, and men hauling up a net and said:

'*Nouvelle-Zelande. Presqu'ile de Banks, 1845. Point dit des charbonners à Akaroa. Peche à la Seine.*'

The other one showed the settlement, with smoke rising from the small houses on the beach, and the bush, with native plants in the foreground. '*Nouvelle-Zelande. Presqu'ile de Banks. Etat de la petite colonie française d'Akaroa, vers 1845; Voyage du Rhin.*'

Madame said, 'There are a lot of things in the attics you will need to go through. Much will be junk, but we were afraid to throw any of it out. But you will know what we should keep.'

Margot was sparkling. For the first time, almost, for two months, the ache because she had lost Jonathan disappeared. He just didn't belong here. And she thought she did.

She said, her eyes taking in evidence of the fact that these downstairs pieces had always been cherished, 'This will be easier than I had anticipated—getting it ready for the tourist season. I've helped at times in restoration, but hours can be spent on one piece even, trying to bring back the patina to something resembling its original condition.'

Madame said anxiously, 'It is not all like this, you understand. We have the main bedroom and kitchen in perfect order, though you may need to reassemble some things, but nothing has been done to the attics. François, would you take Margot up? Four of us would crowd those tiny rooms.'

The stairs were concealed by a door and led up to a tiny recess that served as a landing. It too had a window looking out on to the orchard. There was a spinning-wheel in it and a very ancient sewing-machine. On each side, tucked into the gables, were the attics, with sloping shoulders, beautifully symmetrical, quite different from dormers, which were more common in pioneer homes in New Zealand.

They were just crammed with trunks, chairs, boxes, pictures that stood against the walls with their backs to the rooms, old clocks and ornaments.

Margot said in great satisfaction, 'Ah, here's something I can get my teeth into, sort, classify and restore.' She worked her way in, François Rossignol and his wife, who had followed them, smilingly surveying her from the doorway.

Justine said anxiously, 'Margot, don't get that lovely suit dusty. I've some very enveloping smocks I'll give you. The girls will help you clean it up.'

Margot said, 'Oh, I've got my smocks from the shop with me. What absolute treasures!' She slid the bar of a tin trunk along, and saw a lavender brocade frock with an inserted bodice of French embroidery, with under-sleeves edged with lace of Lille, a frilly parasol, an embroidered pinafore for a little girl.

She said slowly, 'As this is a living house, not a museum, you won't want models dressed in these things ... indeed, there isn't room, but if that little recess at the head of the stairs could have a glass case each side, with a few of these draped on stands, it would give a delightful touch. And beneath the window, a case of these old muskets.'

François nodded. 'We'll see to it—you can just tell us what you need.'

They came down and went through to the other cottage which was rather bigger. 'By then,' said Madame, 'my grandparents had more money. They had a market for their produce in Christchurch which was settled in 1850, and my grandfather by this time owned a timber mill. A terrific lot of timber went round by ship to Lyttelton—in fact sometimes right round and up the Heathcote River—for building. But of course when he first arrived, he was like all the others. He was given five acres of land to make a living from. Oh, the hardships of those first years!

'As their family grew, they added. My father, Etienne, was the youngest son. When the eldest married, he and his wife lived in the first cottage. Come, my dear, see your bedroom, a ground floor one like mine. We use the attics here for spares.'

Margot knew a rush of happiness as she was ushered in. Her window looked down on the dreamy waters of the bay and across to the cluster of houses that was Akaroa. She would sit, she knew, on that window-seat and dream that some day she would pick up a trail, in those narrow *rues* and twisting lanes. Some day, someone would remember a Francis Nightingale who came here, and where he went subsequently.

The room had latticed panes in the windows, and an old-fashioned paper with true lovers' knots entwined among wreaths of rosebuds, and on the wall was a dear round mirror with fat, jolly little cherubs peering over the carved frame at their own reflections. The chest-of-drawers was a later period than most things in the cottage, but had a bow front and beautiful hanging handles and the bed was a sturdy pioneer piece and had a huge puffed-up eiderdown on it in faded rose silk. The bedside lamp had a new shade, but its base was carved alabaster and the table at the other side held a posy bowl of great purple and lilac pansies.

Margot had to control the mist that threatened to gather in front of her eyes as she realised it was going to be very hard, when, mission accomplished, she had to leave here.

That night, in bed, she faced up to the fact she would not want to. It had cast a spell upon her. But if she found her father and found it too painful to stay in New Zealand, if she thought her presence might threaten his happiness, she would have to go.

Besides, she'd want to be gone before one Pierre Laveroux came home. He would smell a rat immediately. To be told a girl had gone to Canada to buy antiques and to find her here would make anyone suspicious. But at least he would stay in England that year his people were there.

The days were full and happy. Justine said to Margot as they tackled the second attic, 'This has given Tante Elise a new lease of life. We were terrified of getting someone who wouldn't be understanding—or loving her. Who might even make her feel that she was the snag in the ointment ... having to look after an old lady as well as managing the museum.

'She looks ten years younger since you came, and the fact you don't mind assisting with the house chores is wonderful. I knew it was going to be all right the moment Tante said, "She not only has a French name, she can cook an omelette like a Frenchwoman." '

Margot laughed. She'd not said she was of French descent, because that would evoke questions of where and how. There had been no time these three days, to pursue her search. But later she would call on the priest at St. Patrick's, and ask, in confidence, if he knew of any Nightingales who had come here from Canada, who might have had a child here, who would have been baptised there. Because if her father had married a French-Canadian, it was more than likely they were Catholic.

Anyway, at church she would meet people. The Rossignols told her she could come with them to St. Peter's Church, Akaroa, on Sundays. This was the Anglican Church. Margot had looked startled. Madame, sitting opposite her at the dinner-table, laughed. 'Do not look so surprised, Margot, nor try to cover it up the moment after. We are as mixed a bunch, in Akaroa, and in this family, as far as religion goes, as we are in nationality. The French and English and German are so inter-married that many families of the same name are both Protestant and Catholic.

'And of late, very happily, there has been much accord and amity. There are three churches here. There is also a Presbyterian Church, established since 1860, called Trinity now, but once called Bon Accord Church. A pity, I think, it was ever changed. It would symbolise our unity more. But relations are most harmonious. Everyone goes to the garden parties that each church holds to raise funds, for instance. In fact, I do as much sewing for the Anglican and Presbyterian bazaars as for our own—but not long ago the first combined service was held. I was very happy. For this I had prayed for many years. François and Justine belong to the Protestant branch of the Rossignols. Even the Irish streak in Justine was Irish Presbyterian. My relations in Christchurch, though, are Catholic. And of course these days, most folk are more ecumenically minded, thank God. I pray that in places where they are not, they will be before long.'

Margot, expressing approval, was thinking, 'Oh, when I find my father, how I hope, whatever religion he is, he has this sensible attitude towards it.'

She asked, 'What religion is Francis Beaudonais?'

'Catholic, though there again the Beaudonais-Smiths, up at Dragonshill, near Mount Cook, to whom he is related, are Protestant.'

François said, 'We must get you round to meet the folk here now. We'll go round a few this afternoon. They're dying to meet you but felt they must give you a chance to settle and didn't want to stop the sorting-out. But you've earned a break. It's a lovely day. Tante Elise, will you come?'

'Yes, it will give me much pleasure to present my *protégée* to them. Where will we go first?'

'Oh, to Partridge Hill. They said they'd be in today.'

'What are their names?' asked Margot, and when François said, 'Murdoch and Flora McTavish,' she laughed inwardly ... at least she would not meet up with her father today.

'We're going over early so we can come back to the Beaudonais'. Frank's up the hill after cattle, but Marie said he'd be back by four at the latest. We'll just wash up and go to Partridge Hill now. They're going to be down at the motels at the foot. They thought you'd like to see them, Margot.'

This must be the elderly couple who were going to run the motels when they retired. No clues there.

They walked. 'It was all part of the Rossignol estate once,' said François. 'Tante's grandfather owned the whole bay then. But we retained this old lane that used to lead up to the sawmill, for easy access—the house is so near, only the shoulder of the hill hides it. The estates have always been run almost as one. Very economical, we share machinery.'

The slope was gentle, and the lane dipped into a patch of native bush, sweet with the songs of birds and the murmur of the inevitable brook tumbling downhill, a brook that was crossed by a corduroy log bridge, bound with iron, and led straight downhill to the corner of the Partridge Hill property where the drive to the homestead began.

Margot saw a cluster of motels where she had expected a row, and for privacy they were set back among a glade of trees and yet faced north for sun. The flowerbeds about them were new and the shrubs and plants just starting to grow, but they gave promise of a colourful summer to come.

There were two mailboxes at the gate, side by side. One said Partridge Hill Motels and the other ... Margot's eyes nearly bulged ... the other said: Henri J. Laveroux!

Laveroux! She said, trying to keep her tone normal, 'I notice this says Laveroux. I thought you said McTavish.'

'The McTavishes run it. Henri and Anne Laveroux are in England. Henri developed a bit of angina and Anne thought a sea voyage might set him up and get him away from the farm. Their son is over there. I believe Henri is much better. They were lucky to have the McTavishes, a splendid young couple. Flora looks after the motels and just loves it. She's a good mixer. Of course it's just a matter of cleaning them out between each lot of tenants, and changing linen and so on. Oh, there they are ... on the steps of the far one.'

Margot made all responses mechanically. Well, she only hoped the Laveroux parents stayed a long time in England

and didn't cut short their visit and persuade their son to come back with them. Just imagine ... she'd thought their homestead safely tucked into the remote Laverick's Bay. No wonder Pierre had said his mother saluted Bossu every morning.

She looked up at the homestead on the ridge, a gleaming white house with green roof and shutters and a row of dormers. This was where Pierre had grown up. He would have the same early morning view as she had from her window. It gave her a strange feeling. Then she frowned. What could it matter to her? She would never meet him again, and didn't want to. *Of course she didn't want to.* Wasn't he a reminder of the most agonising moment of her life ... when she had lost the man she loved?

Frank Beaudonais was another surprise, because he quite definitely had an English accent. He laughed, his broad face creasing into lines. 'My name sounds French, but I'm from the south of England—Isle of Wight, as a matter of fact. Forebears came from France though, fleeing from the Revolution. I was mad keen to emigrate to New Zealand and my father suggested I came out to Dragonshill, where his aunt, Madame Beaudonais-Smith, lives. She's very nearly one hundred years old. That's high country farming, the only access through a river prone to flood. I met my wife up there—she had a year as governess to the children, but she came from Rossignol Bay, so we finally took over her father's estate when he and her mother retired to Akaroa.'

Margot looked carefully round. The others, escorted by Marie Beaudonais, had gone on to admire a mandevillea's progress. She said casually, 'I expect quite a few people who have settled here have come out to look up relatives. Some would come from France, some from England, like you. Akaroa would draw them.'

'A few have, not many. The French ones go to Tahiti or New Caledonia mostly, where they're still in French territory, and need not lose their nationality. A few from England, of French descent, like me, do come. Of course Madame's husband was French, but he was in the Diplomatic Service. A real-life romance, that. And—yes, all right, Marie, we're coming.'

Margot felt disappointed. He might have gone on. Never mind, she'd been here so short a time. She'd see a lot of

64

Frank Beaudonais, and could no doubt lead the conversation that way again.

They had the most delightful children, Angela who was three, with golden curls and soft brown eyes, and Dominic, who was like his father, dark and quite swarthy. Angela sat on Margot's knee and played with her jet necklace. Justine looked across suddenly and said, 'Oh, that must be who you remind me of, Margot. It's been so tantalising. I keep looking at you and saying to myself, "Now you'll remember in a moment who it is if you don't strain after it." It's the same colouring and the same chin ... a perfect oval, except for the dimple in it ... look.'

Margot said, 'What a compliment! If only I were half as beautiful!' Then she looked more closely and said, 'Although I believe there is a resemblance.'

Marie said, 'Angela takes after my mother. We named her for her—Angela Rose.' Margot felt her heart skip a beat then race on. She looked down to see a pulse throbbing in her wrist. And she was Margot Rose. Could this be the clue she was searching for, even if a slight one? But the resemblance——?

She said, 'Where is your mother? Does she live here? Oh, I remember, they retired to Akaroa. Is she a French descendant?'

'Partly. Partly Irish. She was an O'Doherty. In fact, a cousin, although just about forty-second, of Justine's, oddly enough. But her mother was a de Malmanche.'

De Malmanche. One of the first settlers, the name that sometimes appeared in the records as just Malmanche. She might be able to pursue enquiries there, find out if any of that family had gone to England and possibly married into the Nightingale family.

Well, there was one thing. It was true what Pierre had said about the past being alive in Akaroa. No one was going to think it too strange if she liked to delve into the past, especially as she had the genuine background of the antique shop, and now the newly-created Rossignol House Museum. She could say she was trying to trace the possible history of some of the pieces. Had they ever, in their existence, been taken to England, then back here?

Marie took Margot upstairs to ask her opinion on a set of prisms. Angela went up to the attic with them, her little hand tucked confidingly into Margot's. Margot was swept

65

with a longing to identify herself with this family. How sweet to belong to folk like these. But that was silly. Marie Beaudonais was in her early thirties, too old to be a half-sister. But her mother might know if a Francis Nightingale had come here twenty years ago. But how to ask without giving herself away? He might have come looking for a connection called de Malmanche, or Le Lievre, or Eteveneaux ... or dozens of other French names. Patience, Margot. You have need of it.

She caught a glimpse of herself and Angela in a tall mirror that leaned drunkenly against the attic wall. Yes, there was a likeness. But what of it? People who had no connection at all resembled each other so strikingly they looked like twins. Wasn't it said everyone had a double somewhere?

CHAPTER FOUR

BY the middle of December the Museum was almost ready. Margot had worked tirelessly and although she had had no time to really delve into records, or ask vague questions, she had found a happiness in work never before known.

Jonathan's image had faded. At times she almost felt lost without the old romantic ache ... she had meant it to be the one big emotion in her life. Having loved and lost, she had been going to dedicate her whole life to the preservation of beauty. She was almost dismayed to find she forgot to think about him for days at a time. But the healing had come through a sense of being needed, of being part, or nearly part, of a very big family.

Margot felt accepted. Justine took it for granted she was to be included in everything. The greatest boon was that she and Madame had dinner every night at the homestead. François had put his foot down. 'We engaged you as a custodian, not as a cook and rouseabout. We're so grateful that you're with Tante at night, and give her breakfast in bed ... she looks miles better already ... and you can manage a light lunch, which is all anyone her age needs, though Justine says to come up for that meal too, any time your museum activities get you rushed, but you just haven't the time to cook dinners. Justine lectured me about this just last night. We don't want to flog the willing horse, she said.'

Margot giggled. She liked François. He was so good-natured with his turbulent children, and as his wife was just as impetuous and unpredictable as the girls, he seemed to have developed the greatest capacity for being the long-suffering head of the family.

Margot said, 'Know something, Mr. Rossignol? I may be able to whip up an omelette and cook things like poached eggs and bacon, and make a savoury or a curry, but I've had very little experience in cooking dinners, and it was worrying me. My aunt—I told you an aunt brought me up—just hated anyone messing about in the kitchen. It was only after she died I took on any cooking at all, but before my uncle took ill, he and I always had our dinners in town, and we had just a snack at night, sitting round the TV. So if you're sure it won't be too much for Justine, we'll come up for our dinners.'

It worked well. And Justine, primed by François, offered to teach Margot how to cook. No sooner had they started than she averred that Margot had a natural aptitude for it. 'All you're needing is the experience and the confidence that experience brings. But of course always remember that even wives who've been cooking half a lifetime can still burn the pies or undercook the fruit loaves. Trouble with cooking is you must concentrate.

'Take Charlotte, for instance. I've made sure she knows how to cook, because no one can get by without that—but she goes into a trance so often, and seems to have no sense of smell for anything burning, that her cooking is very much a hit and miss affair. I said to her the other day, "If you're after intending to become a writer, my girl, you'd better stay single or you'll drive your husband to distraction!" She was plotting a short story about the French Farm mystery when she was doing the Sunday afternoon scones and forgot the baking-powder! She's really much safer with the ironing or vacuuming. They're mechanical and she can dream all she likes. But I will not be having either of my daughters unable to cook. It is as true as ever, so it is, that even if the way to a man's heart isn't solely through his stomach, it certainly goes a long way to keeping him contented with his woman if he doesn't suffer with indigestion!'

'Fair enough,' said Margot. 'And no doubt Charlotte will be learning to concentrate when she's a little older, especially when she gets married. It's motivated she'll be and all when

67

love takes over.' She stopped, horrified, realising that subconsciously she had copied Justine's Irish way of putting things.

Justine burst out laughing. 'You'll be the death of us, Margot! François and I have been noticing it. When you've been with Tante Elise for a long time, you speak very precisely, almost as if you were not quite familiar with English phrasing. Tante herself, I believe, subconsciously and naturally deepened her slight tinge of a French accent when she married a Frenchman. Oncle Louis never lost his, of course. We nearly died the other day when you came over and asked had we seen the label of the picture of Jean Baptiste Rossignol.'

Margot turned pink. 'Oh dear, I do hope it won't sound affected. Folk may think I'm doing it as a sort of spurious atmosphere for the museum.'

Madame broke in. They had not heard her coming. 'My dear, it sounds perfectly natural. I, too, have noticed it. It is a compliment to us. Is it not always the way? Mrs. Heinrich at Akaroa speaks with the faintest of German accents, yet she was born and bred a Kiwi. And it suits you. You may not know it, Margot, but definitely you have a French air. Have you, somewhere in your ancestry, a trace of French blood?'

Margot was betrayed into an indiscretion. 'I believe so.' She added hastily, as she realised it, 'Not that I know anything about my forebears, but I think there was someone far back. But I don't even know what the name was.'

Madame nodded. 'Probably goes back to Revolution days. So many of the émigrés anglicised their names. What was the natal name of your mother?'

Margot burst out laughing. 'My mother had the most English of all names. And Aunt Ruth was never one to reminisce ... I don't even know my grandmother's maiden name. I always had the feeling that she wasn't a bit nostalgic about the past. I think the happiest days of her life came when she married Uncle Noel and she didn't want to look back.'

Madame did not notice she had not given her mother's so English surname. That had been it—Laura England. Nothing French there.

Margot remembered something. 'Justine, you said Charlotte was writing about the French Farm mystery. A real one, or one she was making up?'

68

'Oh, only too real, Margot. It's never been solved. I've no doubt it will be, some day. I feel a tractor will turn up the skeleton, or some students from Canterbury University unearth it when they're looking for artifacts. Perhaps in some fallen-in cave. It was a terrible thing. Mr. Dicken was one of the first settlers. He went missing in 1857, looking for strayed cattle. They found his horse tied up to some supple-jack—there was a full-scale search. A fortnight later his dog returned, covered with clay. We've always supposed he discovered some cave—the hills were covered with bush, of course, not like now—and explored it and it fell in on him. He may have found some Maori relics and went on searching for more. His poor sister offered five hundred pounds for the recovery of the body, a fortune in those days, but it's never come to light.

'But the searchers did discover the skeleton of a Maori woman in a cave who was probably a refugee from the massacre by Te Rauparaha and his followers at the Onawe Peninsula, and had died either of wounds or of exposure and starvation. All the children from here periodically go on a hunt—they have done for generations, I believe—but it's still a provocative and unsolved mystery.'

François said to Margot some time later, 'Well, when we proposed you came up to the homestead every night, we were thinking of you, mainly, that you mustn't be tied to a stove, and that you needed a bit of young company, but it's worked both ways. It's been marvellous for the girls and Jules. Those girls are so giddy . . . I just hope they'll have your poise when they grow up.'

Margot pulled a face at him. 'Well, as long as you realise it won't be till they *do* grow up! What a pity to expect them to have what you call poise at fifteen and seventeen. And I wonder if you realise how good they are for me? They're so gay and inconsequential and so gloriously natural, they stop me taking myself too seriously. I've never been a member of a family before.' She glanced at him and dimpled. 'You know, you're always decrying those girls, but I'm sure that inwardly you must almost burst with pride. They're so unselfish . . . just bubbling over with the sheer joy of living.'

He grinned back, his brown eyes—the only feature in which he differed from Charlotte—warm. 'You're altogether too astute! I'm always afraid I'll spoil them. I was an only one too, and I think the nicest thing in life is being part of a family.'

'Mr. Rossignol, weren't you lucky to get Justine? She's like Leonie, happy-natured and childlike in some ways, yet so mature and womanly in others. And she has no moods. I think she must have had a very happy childhood. People like that are blest. And they have an aura that envelops other people in their happiness.'

François Rossignol's eyes looked grave. 'She had a happy childhood, yes, and an unshadowed girlhood, and married the boy she loved from schooldays. But he died quite suddenly a week before their baby was born, a still-born daughter. I don't think anyone can guess what the young Justine went through then. She told me once that she just had to rise above it because of her parents. They felt her loss so keenly. I can understand that. I look at Charlotte and Leonie sometimes and long to shelter them from the knocks life may give them. Yet I know one can't and mustn't.

'For Justine it's healed up—mostly—but I know so well that there must be moments—moments I don't know anything about—when something will recall Simon to her, or that little lost baby. Oh, Margot, I've made you cry, *mignonne*. It was over long ago.'

She sniffed and shook her head impatiently. 'Oh, forgive me, Mr. Rossignol. I—I have such active tear-ducts. And it got me by the throat. I'm ashamed of myself. I don't think I'm a jealous person by nature, but subconsciously I think I've been envying Justine. I thought she'd never known anything but calm seas and sunshine. It's very stupid to think like that, just because she's so gay and merry-hearted. Because no one knows what dark secrets other people have or what they've triumphed over.' She blew her nose. 'This makes my troubles seem small. It was just that it happened all within the space of one year ... losing my aunt, then my uncle, then—well, I thought I was going to marry someone, but the girl he had always loved came back into his life again. But that's fading ... since I came here.'

François smiled down on her tenderly. 'No better place to heal a wound than here. Justine and I have proved that.' He reached out and squeezed her fingers. 'Bless you, Margot, I understand. Am I right in supposing you haven't a close relative in the world? Never mind, some day you'll marry and acquire dozens of relatives, probably. But it makes it natural for you to want to belong. And in a very real way you do, here. Not only to us. You must know it.

'Marie Beaudonais loves you to babysit if she and Frank go into town. Flora McTavish said she doesn't feel so tied to the motels now you've said you don't mind taking on the odd office duty at the motels in an emergency, and everyone feels that with running the Museum like this, you'll help pep up the prosperity of the Bay and keep the past alive for us. Jove, I can hardly realise that it's only a week to the opening. I'm glad the French Ambassador can come down to it. Very good of him when it's so near Christmas. And all the bigwigs from Christchurch have accepted.'

Margot was even happier when Justine said one day, 'Margot, I know this was to have been just a working holiday for you, I mean travelling about from one attraction to another, but we've grown so attached. Perhaps it isn't fair, but we would love you to stay. We need you. Tante Elise knew she couldn't live alone much longer and I had the feeling that if we insisted she came here she would lose her spirit, her reason for existing. She has a new lease of life, I'm noticing. Could you stay on? We can arrange for you to take holidays to other parts of New Zealand, when the main tourist rush is over. Would you consider it?'

Margot carefully rolled the pastry she was making for the tamarillo pie under Justine's eye, keeping the bubbles in it intact, and laid down her rolling-pin. She said laughingly, 'If I wasn't covered with flour, you darling, darling thing, I'd fling my arms around you and hug you. I don't think I could bear to leave. I love this place, you, Mr. Rossignol, the girls, Jules and Madame. And my job.

'Although, back Home, I loved saving antiques from being consigned to the scrap-heap, I never liked having to bargain for them. It made me feel an arch-sneak. But getting the Rossignol Museum ready has been heaven. I don't want to move from here for a year at least. Justine, I hope I make a go of it. Oh, I've been so lucky. I can't imagine why you're all so sweet to me.'

Justine hesitated, said, 'It's easy and all. I—I—for me, most of all, perhaps. Partly because of what you are, yourself, and partly—Margot, this is something I hardly ever talk about, but François is my second husband. I was married at twenty, to the boy I loved when I was twelve. He developed

71

an incurable disease just before our baby was born. They operated immediately, but he had only a week. We knew he wouldn't see his baby, but we planned a future for that baby. It was to be called Simon if a son, but Margot, after his French grandmother, if a daughter. It was a girl, but she never drew breath. But she's never been just a still-born child to me. How could she be? I had carried her for nine months, had felt her moving. She has always been Margot St. Laurence to me. I look at girls of her age, often, and think, "She would have been like that ... at that stage ... and this ... she would have been twenty-five, Margot. Your age, even to the very month."

'She was born in February. You must have been two weeks old. Sometimes when I say your name I get the most exquisite pleasure. As if you'd been sent here by God. So—without wanting to be in the least possessive, because it's your life, if you *could* stay here with Tante Elise, it would fill up that little gap in my heart. I mean that *big* gap. Oh, dear, you'd better put that pastry on the fruit. I picked a bad moment as far as our pudding is concerned, didn't I? Cut it with the kitchen scissors, but overlap a little, because it shrinks in the cooking. Now sort of work it back on, press it down with a fork, right round ... so; open it over the funnel and make a couple of pricks each side. Now, let me see ... yes, the oven's at four-fifty ... pop it in and switch from preheat to high-bake.'

Margot got it carefully in, put down her oven-cloth, put her arms round Justine and kissed her on the cheek. 'Thank you for telling me that, Justine. You see I've a gap in my life too. I never knew my father or my mother. Mother died about exactly the time you lost your Margot. And my father and she were separated.'

'And did he leave you to your aunt to bring up? Or did he die too, later?'

Margot said, 'He didn't even know there was a baby on the way. He never knew. Justine, I'll stay just as long as Madame needs me.' And she added to herself, 'And may Pierre Laveroux love England so much, and his job there, that he never wants to come home.'

The days raced on to the opening of the museum. The project had snowballed. It had a deal of publicity in the Christchurch papers and on TV and radio, and stuff kept pouring in. Almost every family in the neighbouring bays found relics of the past and to Margot fell the task of classifying and labelling them.

She dreamed now, when all this hoo-ha was over, of putting out a catalogue, because some of the pieces had such delightful histories. And they had been handed down by word of mouth, which made them vivid and real.

She did an interview on TV and it was so successful that one of the officials from Canterbury Museum asked if she would speak from the platform at the opening.

Margot shrank from this. François Rossignol looked at her kindly. 'You just don't want to push yourself forward, do you? You feel it should be a member of the family or of the Bay. But none is better qualified than you. You can link up what we have here with stuff in the great museums and salons in London. It will make the public realise we have a gem of a museum. And it's going to make a tremendous difference to Henri Laveroux's motels. It was tough on Hal having to give up farming. I'd like to see him make a real success of his venture. This museum is going to be a great tourist attraction. How about it?'

She could not say no. There were times when, thinking of Pierre Laveroux, she knew a sense of guilt. And she had been grateful to him for filling in those first few empty days when she had, in effect, given Jonathan to Betty. He would never know, of course, but this much she could do for his father and mother.

The day of the opening dawned gloriously. At five Margot woke and went across to her casements that had stood open all night to the breezes of the hills and the Bay. The sun had risen and was slanting down on Purple Peak above the sleeping gables of Akaroa. Old Bossu would be smiling above them, she knew.

Below her, beyond the vivid colours of the garden, the green turf swept to the road and the tide came curling up to the verge at the other side of it. Gulls were wheeling above the bay, a *tui* twanging a woodland harp in the tallest *totara*, bees tumbling in and out of the roses; delphiniums raised indigo and azure and rose-pink spikes against the grey palings. Honeysuckle was almost unbearably sweet on the sun-drenched air, and the clove-scented pinks and stocks wafted their fragrance towards her ... the gillyflowers ... it was fitting the world should be so beautiful on this, Madame's big day.

Madame had decreed that Margot should be dressed in a soft rose-pink frock of her choosing. Apart from the length of its skirt, it might have been what Madame herself could have worn in this old-world garden when young Elise Rossignol had met for the first time her distant cousin, Louis, from Normandy.

Margot had scarcely seen Flora and Murdoch McTavish for days. They had had heavy bookings at the motels, naturally, and Margot had thought, in a vague way, that Flora looked harassed, but so much had crowded in on her, she had not enquired why. All Margot was worried about was that this excitement might not prove too much for Madame.

François had admitted he was impressed by the way his three children had entered into it all and how much they had done. 'One doesn't expect teenagers to be quite so thrilled over historical events—one develops this later in life—especially when they're not in direct descent—but they've got a real kick out of this.'

Margot knew what he meant. Tante Elise had no grandchildren. Her two sons had given their lives in World War Two. One had died in the Pacific War, and one on the beaches of his own Normandy on D-Day. Neither had been married. She had spoken of this to Margot. 'But François is as a son to me. And it is wonderful that he bears our name.'

Margot said teasingly to François, 'Don't you think that you must now admit Charlotte and Leonie have achieved poise? I think you're going to be very proud of them today. They've worked like Trojans. The way Leonie was determined to get every bit of dirt out of that iron filigree necklace that was dug out of the dump did her credit. I mean, it had been buried in fish refuse, a horrible task, but now, on its bed of white satin, no one would ever know.'

The Big Moment was upon them. The Bay was lined with cars, all the spare space of the homestead lanes used for parking, and the first guests were coming in through the gate and making their way to the seats on the side lawn. Thank heaven it had not rained ... they had been incredibly lucky ... just the lightest of zephyrs was stirring the whispering poplar leaves, and the bell-birds had got word that this was a day to remember and were chiming, chiming, from the honey-sweet red gums. The pungent scents of lavender and lemon

74

verbena rose from the narrow paths as the people brushed by, and a carpet of rose-petals from yesterday's breezes patterned the lawn. Broom blossomed in fountains of living gold and a bed of clarkia, as rosily pink as Margot's frock, with its old-fashioned bows of brown velvet, was a solid block of colour. Candytuft flowered in rainbow drifts, bougainvillea cascaded in magenta and coral and purple from the trees it had climbed, arches burgeoned with the huge trumpets of pink and white and orange bignonia, Madonna lilies bloomed in scented purity, making Margot realise Christmas really did come in summertime here, clematis and rambler roses outvied each other in prodigality of blooms, and everywhere were the gnarled old *ngaio* trees that Margot loved so much, with their tiny, daphne-like stars of flowers.

François appeared in the sitting-room of the cottage and said, 'We must go on to the dais now. The official cars are just drawing up. Jules, give Tante Elise your arm.'

It was a tribute to Madame that a gasp of admiration went up as Jules escorted her to the dais. Justine had asked her to be in costume dress for the occasion. Margot thought she had never seen anything so elegant, so perfect, as Madame Rossignol in the lavender brocade that had been her grandmother's wedding-gown. It had an inserted bodice of French embroidery and knots of silken roses caught it here and there in the over-skirts, and lace embroidered under-sleeves came right to her wrists. Her diamonds and opals blazed on her white hands. Justine had piled her luxuriant silver hair high, with combs, and had added a trace of rouge to the high cheekbones. Her brows, black as her eyes, gave character to her face and she rustled as she walked, smiling, acknowledging the folk she knew.

Justine's eyes were misty as she looked at her son. Jules was not in period dress, but he had gone to Christchurch and had come back with a soft black silk stock that with the narrow trousers of present-day fashion gave him an elegant air.

Charlotte in azure blue, and Leonie, in a golden frock that set off her coppery hair to perfection, followed them, then Justine turned to Margot and said, 'You're to walk between François and me.'

Margot said swiftly, 'I'll follow, Justine. This is for Rossignols, this procession.'

Justine's eyes flickered just a little. 'Please ... it would so gratify me to know that someone called Margot walked with me this day.'

She saw François's hand go out to Justine's in a quick gesture, then release it. Margot walked between them. The head of the tourist and publicity department brought the French Ambassador on to the dais, and there was spontaneous applause as he kissed Madame Rossignol's hand.

At the end of the official speeches, François got up to reply on Madame Rossignol's behalf and then said briefly that the success of the whole venture had depended on one person and one alone, Margot Chesterton, who had come to them quite by chance, on a tour of New Zealand, straight from the museum and antique world of London, had fallen in love with this little out-of-the-world place, and more for love than for money, had stayed to re-create a corner of yesterday, for today's people. Now she would speak to them herself.

Margot was glad of that faint zephyr from the Bay to cool her hot cheeks, but she spoke very naturally, then, warming to her subject, very enthusiastically of the heritage Banks' Peninsula had, of the future it would encompass, when it could become an idyllic and better-known beauty spot where jaded people could recapture a romantic past.

'You have, as Mona Tracey so beautifully put it in her poem on Akaroa, such kindly ghosts. I'm sure they come, because they must have been very happy here. We have put that poem into the souvenir booklet issued for today. I hope you'll let your imagination have full rein and get a little glimpse into the past ... that you too will see as Mona Tracey did, when at dusk in Akaroa Town

" ... the kindly ghosts move up and down."

that you will see

"If laughing lads and girls come yet
To dance a happy minuet;
If Grandpère muses still upon
The fortunes of Napoleon,
And Grand'mère, by the walnut tree,
Sits dreaming on her rosary?"'

76

She waved a hand towards the garden. 'I think you will find that:

> *"Still in gardens there are set*
> *The gillyflower, the mignonette,*
> *The rata on the oak tree hung—*
> *Ah, sweet it is ... so old, so young!*
> *The jonquil, mocking kowhai's gold—*
> *So blithe, so new! So triste, so old!"* '

It was just as Margot uttered the last line that she saw him. He was standing at the very back, with Flora and Murdoch.

Pierre Laveroux! And his face was the only face that did not wear a smile. His eyes were full of hostility and contempt.

She finished the line without pause or tremor. Then she stepped back as the crowd applauded. The head of the tourist and publicity department intimated that Madame would now unlock the door into the cottage museum and declare it open, and he added that as it would take time to get a crowd as large as this moving through Maison Rossignol, that say seventy-five per cent of them should take this moment to go up to the terraces at the new homestead, where refreshments would be served.

This had been an admirable communal effort. The three churches had decided their women's committees could handle this. They had baked all week—a splendid example of what a small town could do. Justine had been told she was to have no responsibility in this matter at all. She had to be free to meet people.

Madame wanted Margot at her side. 'If not,' she had said, 'I'll get mixed up in the periods. At eighty one's memory plays tricks.'

So Margot was not free to go to Pierre. No one had said he was coming home, not so much as a hint. And he'd be bound to say he had met her in London. And they would think it peculiar, even suspicious that she had never mentioned meeting him. Oh, how she wished she had! One half of her mind dealt automatically with everything she had to do and say, the other half was numbed, uneasy, waiting for the blow to fall. It even made her forget completely the fact that if her father lived in Christchurch, he might have come across, and someone might greet him by name in her hearing.

The French Ambassador said, 'How surprised I was, *mademoiselle*, to find you were not a Rossignol. You have so much the look of a Frenchwoman. I thought this is, for certain, their eldest daughter. What a coincidence that you should have come here, to this far-flung corner of the earth, where you were so much needed and to—to suit so well.' Margot flushed with pleasure, and embarrassment.

Someone else claimed the Ambassador's attention and Margot turned away to look directly into Pierre Laveroux's narrow dark eyes.

'Yes,' he said softly, but intensely, '*what* a coincidence! But we—you and I, *mademoiselle*, know different, do we not?'

Margot flushed deeper still, then the colour ebbed away. She said in a whisper, 'Oh, don't. He might think you were mimicking him.'

'Well, why not? Other people mimic. You, for instance ... you have so much the look of a Frenchwoman! Pah! And *how* you've disarmed them all!'

She said nothing.

He continued, still in that sarcastic tone, 'Imagine my surprise ... all the way from the motels to the museum Flora and Murdo sang the praises of this girl who was looking after Madame. A wonderful girl who had simply appeared out of the blue and had lost her heart to the Peninsula and had given Madame a new lease of life. A girl who didn't care for money, who was content with a wage that must be just a fraction of what she had commanded in London ... a girl who could cook omelettes like a Frenchwoman. Who was like a sister to Sharlie and Leo, who had proved a very natural horsewoman, so that by now she could jump fences almost as well as Jules ... oh, how I longed to meet this paragon!

'Though nobody likes paragons, really ... they induce inferiority complexes in other people ... but at least one can respect them, usually. They mostly have integrity, even if they are unbearably smug. And what happens? I join the crowd at the very moment this model of all the virtues is being introduced. I was here from the moment François said the success of this had depended upon one Margot Chesterton who had come to Akaroa *quite by chance*.

'Faugh! It makes me sick. But you and I, now, we know different, don't we, Miss Chesterton? We know you had a *very* important reason for coming here—an underhand

78

reason. And let me tell you I know full well it was because *I* opened my mouth too wide! I know why you're here. Do you think if these people knew what your real motive is in worming your way into their friendships, they'd have applauded you? But you won't get away with it. I'll see to that. We're a close-knit community here and I won't see you do any family any harm.

'Oh, you've pulled the wool over the Rossignols' eyes all right, and I can't blame them. After all, I too, fell for you in a big way, more fool me. But perhaps it will only tickle your vanity to know I was deeply hurt when you cleared out with only a note, an unfeeling note, to say goodbye. But when I found out later what a beastly little two-timing, double-crossing girl you were, I thought I'd had a lucky escape not to have got more deeply involved!'

He swung on his heel. Margot hated having to do it, but she just had to know. She clutched his arm. 'Mr. Laveroux, please tell me, does anyone here know we've met before?'

His lip curled. 'No, they do not. And they won't hear it from me. I don't particularly want any of them to know what a sucker I am. They'd think: "Poor Pierre ... he never learns!"'

CHAPTER FIVE

THE bubbling enthusiasm of the girls, that even spread itself to Jules, helped carry Margot through. And she was endlessly in demand for information. It was amazing how many people from as far south as Dunedin and as far north as Nelson, with long-ago ties with Akaroa, had come for the opening. It seemed as if a good many heirlooms were to find a permanent home here in Maison Rossignol, and in the Akaroa Museum. These folk felt it would preserve them for all time, and for the public.

At last it was all over and the guests had departed. Dinner was to be just a buffet meal tonight. It had all been prepared the day before. Just as well, for so many neighbours stayed on, to please François and Justine, that no table would have held them. They had put the huge extension table against a wall, arranged boxes on it in a tiered effect that was very pleasing and had spread snowy cloths on it. The delectable food thus made a pyramid of colour, and Leonie and Charlotte had decorated between the dishes with dainty trails of ferns and vines from the bush. The effect was charming. Curls of pink ham and Scotch eggs nestled in beds of crisp lettuce curls, tomato baskets splashed a vivid note, gherkins and sweet corn, celery and cheeses, crusty brown loaves of Justine's Irish soda bread, bowls of soused native trout sprinkled with parsley, and with mayonnaise and paprika; local crayfish flaked into a potato salad and tossed in French vinegar, curried savouries and pastries, pavlova cakes oozing strawberries and cream, all made the mouth water.

Margot, to her great surprise, found she was hungry. She sat down on a window-seat, with Dominic one side of her and Angela the other, carefully selecting for them dishes they wouldn't find too spiced for their delicate palates. She tucked a handkerchief under Angela's chin but decided wisely, lest she offend his manly five-year-old dignity, not to press one upon Dominic. She finally went off to the kitchen to get them some icecream and fresh red and yellow raspberries out of the fridge. When she came back Pierre was occupying the window-seat with them.

She kept her voice low. 'I'm quite sure you don't want to stay here, Mr. Laveroux. Perhaps you didn't realise I was looking after the nips?'

His voice was sardonic. 'Indeed I did. I got so tired of Frank and Marie singing your praises I left them and decided—since I'm so consumed with curiosity at the way everyone speaks of you—to come and find out exactly how you've done it. What your secret is.'

Margot busied herself getting the children settled with their bowls, then picked up Angela Rose and sat down with her on her knee. She said smoothly, 'Well, I must just leave you to find that out for yourself, mustn't I? I had a good start, of course. I just happened to have the qualifications that were needed to give this a start.'

His voice was hatefully suave. 'And that's all you intend ... just giving it a start? Then you'll go, leaving them in a quandary, seeing your being here has made them so ambitious. Better for them not to have done things on so grand a scale than to give it a boost like this, then let it flop!'

Margot dabbed at Angela's chin. 'I've by no means put a fixed time on my stay in Akaroa, Mr. Laveroux. I find

Akaroa's—er—charms almost inexhaustible. And I fail to see that it has anything to do with you.'

'How can you say that?'

'Because I work for the Rossignols, not for you.'

His eye glinted. 'Do you not realise how closely-knit we are here? Do ties have to be of blood? These people,' he touched Angela's golden crown fleetingly, 'are very dear to me. I don't want any fossickings of yours to harm them.'

Fossickings!

She said, breathlessly, 'What do you mean?'

'You know exactly what I mean. Your coming to Akaroa was for your own selfish ends, wasn't it? Admit it now?'

Margot spooned some cascading raspberry juice off the handkerchief, gave Angela back her spoon. 'I didn't consider it selfish. After all, it's my life——'

'Yes, it is. There are girls like that, I believe, who can think of nobody but themselves. Who come and go, leaving havoc behind them. It's so irresponsible to set off for the other side of the world like this to——'

Margot said, 'But how did you know? How did you find out? I mean you said this afternoon that——'

'That I got a shock when I found this paragon was none other than you? It wasn't true. I was trying you out. I thought you might admit then what you were here for, thought I might sting you into honesty. But apparently not.'

Anger replaced Margot's dismay. She was glad of this. She'd rather feel angry than afraid. 'I think you're being ridiculous! It would have been pretty stupid of me to tell anyone why I was here. Surely you can see that!'

'Oh, I can see it all right. You wouldn't have much chance of ferreting out things if people had known, would you? After all, we are a closely-knit community, and we protect each other.'

'Then why did you expect me to blurt it out to you today?'

'I thought the shock of seeing me would do it.'

Margot took a rein on her temper. The children might notice—even if they were speaking in low, intense voices and there was such a buzz of conversation it drowned them out.

She said intensely, 'I think anyone in my position would have taken the chance I did.'

He made a strange gesture. As if he despised her.

She said: 'And you haven't answered me. I asked how you

81

found out?' She swallowed. 'Only one person knew and I'm sure she——'

He said coolly, 'You mean Roxanne Gillespie, of course. Yes.'

Margot stared. 'But—but I asked her not to tell anyone. I——'

'She didn't really want to, but I was very insistent. I demanded the truth. Wanted to know where you were.'

'But she need not have told you. She promised. I didn't make any exceptions. I said no one was to know. Why should she tell you?'

He smiled wryly. 'Oh, there's always one reason that undermines a woman's resistance ... I persuaded her I was romantically interested in you. So I got the truth.'

Margot's voice was derisive. 'How despicable of you! But—but I've been gone so long and you've only now done anything about it. And was it necessary to do anything as drastic as coming all the way here?'

His sarcastic amusement bit. 'My dear Miss Chesterton, you aren't naïve enough to imagine for one instant I'm here because of you? Really, that's too funny! How important do you think you are?'

Margot said, 'That's what's so strange. It's none of——'

He broke in. 'It wasn't till I decided to come home, that I was needed here, that I began to make enquiries. I could laugh at myself now, of course, but after I got over my soreness at being ditched so suddenly with nothing but a curt note, and the need for returning to Partridge Hill cropped up, I had the quaint idea that I would like to see you on the way home, fly to Canada first. I even thought you might be glad to see me, that you might not have realised in England I was—rather serious. Have a laugh over that some time! I've laughed about it myself since. I asked Roxanne Gillespie for your address in Canada. When she was cagey I laid it on— the romantic angle. So she had to tell me why you had come to Akaroa. I was more glad than ever that I was coming home. It seemed to me the families here needed protection— and one family in particular.'

Margot's brain reeled. Then ... then *he* ... the only one so far ... actually knew the family her father was connected with. And—she looked at his set jaw—there was going to be no help for her here. He must know that if she revealed herself to her father it would bring unhappiness to him and

82

his. Well, there were no Nightingales here, but they must not be very far away. It must be the Christchurch Nightingales. A thought struck her. He had said *here*. Now did that mean at Rossignol Bay, or Akaroa Harbour in general? Probably Akaroa Harbour. It didn't narrow the limits for her.

She said, a little unsteadily by now, 'I'd have thought you'd have been sympathetic to my quest. And understanding. I mean, knowing what I am—you'd have thought it natural for me to do this. I mean, what's wrong with it? I'm not going to——'

She had not thought those laughing dark eyes could hold so much anger. 'What's wrong with it? Heavens, what's *right* with acquisitiveness? It boils down to money, doesn't it? It's absurd to say you aren't doing it for money. Nobody would believe that!'

Margot untied the handkerchief from Angela Rose's neck, wiped Dominic's mouth with it too and let them go.

She said quietly, 'Then I won't try to make you believe anything. What are you going to do? Warn them?'

'No. This is their supreme moment. I don't want to be the one to brush the gilt off the gingerbread. I don't want Madame to be disillusioned. I imagine it hurts just as much to be disillusioned about someone when you're very old as it does when you're very young. But I'll be here, and I'll keep an eye on you to see you do no damage.'

'You mean you'll block me in what I want to do—if you can?'

'I most certainly will.'

A thought struck her. 'You're here to stay then? It's not just a flying visit?'

'Is that what you hoped it might be? Why, in that case I'd have had to issue a warning. It seems you've missed out on a bit of news. Flora's uncle, an old bachelor who owned a farm in North Canterbury, has left it to her, on condition that she and Murdo take it up right away and work it themselves. Murdo wrote my father asking if he should get one of the firms to appoint a man, but with running motels too, it's awkward. Dad is picking up so well I wouldn't let them cut their year short, so I'm home for good.' He looked up. 'Here's François ... wanting either you or me. I'll leave you now. See you later, Miss Chesterton.'

François caught only the last sentence. He grinned. 'It won't be Miss Chesterton for long. Margot is one of the

83

family, Pierre. You can drop the formality here and now. I mean it. Margot, there's an old man over here who wants to tell you something about the whaling days. He's heard you're going to put out a catalogue. His grandfather was a whaler here. Pierre, you know old Jasper, come on over with us. He dearly loves an audience.'

Margot said quickly, 'I must get Charlotte. She's the one who should write up the stories. Excuse me, please, till I find her.'

At night Margot lay for a long time without sleep. Pierre Laveroux wasn't the only one to feel disillusioned. In the short time she had known him in England she had taken him for a kindly type. But he had no sympathy whatever for a solitary girl who had come seeking the father who didn't know she existed. He must have a streak of granite in him. Oddly enough this seemed to sting more than the knowledge that he thought it would upset her father to have a daughter suddenly appear in his life. That was quite ridiculous. What did Pierre Laveroux, evidently a man of hasty judgement and quick temper, matter to her?

In spite of that thought, an unexpected wave of regret scalded her. Why had she not taken Pierre Laveroux into her confidence? Why had she not asked him that idyllic day as they walked under the trees in Osterley Park? At least then he wouldn't have thought her deceitful about it, might even have helped her. But would he have done so? It hurt terribly to know he thought she wanted to find her father only for the material gain it might bring her. That meant her father was a wealthy man, or reasonably so. It meant Pierre thought she would claim from him. Perhaps that was how most people would view her search . . . trying to cash in.

Margot tossed and turned, her mind a jumble of chaotic thoughts. She really did whip herself for not having been frank with Pierre. Then common sense prevailed. That walk at Osterley he had simply been someone she was meeting for the second time. Practically a stranger, and she couldn't have told, on so brief an acquaintance, whether or not he was the type to keep a secret. Heavens, no—why, she'd worked with Roxanne for years, yet *she* had betrayed a trust. Margot decided it would be a long time before she wrote to her former employer again.

No, it would have been foolish. She would have taken the

risk of having him write to someone in Akaroa, 'What do you think? Met a girl the other day who turned out to be Francis Nightingale's daughter. Not that Francis knows that. She's his daughter by a former marriage that split up. Francis didn't even know a baby was on the way.' Oh no, you didn't tell strangers things like that. She had, after all, acted as wisely as she had known. And she had thought to come, trace her father, and, if it had appeared wiser to keep her secret, have departed, unknown.

Margot felt a little better. Then she thought of something comforting. If Pierre knew who her father was, then Francis Nightingale must have been here for some time. After all, how old would Pierre be? Thirty at the outside. Then he must have been only ten when her father was here, receiving that case of goods. So Francis must have stayed on for Pierre to remember him. Now she was almost sure Christchurch would yield some clue. And it was pretty certain one of these French families in Akaroa was related to him. Could it be through Angela's grandmother? Because Angela *was* like herself.

Well, she could not be away by herself in Christchurch for any length of time till the peak of the season was over, but after that she would try. Perhaps the electoral roll was the best bet.

By now she had asked the three clerics, the priest at St. Patrick's, the vicar at St. Peter's and the minister at Trinity, if any of them had a Nightingale on their baptismal registers and had sworn them to secrecy. She had simply said, 'I'd like to tell you why I'm asking, but I can't. But it would help me if you found one.' There had been no result. And that visitors' book at the Museum had yielded nothing, though it had a terrific crop of Francis's and François's.

Margot decided sleep was out of the question and that she'd get up and make herself a cup of tea. She thought she'd moved so silently that Madame would not have heard her, but suddenly she appeared, her silver plait hanging over her shoulder and tied with a blue ribbon, a delightfully feminine and frilly dressing-gown over an embroidered nightgown. Madame's eyes looked mischievous.

'I was so glad when I heard you moving about, *mignonne*. I think we have had too much excitement today, you and I? My brain is too active by far, and so is yours. So we will have a cup of tea together and talk, yes? And we will sleep in

85

tomorrow, an extra hour. We deserve it.'

Odd how company could dispel one's worries. Madame was in a relaxed mood and a reminiscent one. She talked of France and the journey she had made, with her husband and the boys, before the war. 'These are the things that remain. Someone said before we left that the enormous amount of money we were going to spend on the trip would go a long way towards setting the boys up in farms of their own if and when they married.

'I did think myself this might be so, but it meant so much to Louis to be able to show the boys where he had grown up and to present them to his brothers and aunts and uncles. And Philippe and Eugène so loved France. It was the happiest time of their lives. I think of it often and am glad in my memories, so glad for them that they had this carefree time. Because so soon they had to take on men's cares, men's responsibilities towards their world. And nothing can take from one the felicity of memories.'

Margot felt a warmth take possession of her. What did it matter if Pierre Laveroux despised her? Madame loved her enough to open up her heart to her, and needed Margot, needed her here in this house. She asked a leading question or two. Madame began speaking of Louis, of their courtship set in this very garden, and in diplomatic circles in Wellington. 'It made my father very happy indeed that the name of Rossignol would not die out. I took this to augur well for our lasting happiness. And it did. And even though we lost our sons, the sense of fulfilment was still there ... we had borne them. There is just something about experiencing birth-pangs and showing his offspring to your husband ... it is incomparable. Then we had François and Justine to carry on, and later, just before Louis died, small Jules, who is so like my husband. So very like. Odd how these family likenesses persist, generation after generation.'

It was only when Margot was back in bed, relaxed and ready now for sleep, that she wondered about that likeness ... she had taken it for granted that François Rossignol was the son of one of Madame's brothers—but she must have been an only child. So he must have been Louis's nephew. Though he had never mentioned France. Justine had, but then she had come from Ireland, and France was so close. What matter, anyway? Madame had married a distant cousin, so perhaps she'd only meant family likenesses can crop up in distant branches generations later. Indeed, people often saw likenesses where there were none. Wishful thinking. Because Charlotte and Leonie had said Jules was like Justine's brother. Margot fell asleep.

There was a lull in the stream of visitors to the museum, of course, because now was the busy commercial time before Christmas, busier even than in the Northern Hemisphere, because in addition to the festive preparations, summer holidays were upon them.

Schools were breaking up for the year and wouldn't resume till the beginning of February. Margot found herself going to all the break-up functions. Dominic Beaudonais insisted on Mard-o, as he called her, coming to the Convent Concert, Charlotte and Leonie took it for granted she'd go to the High School prize-giving and Justine asked her one day to go across with the girls and look at some flats they'd seen advertised in Christchurch.

'I can't. It's Aunt Rose's birthday—Marie's mother—and Marie is giving her a little tea-party, across in Akaroa. But this flat sounds ideal. I rang Bridget Connolly's mother to see if she could take them, but as luck would have it, she's going to the party too. But you'd have far more idea than the girls if this would suit. They're so taken up with the idea of flatting when they are at Teachers' College, they'd close with the first one they saw. This is being done up, it says, and will be ready by the middle of January. We could take it from then. Would you, Margot?'

Madame was going to the party too, so it suited everybody. François was driving them because he had business in Akaroa. At the last moment they discovered Margot's Mini had a flat battery.

François, investigating it, because he was doubtful any woman could decide what was wrong with a car, pronounced it flat indeed, said, 'I know,' and tore back to the house. He came back smiling.

'Pierre told me yesterday he was going to town this morning. He's on his way right now. I caught him just as he was leaving.'

Margot was dismayed. 'But it will take time, we might hold him up—one flat is in Merivale and one at upper Riccarton.'

Charlotte said, 'Don't be daft, Pierre won't mind. He'd better not. I cleaned out two motels for him three days ago.

Flora was busy packing. Besides, we could take taxis from the city if he's too busy, and Bridget will be thrilled.'

Margot said, 'Why?'

Leonie giggled. 'She's got a crush on Pierre. She thought he was terrific turning up for the school break-up. We don't get many men of that age. Gives the girls a lift.'

Margot suppressed a smile. But she'd been giving Pierre a wide berth. Justine came out to say goodbye, kissing all three girls.

'Quite one of the family, aren't you?' commented Pierre as they drove away, and only Margot knew it was meant to be offensive. 'Of course she is,' said Charlotte from the back seat. 'We can't imagine life without her now. She solved all our problems. Mum and Dad were terribly het-up about Tante Elise being on her own so much. And Tante thought it disturbed our homework routine to have one of us go down there every night.'

Pierre said, 'What's Leonie giggling away to herself in the back seat for? Leo, I can see you, and if you're up to any mischief you can come out with it now! I know you of old. I hope you haven't been plotting some ghastly schoolgirl prank with Bridget?'

He said to Margot, sitting beside him, 'Bridget is the biggest tomboy you ever met. Incidentally, I hope she's properly dressed for town. I don't remember ever seeing her in anything but jeans and huge sloppy jerseys. And you've got to make a good impression on a future landlady. Some have a prejudice against students.'

This had the effect of sending Leonie into more giggles. Margot thought it was probably at the thought of the surprise Bridget would get when Pierre turned up. Margot said, 'Yes, I thought it would have been nice if Tante Elise could have come today. She'd impress anyone. She has the air for it.'

'Oh well,' said Pierre sarcastically, 'you'll be a fair substitute. You seem to have the knack of impressing people, even to the extent of having flowery speeches made about you, so perhaps we'll not miss Madame, or should I too say Tante Elise? It seems to be the custom!'

Margot's cheeks showed a flake of pink. 'I always call her Madame,' she said tartly, 'even though she has asked me to call her Tante Elise. But I do sometimes speak of her as Tante Elise to the girls. I'm sorry if it doesn't please you.'

Charlotte's voice sounded bewildered. 'You two are quarrelling,' she accused, 'what's got into you? And what does it matter what she calls her? I didn't think people ever quarrelled the second time they met.'

Margot decided she'd better lighten the situation. She laughed. 'Perhaps it strikes like lightning. You know ... the opposite to love at first sight!'

Leonie had stopped giggling and was on the defensive. 'I don't believe it ever acts like that. I never heard of it before.'

Margot went wicked. It would serve Pierre right, the sardonic beast. 'Oh, but it does. Shakespeare even wrote about it. Don't you remember this bit ... "No sooner met than they looked; no sooner looked than they hated; no sooner hated than they snorted; no sooner snorted than they fell to fighting!"'

Charlotte said, 'I don't believe it. I just don't believe it!'

Pierre's voice was suave. 'You don't have to. Miss Chesterton has a very fertile imagination. I imagine she once played Rosalind in "As You Like It"—well, it's just too bad for her that at Lincoln College I once took the part of Orlando and a most bewitching Rosalind said to me "No sooner met than they looked; no sooner looked than they loved; no sooner loved than they sighed; no sooner sighed but they asked one another the reason."'

Margot giggled unrepentantly. 'I couldn't resist it.'

'Anyway,' said Leonie soulfully, 'what Pierre said sounds more like it.'

'Like what?' demanded Pierre.

'Like—like—like the sort of thing that ought to happen. We thought—ouch! Charlotte, keep your feet to yourself ... oh——' She stopped dead.

Pierre sighed. 'I've no idea what she's burbling about, have you, Miss Chesterton?'

She had. Only too well. She said calmly because she was going to scotch this from the start, 'I have a strong suspicion they've been matchmaking. Girls of this age are like that, I know. I was like it myself. We once tried to make a match between two of the teachers at our High School—with the result they detested each other from the word go. You happen to be the only bachelor in the Bay. I'm the only spinster. You have been warned, Mr. Laveroux.'

To her surprise he burst out laughing. They came into Akaroa and pulled up at the Connolly house in the Rue

Balguerie. Pierre blinked at the elegant figure waiting at the gate, a figure with ash-blonde hair swirled about the shoulders, and that wore a mulberry suit in softest shantung with a bright splash of turquoise blue in bracelet, bag and gloves.

'Is that a cousin of Bridget's?' he asked. 'I can see a certain resemblance. She really is something, isn't she?'

Leonie shrieked, 'Oh, Pierre, it's not your day. That *is* Bridget, you idiot! You poor man, you thought we'd all stood still the three years you were overseas ... though I admit, since at the break-up she was in a gym frock, you had some excuse.'

While Pierre recovered himself, Margot slipped out of the front seat and in with the girls. 'I want them to show me all the landmarks on the way, and name the trees,' she said sweetly, 'and I never believe in distracting the driver.' In the mirror she met Pierre's eyes, malicious amusement in hers, and defiance.

It was impossible to stay sombre in the presence of these three light-hearted young things. Bridget had the sense not to reveal she had a crush on Pierre and they all teased him mightily. Pierre lunched them well, said he'd take them out to see the flats if they could amuse themselves for an hour in town. He just had to see the firm and do some signing up.

The Riccarton flat proved too large and too expensive so they cut round Dean's Avenue and Harper Avenue towards Merivale. 'If this one is right, it would save you a lot of transport, girls, it's very close to the College.' He looked towards Hagley Park and spoke over his shoulder to Margot, without thinking, 'Doesn't that remind you of Osterley Park, Margot? Only it's high summer instead of early autumn.'

There was a stunned silence. If only he hadn't fixed the time she might have wriggled out of it by saying they'd discovered they both knew Osterley House!

Then Leonie said triumphantly, 'You knew each other in England! Don't deny it. I was right. People *don't* fight the moment they meet. Why didn't you tell us? Though I knew there was *something*.'

Pierre said, 'Little Miss Omniscience, in fact. What is it, Leonie? Second sight? Are you the seventh child of a seventh child and all that guff?'

Leonie said calmly, 'You're trying to sidetrack me. What happened? Did you have a lovers' tiff? And did Margot——'

Pierre said: 'Get those romantic notions right out of your

head, infant! I can almost hear the cogs fitting into each other. We did not have a lovers' tiff ... I did *not* chase her across the world. Why, when I first met Margot she was all but engaged to someone else, weren't you, Margot?'

His eyes, challenging, met hers in the mirror, mocking, demanding. Enjoying seeing her squirm. 'I was,' she said huskily, trying not to sound as if she'd been put on the spot. 'But I decided marriage wasn't for me. I don't like the male species enough for that. So I settled for travel.'

Charlotte came in with a most unexpected and mature grip of the situation. 'That'll be enough of this. Margot's life in England is her own affair. If she was almost engaged but broke it off and came out here to get over it, it was jolly lucky for us. Look, Margot, there's the old mill. This is a very old part of Christchurch, pre-Canterbury Pilgrim stage. The Deans brothers settled here before the Pilgrims came. Christchurch, isn't as old as Akaroa, of course,' she added with endearing and partisan pride. 'Pierre, if you're going over the Carlton Mill Bridge, I think you should cross right over into Bealey Avenue when the lights change and then turn left up Springfield Road to come into Merivale. Pananui Road is so busy you might wait ages for a turn.' Margot could have hugged her.

But Pierre was unkind. He didn't let it drop. He said sarcastically: 'I might have known you would romanticise it too. All in the style of a budding writer. She didn't have a broken heart. Somebody else did. *She* did the ditching. Blast that chap ... where does he think he's going? He's in the wrong lane.'

'That's easily done,' said Margot. 'You might do it yourself some day ... take a wrong turning, and have to rectify things. Just as I did. You ought to cultivate a little tolerance, Pierre—especially in driving.'

The flat was delightful. True, they had a setback when they found it was mainly unfurnished. The landlady said, 'Well, I don't usually let to students, but when your mother rang and I realised she was a Rossignol from the Bay, I was willing to let it to you. I like, as a rule, tenants for a longer period than students want. But it has all fitted carpets and linoleums and drapes.'

There was bright orange matting on the floor, pale green walls, a dear little porch big enough to take a couple of desks, and it had, of all things, a porthole each end. The woman smiled at their surprise. 'We built this on for my father and mother in their last years. Dad was an old salt and he went to Lyttelton and bought up some marine disposal stuff and incorporated it.'

The flat would get the sun all day, was small enough to be manageable, but big enough for comfort. Best of all it was surrounded by a charming garden with a tiny stream running through it on its way to join the Avon. They could just picture the girls sunning themselves on the bank behind a screen of rhododendrons and lilacs and a huge magnolia.

For once Pierre and Margot were at one. They both spoke at once. 'There's plenty of furniture to spare at the Bay.' Then Margot said, 'Would it be very expensive to get it over?'

Pierre shook his head. 'François has his truck, I've got mine, and if necessary I reckon Frank Beaudonais would bring his. There's a lot of more modern stuff that was cleared out of the cottage when the museum was first mooted, and we've got some in the big loft—brass bedsteads, single ones. I hear they've come in again. And you girls could cover a couple of the old chairs that are there. I expect your folk would have some bits and pieces too, Bridget.'

The landlady said the only thing was that she must let it to the first person who made a firm offer for it Margot said, 'Of course. I think I ought to ring Mr. Rossignol at Marie's mother's, and ask what he thinks. We don't want to miss it, but on the other hand, they thought it was furnished. Of course it's cheaper than a furnished flat. Could I use this phone?'

'It's not connected. I had it cut off when the last occupant left. But you can use mine, the front flat. Just below me.'

When she took Margot in, she discovered she had a visitor, her sister. 'Oh, hullo, Marion. I thought you weren't coming till tomorrow. This is Miss Chesterton, who wants to use the phone. Miss Chesterton, this is my sister, Mrs. Nightingale. Didn't Doug come with you?'

Mrs. Nightingale ... Mrs. Douglas Nightingale. Not Mrs. Francis Nightingale, but still——

The landlady, Mrs. Kealey, said, 'Oh, I'll be back in a moment. I just saw Miss Robertson from the other flat pass. I've a message for her.' And she left them.

Margot thought it was now or never. It was too good a chance to pass up. She said, 'I wonder if by any chance you happen to know a Mr. Francis Nightingale? I'm from London, and years ago, when I was quite small, in fact, my people knew a Mr. Francis Nightingale who was coming out here to look up relations. Have you ever heard of him?'

'No, I'm sorry, I haven't. I've lived here all my life and knew all the Nightingales in Christchurch, from kindergarten days on. So he can't have come here. Have you any idea which part of New Zealand he came to?'

Margot shook her head. 'No, none at all. It's not important, just that hearing your name recalled this man. Well, I'll ring Akaroa now. I've just lived there since October. Interesting place, isn't it? With so many people descended from the French.'

(If this woman's husband had French ancestors, she would probably say so.)

'Yes, we're very fond of it. We've had a couple of holidays there. Nice and peaceful.'

No lead there. And she thought she could forget about contacting the Christchurch Nightingales. Margot spoke to François and Justine and found them very much in favour. 'Bridget's mother is here, I'll ask her.' Justine came back to say pay a month's rent to secure it.

When they arrived back at the Bay, after dropping Bridget, Pierre said to Margot, 'You've never seen through the homestead at Partridge Hill, have you? Care to come up now?' His eyes issued a challenge. No doubt he had something to say.

As they drove to the green-shuttered house he said, 'You surprise me.'

'Do I?' She did not ask why and her tone relegated his opinion to the realms of no importance.

'Yes.' Then when she still didn't rise to the bait, he added, 'Don't you want to know why?'

'Not particularly, but I don't doubt you'll tell me just the same. You don't appear to be able to put a curb on your tongue whatever.'

She expected that would thrust home, but he chuckled in the most maddening way. 'I'm beginning to enjoy you as an antagonist, Margot Chesterton.'

'I'm sorry I can't say the same about you. You're seeking

to destroy my image in the eyes of those girls.'

'Let's say, rather, that I'm trying, without giving you away completely, to warn them that you're not the angel of sweetness and light you appear to all the inhabitants of this bemused bay.'

She said steadily, looking him straight in the eye, 'Well, you didn't succeed, did you? Charlotte flew to my defence. Which means she is now mature enough to trust her own judgement. I think all you did was to damage *your* image in her eyes. Those girls think—thought—the world of you. Serve you right if they're now thinking your years away haven't improved you. They didn't like your sarcasm. Better watch it. I'll do nothing to decry you—it's not my way. But you might do it yourself. They were disappointed in you. And—as far as my—my near engagement is concerned, it has nothing whatever to do with you!'

His lips thinned. 'It did have something to do with me once. I'm not in the habit of taking out other people's fiancées, believe me!'

Margot lost a little of her air of maddening calm. 'Pierre, did you meet Jonathan, then? He doesn't know I'm here, does he? I mean he might wonder——' She broke off.

His lip curled. 'Rest assured he did not. I doubt if he has ever heard of me. I heard of him through a chap I worked with. It so happened the two of us went off together on our concessions when we had three days off—to Zurich. So we spent the time together, and during that time he told me of a friend of his with another airline, who'd just been jilted. The word he used was inexplicable. Inexplicably jilted.' He looked at her, one eyebrow raised.

Margot said, 'But you *knew* why I came here. Roxanne told you.'

He shrugged. 'I didn't think it a strong enough reason. I can only suppose that the money in this lured you into pursuing it. I just don't understand it otherwise.'

Margot thought sadly that her father must be a very wealthy man then. She'd hoped he might be an ordinary working man, so he could never think she wanted to cash in. If he was really rich then she would never make herself known.

She said, with a hint of a break in her voice, 'It's not the money, it's the quest, the satisfaction. No, you don't understand, how could you? Something drives me.'

94

He stared at her and she thought his antagonism was replaced momentarily by puzzlement. Then he said, 'Well, if you feel driven, why on earth are you here wasting time? I don't get it.'

Margot said, 'I thought you, of all people, would understand why I linger. Over in England you suffered, you said, from *mal-du-pays*. Perhaps you'd think it foolish of me, since I wasn't born here, to say the Bay has cast a spell on me, that it drew me like a magnet. Although I came here with a definite purpose, I don't want to leave. Have you never heard Madame at the piano singing:

"*O, le beau ciel de Normandie,*
C'est le pays qui m'a donné le jour"?

singing it as if indeed the blue skies of Normandy were the skies she was born under. As if it was indeed the country that gave the light of day to her! You said yourself you had fallen in love with England, with the little villages outside the built-up areas, villages that remain so unspoiled ... some people even love them so much that when they come from, say, Australia or New Zealand, they stay for ever. Is it so strange then that I love Akaroa like that? I had only one thing in my mind when I came here, but now it doesn't seem quite so important. I just can't leave it yet.'

His brow darkened. 'I wonder if you know just how selfish that sounds. You're thinking of it solely from your standpoint. Can't you see it's an abominable type of selfishness to make yourself indispensable to people, then move on, leaving a gap that wasn't there before?'

'Had you not arrived to run it I doubt if the museum might have been completed on so ambitious a scale. Madame is delighted—she can stay on in her own home, be independent, gloat over her treasures and become a very important person in the eyes of the public, which must be very gratifying when you're eighty. Then, some day, when you're tired of the novelty of this ... when you've exhausted all the possibilities, and you long again for the elegance of the antique world in London, you'll be up and off, leaving a big gap in their lives. Just as you left a gap in Jonathan's, even if he did appear to be consoling himself very quickly, or so Tod told me in his last letter. Tod was glad.'

The colour surged into Margot's cheeks. She'd damned well tell him the truth about it—that she had done it for

Jonathan's own sake and had even concocted a stupid story about preferring a career so he should not feel guilty in any way, or suspect he had caused her great pain. She'd tell this condemnatory Pierre Laveroux! Then, providentially, she thought, her anger evaporated and common sense prevailed. If she did, then Pierre might tell this Tod. And through the airport grapevine, it would reach Jonathan and Betty, and it would make them unhappy. As it was, they probably rejoiced in the fact that things had turned out as they had done. No, better nobody should know. No risk that way.

So she said quickly, 'I'm glad he's consoling himself. That was what I hoped for.'

'And when you leave here you'll piously hope—even say— someone will turn up to take your place.'

Margot said quietly, 'Suppose we leave that now. I'm not considering moving on soon. All I want to do is to live life from day to day looking after Madame and Maison Rossignol and being made to feel a member of the family by Mr. Rossignol and Justine and Jules and the girls. It's enough for me.'

'Enough for you at present ... till the novelty wears off. Well, I just hope you don't leave emotional havoc behind you, that's all.' Something struck him. 'Don't you call him Frank or François? I mean, you call his wife by her Christian name.'

Margot lifted her shoulders and spread out her hands in a shrug. 'How should I know? Perhaps because he engaged me I look on him as my boss. But Justine asked me to. She and I——' She stopped.

He looked at her curiously. 'Go on. She and you——?'

Margot shook her head. 'No. You've jeered enough. You would certainly jeer at this, say it didn't mean a thing, and you would think it was just one more way in which I'd ingratiated myself with the Rossignols.'

'Why would I jeer?'

'Because it's rankly sentimental.'

Pierre snorted. 'What makes you think I despise sentiment? Why it was because I thought you didn't have enough womanly feeling in your make-up that I despised you? What——'

She said slowly, 'Justine didn't say it was to be a secret. Did you know that she had been married before? That she had a stillborn child who would have been called Margot?

You did?'

'Well, not that she would have been Margot. But I did know the rest.'

There was a silence, then Pierre said, 'You do me wrong if you think I would sneer at that. Well, come and have a look over. Mrs. Grendon comes every day, so it's much as Mother keeps it.'

Margot said, 'Is there any need to, now? I thought you'd just made this an excuse to get me alone so you could read me a lecture!'

'So I did, but you'd better take a look because if I know anything of the talkative Rossignols, they'll be bound to bombard you with questions. And you'd better be able to answer them. Be able to say, yes, you did see the rosewood escritoire, the walnut bureau, the wig-stand.'

Margot said, 'I should like to see those things. They are the things that interest me.'

'Of course. Yours is a professional interest.'

She said, 'You have a curious note in your voice—as if it held a double meaning. Why should you make it sound as if a professional interest were rather less respectable than an amateur one?'

'Oh, just that I mean an amateur loves the antique for its beauty alone or its associations. The professional weighs up its value, sees it in dollars and cents.'

Margot whipped round on him. 'This time you really have got me on the raw! That's about the most uninformed remark I've ever heard passed about the trade. Don't you realise if it were not for antique dealers, some priceless possessions would have been lost to the world of art and museums for ever? That apart from a very few, who are inclined to be unscrupulous, and see nothing but profit and loss, most dealers love handling this stuff?

'They take an exquisite pleasure in rescuing something from a junk-room, spending hours scrubbing, scraping, polishing and rejoicing in a thing of beauty. Don't you know it is wicked to have good Victorian mahogany stored in filthy old attics and to have cheap, mass-produced stuff in its place?

'A remark like yours is unintelligent. You haven't met many antique dealers, have you? No, of course not. Or you wouldn't have made such a sweeping statement. I've seen many a one forfeit a handsome profit for the sheer joy of

97

keeping some choice piece, or even buying a piece without real value because of its history. In Canada, I bought for more than its worth a curved, silky brush in very poor condition, because a Scots-Canadian said it had been brushing top-hats when Napoleon was off the coast of Scotland.

'And in London I bought a box for holding those ridiculous high collars they wore in the Prince Regent's days. But no doubt you'd sneer at the Prince Regent too ... think of him only as a fop, and a fat, self-indulgent fop at that, as having too many *amours* ... yet I bought that box as a memento of his times, because someone at St. Sepulchre's Church in London—opposite what used to be Newgate and is now the Old Bailey—told me that the Prince Regent was largely instrumental in abolishing public hangings. They used to erect seats for watching, right by the church! That started me off finding out his other good points. I found that later, as George the Fourth, he greatly encouraged Walter Scott. I—ohhhh!'

She gritted her teeth at him.

To her immense chagrin Pierre burst out laughing. She couldn't mistake something else ... there was actually admiration in his eyes. She widened her own in surprise.

He grinned, recognising her astonishment. 'I do so like people to get worked up over things ... to fly to the defence of the things they believe in, even if one gets withered in the blast. It's your ruling passion, isn't it, a love for the things of the past? Oh, how my fond mamma would like you. She sees everything through a haze of history. It's fantastic. It's also embarrassing going to church with her. She's singing madly away and suddenly she stops and goes into a rapturous trance and either sings the wrong word or the wrong line. Dad and I exchange exasperated looks over her head—we know her eye has wandered to the dates under the author's name. We're Presbyterian, as you probably know, and all our hymns have the author's life-span beneath.

'Then, as we drive home round the harbour, we get a sort of lecture. Mother says enthusiastically, "Did you notice that that magnificent hymn about beating the swords into ploughshares and the spears into pruning-hooks was written by a young man who died when he was only twenty-one, Michael Bruce? No wonder he wrote like that ... he was born the year after Prince Charlie was defeated at Culloden .. people's minds would still be scarred with the barbarity of war." Or we sing, "Jesus, Thou joy of loving hearts", and Mother asks us didn't we get a thrill out of singing a hymn by Bernard of Clairvaux—who was actually born in the reign of William Rufus?'

Margot chuckled. 'I'm afraid I do that too. Like the other day wandering in the cemetery. I was muttering to myself, "Fancy, he was born at the time of Waterloo, lived in the reigns of George the Third, Regency days, George the Fourth, William the Fourth and Queen Victoria, and died in the first year of Edward the Seventh's reign." Your mother certainly sounds a kindred spirit.'

Pierre's mouth twitched. 'You needn't sound so reluctant to admit it, so surprised. As if you couldn't possibly like anyone belonging to me.'

Margot gave him a steady look. 'I've never said—or thought—I didn't like you, Pierre. You loved the things I did, history and antiques and England. But you've disappointed me. You've been very scathing, have sat in judgement on me and my—my reason for coming here. You've even thought I was two-timing. You said so. But I knew, even when I was out with you, that I wasn't going to marry Jonathan.'

He looked at her curiously. 'I still think that was odd. But——?'

He obviously thought she might explain, but she wouldn't attempt to. He thought it a cold, stupid thing to do, to put a father before marriage, to set out to look for a father who didn't know you existed and who now had dearer ties of flesh and blood. That much Roxanne must have told him, but she couldn't have told him about Jonathan and Betty. And it mustn't get back to Jonathan that she had known.

Pierre said irritably, 'Don't go into a trance. Aren't you going to explain it?'

'No. You wouldn't understand that any more than you understand the love an antique dealer bears for the things of the past. You seem to think one should be fond only of the things that belong to one's personal past, to one's own family, and would deliberately block me in my attempts——'

She had been going to say, 'to find my own father.' But he broke in, harshly, 'I certainly will. I'll be quite frank in my opposition to that. I don't want anyone here to be deprived of what belongs to them.'

He must have seen the blank look that came into her eyes.

But what did that matter? He was so certain of his ground in this, it must mean the clue lay very near home. But how? But who?

She said desolately, 'Well, if you take up that attitude, I can do nothing about it.'

There was a silence between them. She had an idea he was at as much of a loss as she was herself. Then she roused. 'Well, that's that. We have stated our minds to each other, but for the Rossignols' sakes, and the fact that through their great kindness we must spend many evenings together, we must appear, outwardly at least, friendly. I too would not want them hurt. For heaven's sake show me what you want to show me and then we'll go back to them.'

CHAPTER SIX

PARTRIDGE HILL was beautiful. It had been built in a slightly more prosperous era than Maison Rossignol, which was natural, because Pierre Laveroux's ancestors had come out later than the original settlers, who had had to wrest a living off five acres of land each, who had had to wait a year before they could grow their own potatoes and corn; who had been very poorly treated by the promotion company of their own land and had arrived without livestock to find themselves in an area so isolated it was difficult to come by. They had had to rely on the fat wood pigeons in the bush, and fish, and when they did begin to produce, their only markets for this, for long enough, were the whaling ships that came to the Harbour for supplies.

But apart from that, it was evident the Laveroux's were certainly more supplied with this world's goods than Francis Rossignol, because some of this stuff was really good. 'Mother fancies herself as a collector,' said Pierre, supplying the answer even as she thought it, 'and she was left a bit of money by an old uncle. And put it into some of these things, mostly the non-French stuff. She used to go up to the antique sales in Auckland and Wellington.'

Margot appraised a Sheraton drum-top writing-desk ... she guessed it was worth eight hundred dollars ... and she stopped, entranced, in front of a hanging cabinet in walnut, with glazed doors and splayed sides. It had a swan-necked pediment top and one drawer and she guessed it would be about 1710. She touched it lovingly.

Some of the furniture had come direct from France and had been preserved by generations of women who had loved and cared for it. Flora McTavish had been delighted to be entrusted with it, and Pierre was fortunate in Mrs. Grendon, who did everything for him and his two single men, except cook their breakfasts. Pierre did that himself and piled the dishes into the dishwasher. No wonder he had flown home when Flora and Murdoch had to leave! You could not leave treasures like these to some unknown housewife.

She pushed the recent discussion to the back of her mind and revelled in her inspection. Pierre's room was very much a man's room, with the sturdiest of walnut furniture, not made in France but here, with the French styles excellently copied. It was a good blend of old and new, with a small exquisite table of heart of *totara* and another of Southland beech, beautifully grained.

There were silver cups, awarded by his tramping club, photos of Pierre from schooldays on, a picture that was a coloured photograph of a French village. He had taken it himself and sent it home when he had visited it, the village of his ancestors.

'They gave me a wonderful time. I had to brush up my French, of course, though Dad did insist I took it right through High School days, despite the fact I was lazy about languages and wanted to drop it. But I got a tutor in London. It gives one a great kick to meet one's kin, however distant.'

Margot turned her face away. Yet he would deny her just that. How maddening to think that he, and he alone, held the clues she sought. But she would never beg him to assist her. What she found out would be due to her own efforts. But he must be very sure it would be undesirable for her to reveal herself. Had her father then talked about the unhappiness he had had with his first wife? She felt a little sick. He was so sure that her appearance to her father would mean only discord. There must be some strong reason for this. He must know that the second wife would resent her bitterly. Well, she'd never tell, but she still wanted to find out who he was, to just see him. And of course she might not *want* to tell. She might not even *like* her father.

She picked up a small box, beautifully enamelled. 'I use it for my cuff-links,' Pierre said. 'Dad gave it to me on my twenty-first. He didn't know how old it was, just that it had been in his family for generations.'

Margot examined it closely. 'It's eighteenth-century. It's a patch-box. Did you know?'

He shook his head. 'You mean——?'

'They used it for keeping the patches they wore—the beauty-spots.'

Pierre laughed. 'Wasn't it the oddest fashion? Wonder what started it. I suppose someone saw another woman with very well-placed moles that enhanced the fairness of her skin and decided to help nature along.'

'Oh, it wasn't just the ladies. The occasional fop wore them, just as the men sometimes wore an earring.'

Pierre said, 'You'd have a head start on everyone else if you went to an eighteenth-century costume ball. You'd need only one patch ... you have one beside your mouth. You'd need one only on your cheekbone. Like that oval picture Madame has in the museum bedroom, a girl in blue with pale golden hair. Ever noticed how like Sharlie that picture is? And incidentally, when you get in a royal rage ... like before .. you look just like Sharlie in one of her tantrums. Ever seen her in one? She's so placid most of the time, but really loses her block when she gets properly upset.'

Margot ignored that. 'Yes, that likeness of Sharlie's to the picture is striking. I've always thought if we had a grand affair here, provided we could think up an occasion for it, that Charlotte would create a sensation if she appeared in a blue brocade gown like that.' She put the patch-box down. It was the same period and maker, though not the same design, as the snuff-box in her possession.

At that moment they heard Sharlie running up the stairs, calling out for them. 'Dinner's almost ready. I offered to come and get you.'

Pierre looked at her impatiently. 'Why belt up here? Is the phone out of order?'

Charlotte set her mouth. Hers was an ethereal type of beauty but when she did that, it squared her chin and she looked very like François. She said without hesitation, 'I thought this might need breaking up by now. I hope you didn't bring Margot over here to lecture her, Pierre. I don't want you upsetting her.'

Margot knew a lift of the heart. Dear Charlotte! Margot had never had anyone to fight her battles for her before.

She said quickly, 'Oh, Charlotte, it's sweet of you, but don't quarrel with Pierre on my account. It's nothing—just that Pierre and I rubbed each other up the wrong way in England. It happens sometimes. We got off on the wrong foot. But we've now talked it out. It was a good idea for Pierre to create the opportunity. Just a misunderstanding. We understand each other very well now. No need for anyone to be partisan. We were both to blame. And Pierre has given me a wonderful half-hour examining the family treasures.'

Nevertheless she expected Pierre to look put out because definitely Charlotte had put him in the wrong. That would make anyone mad. But he ruffled her hair as a brother might. 'Good for you, Sharlie. I like people to take up the cudgels for other folk. And I like the way you've matured. I also like your extreme frankness.'

His eye flickered to Margot's and she got the message. He thinks I am secretive, she said to herself. Well, so I am in this one thing. And anyway, who cared for Pierre Laveroux's opinion?

But she did.

Ever since his return Pierre had dined at night with the Rossignols, for Mrs. Grendon had to be home for her own family, and Pierre's men cooked their own in their quarters. It annoyed Margot to find that though the days were full of singing happiness she looked forward most of all to the evenings.

Justine was always keen for Pierre to stay on, saying to Margot she admired him so much for cutting short his time in England and tackling what was a very big job. 'His heart has always been more in the tourist trade than farming, though he's a good farmer and all, went to Lincoln College and very much improved methods at Partridge Hill the year or two before he went overseas. That was his own idea, a sort of investment for the years ahead ... to visit all the resorts of Europe and return to put into practice here what he things would suit Akaroa best. But he must miss that huge staff at London Airport, and with you here as well as the children, I feel he gets some young company.'

Margot couldn't help enjoying those evenings. She felt

lulled into contentment and the search for her father was something she seemed to be getting more and more reluctant to pursue. It had brought her here where she had known more happiness than ever before. Her existence with Aunt Ruth and Uncle Noel had been very pleasant indeed, but this—oh, this was different. In this lull before Christmas and the January tourist trade, the museum work was very light and the girls included Margot in everything, from gathering shells and fishing to studying birds.

But the evenings were loveliest of all, from after dinner, when the sunset stained the harbour with the living fires of coral, amber and crimson, till nearly midnight, when the moon had paled to silver and the Southern Cross shone above the horizon.

They watched what programmes they were interested in on TV, but they were all great readers and talkers and the bookshelves at the homestead were full of riches. Jules had a special affinity with Madame. He was always talking French history with her. They were asking Margot about Madame Tussaud's one night. Jules asked if she liked it.

Margot hesitated. 'It ties in, mainly, with my work, so yes, I do. Only some tableaux bring too vividly before one the horrors of the past to say one likes it. Yet I've visited it many times. What always gets me is the fact that Madame Tussaud, as a very young woman, and after being closely associated with the Royal Family as Art Tutor to Louis the Sixteenth's sister, was forced to model death masks of Louis, and later Marie Antoinette, people she had known and loved, from their severed heads. It brings that side of history too close for mental comfort, as does any cruelty. Oh, perhaps it's silly to let it become too real to one.'

Madame said softly, 'But easy to understand, *mignonne*, I know. I felt much the same once when I read something Burke once said. It got me by the throat, even if my people were probably Republicans. Jules, would you pass over that Everyman's Dictionary of Quotations from the end of the shelf near the fireplace? That is where I saw it.

'Listen, children. Burke says : "It is now sixteen or seventeen years since I saw the Queen of France, then the Dauphine, at Versailles; and surely never lighted on this orb, which she hardly seemed to touch, a more delightful vision. I saw her just above the horizon, decorating and cheering the elevated sphere she just began to move in—glittering like the morning star, full of life, and splendour, and joy ... Little did I dream that I should have lived to see such disasters fallen upon her in a nation of gallant men, in a nation of men of honour and of cavaliers. I thought ten thousand swords must have leaped from their scabbards to avenge even a look that threatened her with insult. But the age of chivalry is gone. That of sophisters, economists, and calculators has succeeded." '

They were all silent for a moment. Then Madame Rossignol said, 'And all that pride and *joie de vivre* was brought so low she even apologised for treading on the toe of her executioner, Sanson, as she hastened up the steps of the guillotine, in order to get it over as soon as possible.'

In the half-light Margot saw a tear gleam in Madame's eye and felt immeasurably moved. There must be something in racial memories. These people here, who had so identified themselves as New Zealanders, in whose blood mingled English, Irish and other races, could still sit here in the twilight and dream of France.

It was like that with Pierre, with a very mixed heritage. Yet he had such an endearing affection for the British Royal Family. 'It holds us together,' he said once. 'Our loyalties are constant. Elections cannot change our Head of State. The Queen is there, ours, the Head of our Family, whatever our political affiliations may be.'

Oh, how Margot wished there wasn't so much to like, to admire in Pierre Laveroux! So much that was warm-hearted, impulsive, generous ... above all, kindred in spirit, loving all the things she herself loved so passionately ... the beauty of the world about them, this small world locked in by the hills of the Peninsula, the larger world overseas, the same sort of ancestry ... yet to her own quest he was unfeeling. Indomitable in his opposition.

Margot got up and moved to the bookcase. She must stop dreaming. She picked up Buick's *The French At Akaroa* and said, 'I read something here the other day that pleased me. Listen. Evidently Lord Lyttelton's son visited here with his father in 1868, walking and riding over the hills from Pigeon Bay, and the beauty of the harbour so impressed him that twenty years later he declared that if ever he should be crossed in love he would return to Akaroa to repair the damage. That's a great tribute to Akaroa.'

She looked up to find Pierre's eyes upon her and she

didn't understand at all the look in them.

He said abruptly, 'When did you first read that? Was it before you left England?'

Margot's lids flickered over the pansy-brown eyes, then she conquered her hesitation and said firmly, if lightly, 'How could I? I never saw this book in my life till I found it here. But I thought that was charming. I wonder if he did return ... even if not because of a broken heart.'

Pierre said, 'A descendant of his did, anyway, whether a direct descendant of his or not, I'm not quite sure. Returned as our Governor-General. A much loved Governor-General, Lord Cobham.'

Charlotte said, her eyes on Pierre, in such a way that her mother looked at her curiously, 'But of course, that depends. About coming back here if you've been crossed in love. I've known it act the other way. People leaving here.'

Justine said sharply, 'Charlotte, that's too personal by far. It's one thing and all to discuss abstract things, and another entirely, so it is, to be specific. Pierre, you will excuse my daughter, I hope.'

Margot was startled and looked from one to the other. Oddly enough Charlotte seemed completely undisturbed by this rebuke from her mother. Her eyes held Pierre's and for the first time, since their colouring was so different, Charlotte looked like Madame. Her eyes, blue as the harbour waters, held a little of the native shrewdness of Madame's black ones.

Margot expected Pierre to make mincemeat of her, but he didn't. He grinned, the lines grooved in his thin cheeks deepening, 'Leave her alone, Justine. Sharlie had always been the direct one of the family. You've been dying to know if fresh scenes and other interests worked, haven't you? The answer is yes, my little sister-in-all-but-fact. I went slap-bang into Lisette at Harewood Airport when I flew in, and couldn't have cared less. She's a feather-brain. Honestly, despite marriage and a youngster, if you shook her, she'd rattle. She's completely immature. I must have had no discrimination whatever. That satisfy you, Sharlie?'

'Mostly.' Sharlie grinned, Pierre's lack of resentment giving her courage.

He sighed in brotherly fashion. 'What else do you want to know?'

Even Leonie was looking apprehensively at Charlotte. But

that one had no inhibitions. 'I'd like to know was it when you saw her you knew, or——'

Pierre's dark eyes danced. They were like narrow slits when he laughed. 'Long before that, Sharlie. But I won't give you chapter and verse ... or, more correctly, the time and the hour.'

Justine said, 'I should just think not! Let's change the subject. I hardly know what to make of my own daughter.'

Pierre spread his hands out in a gesture that was wholly French, his shoulders up. 'Justine, you're not to take Sharlie to task. Half the trouble in this world comes from people not being open.' Margot flinched inwardly but would not look at him. He added easily, 'And if we can't be frank in this intimate little family circle, when could we be? Because it *is* a family circle, isn't it? We live so closely here at the Bay. And I think it would please our forebears. It was all one property once, Margot. And Dad told me once that when the first Rossignol had to sell out to my great-grandfather, a comparative newcomer, there was no resentment.'

'Which is as it should be,' said Madame. 'It makes a small community very unhappy when landowners quarrel over boundaries or straying stock. My grandfather said once that when Eugène Laveroux took that shoulder of the hill off him, it solved a great financial crisis for him. Just as Margot's coming solved the problem of Maison Rossignol and made it possible for it to be preserved fittingly. And please, children, let no one say what a coincidence that she—with her specialised training—should come here. Some things are coincidental, I know full well after a generation of living, but other things are arranged by *le bon Dieu*. I *know*. This is one of those.'

François Rossignol knocked out his pipe in the little silence that followed and looked across at his wife. 'Justine would say amen to that, Tante.'

Margot's smile was misty. 'Thank you, Mr. Rossignol. It means a lot to be included in a family like this, especially when you have no one of your own. Oh, sorry, that sounds all pathetic and Little Orphan Annie-ish. I didn't mean to sound that way. Since coming here I've quite forgotten to be sorry for myself on that score.'

And even though she looked for a derisive curl to Pierre's mouth, she did not find it. He even smiled back at her, the first unguarded smile he had given her in New Zealand. Perhaps that was his way of making amends.

He said crisply, 'Well, from now on the pace is going to be hectic. Thank heaven I've such good lads on the farm, and also that the bookings for Christmas are long-term ones. Of course here we tend to get that sort. People come to stay. Out on the main roads they get a lot of fly-by-nighters. No one here is booked for less than three weeks.'

'No wonder,' said Margot. 'Rossignol Bay casts a spell.'

How strange to be celebrating Christmas in high summer ... but she was getting used to the idea, just as she'd got used to the sun going round to the north for most of the day, and the cold weather coming up from the south, sweeping over Mount Bossu, who hunched his shoulders to the Antarctic storms and faced the sun all day.

Leonie loved to hear of the differences. She said to Margot, 'In June, over there, under the rhododendrons, will come up what you will think of as Christmas roses—so Dad said—and what we call winter roses.'

Yes, of course, for here on Christmas morning Bourbon roses nodded in at her sill and great lumbering, gold-dusted bees clambered in and out of a score of exotic-looking creepers such as Margot had seen before only in the South of France and Italy.

Justine was in her element, cooking, had been for days. Margot was glad there was a cooling east breeze coming in through the Heads, for the early morning, still and breathless, had given promise of the same almost heat-wave conditions of Christmas Eve, and she wondered how they would have done justice to the huge puddings Justine had prepared, had it been as hot.

Mrs. Grendon had asked the two farm lads to her house for the midday dinner, so there was just the Rossignol family and Pierre and Margot.

At eleven-thirty Charlotte arrived. She whisked Margot off by herself and whispered urgently, 'Pierre has put something on the tree for you. Thought I'd better tell you. You didn't seem to be buying him anything that day we did our shopping in Christchurch. Or——'

Margot bit her lip. 'I didn't. Oh dear, now what——'

Charlotte said, 'We got a lot of little presents for Dad. He said not long ago that no big present is half the fun a Christmas stocking is, so just for fun, Leonie and I made a huge one out of some net, and filled it up. There are hankies and tie-pins and socks and ties and cuff-links. Would you like me to sneak something out? I can easily snip the gold thread and sew it up again.'

Margot said, 'That's sweet of you, Charlotte, but I've an idea. I've something I picked up in Quebec. It would almost match that patch-box he keeps his cuff-links in. Same period, how would that be?'

'Oh, wonderful. That would really appeal to him. You two are okay now, aren't you? By the way, I swore Leonie and Bridget to secrecy that you'd ever met. In case anyone thought it peculiar, but if you two had been at cross-purposes over there, it was only natural you didn't say you'd met him—especially as you didn't know he was coming home. Wrap it up and I'll tie it on the tree, and he'll never know he was an afterthought. I'd better not waste time, I'm supposed to be making the sauces for the puddings—butterscotch and caramel. Wrap it up right away, Margot.'

Charlotte whistled when she saw it. 'It certainly is beautiful. Had you wanted to keep it for yourself?'

'No, in my trade we just can't resist buying. Nothing personal about that.' It wasn't quite true. She had bought it because it was the same period, though a different design, from that snuff-box she had found among her aunt's things. She knew a queer sort of painful pleasure in parting with it. But because it was for Pierre—she shut her mind to the implications of that ... enough, Margot, enough. He doesn't even want you here.

Charlotte rushed back. 'Oh, Margot, what are you wearing?'

Girls Charlotte's age were always intensely interested in clothes. 'That cream shantung, I thought. The sleeveless one.'

'Oh, do wear that frock Tante Elise made you buy—the bluey-green one. And tie back your hair with green chiffon. You will? Good. Dad said the other night how much it suited you. Bye-bye,' and she was gone.

As Margot and Madame came up the terrace steps and into the wide hall, François Rossignol appeared and kissed them both. Madame looked up and said, 'Oh, the mistletoe, of course,' kissing him back.

Margot, looking up, said, 'Mistletoe? It's red!'

They all came into the hall then, laughing. François, one

arm about Margot's shoulders, hugged her. 'It's native mistletoe—always red. A lot of people mistake it for *rata*.'

Then Margot was surrounded, but when Pierre bent his head, she turned a cool cheek to his lips.

When they finished the superb dinner and washed up, they all came into François's den where the Christmas tree stood in all its splendour. 'It's traditional by now,' said François, 'not to have this till after dinner. When the kids were small we used to give them stockings at the end of their beds, full of small things, then had this after dinner, mainly to keep them occupied for an hour or two after the heavy meal, so they weren't pestering us to go down to bathe before their meal was digested. And it has persisted, even though they have more sense now.'

Leonie giggled. 'Dad told us the other day we had matured since Margot arrived. He thinks she's had an effect upon us, that she's just enough older for us to respect her and young enough for us to feel she's one of us.'

François groaned. 'This habit of repeating conversations is the most humiliating I know!' He caught Margot's eye and grinned. 'And I'm darned if I know why I said it ... Pierre, Margot is as big a limb as any of them. The other day I was going up the gully and thought I heard a noise above my head and here's Margot, bless my soul, in the kids' old tree-house, all by herself.'

She laughed. 'It was an irresistible temptation. I've always wanted a tree-house.'

François said, 'Let's get at these presents, I'm getting impatient myself. Especially for that outsize stocking with my name on it.'

Leonie beamed on him. 'That's the way it ought to be. When you stop getting impatient about opening presents, we'll know you're getting old, *mon père*. Here, you can open one of yours first, catch this, you great baby.'

It was Margot's present to him, a book on trout fishing. François's eyes began to sparkle. Charlotte snatched it off him. 'You needn't think you're going to get immersed in that, pet. You can maintain your interest in all the other parcels to the bitter end, then we'll let you have it.'

Margot couldn't remember a more happy Christmastide; even though her aunt and uncle had been so good to her, there was nothing to compare with a larger family at such times.

Pierre got a rapturous hug from Sharlie, who was starry-eyed over his package of blank paper, carbons, folders and a new typewriter ribbon, given, as his card said, to inspire her to get cracking on the family history.

Leonie said, 'Me, I'm not one for all this embracing, Pierre, but thanks a million for this book on New Zealand birds. It must have set you back quite a packet with those wonderful plates in colour. Oh, thank you, Jules ... the one on trees to match it! Oh, what bliss!'

He had a rosary he had bought in France for Madame, whose eyes softened with pleasure, and some Irish linen for Justine.

Margot felt tears rise when Justine tossed over three identical boxes tied with coloured ribbons ... 'For my three girls ... I bought my presents in bulk, by the quarter dozen; it's cheaper that way.'

Three negligées, in softest gauzy nylon, blue for Sharlie, green for Leonie, with her red hair and green eyes, rose-pink for Margot. Margot looked down on the card and knew what pleasure Justine had known to be able to inscribe on a card, 'Merry Christmas, Margot.' Something she must have dreamed of twenty-six years ago, when her young first husband was alive, and their baby expected.

Margot handed her own gift to Justine ... something she had scoured Christchurch antique shops for, to remind her of Ireland ... a bit of Waterford glass. Then she had the exquisite pleasure of seeing Madame bend over a tiny package. This had come by air. Margot had broken her vow not to write to Roxanne, because she had so longed to buy this for Madame ... a miniature of Marie Antoinette. Madame, for once, was speechless. After she had taken out a lacy handkerchief and blown her nose fiercely, she said, 'Chérie ... forgive my sentimentality, but it is so sweet ... and quite valuable ... and I, too, am still a child about receiving presents. Tell me, was this the small registered packet that came by air last week?'

Margot nodded, well pleased, and was conscious that Pierre had picked up her gift to him. But he paused and tossed neatly into Margot's lap, a package about the same size. She was conscious her colour had heightened and bent over unwrapping it. There lay the most beautiful *paua*-shell necklace she had ever seen, an iridescent star, rimmed in silver and hanging from a slender silver chain. It sparkled up at her, with all the colours of the ever-changing ocean, blues, greens, mother-of-pearl, amethyst, rose.

François said, 'Oh, how perfect for your frock, Margot,' and came behind her to fasten it on. Charlotte beamed. 'That was my doing. She'd been going to wear her cream shantung, but I said wear this and got away before she could ask why. Wasn't it clever of me?'

'Very clever, Sharlie,' said Pierre, and stripped off the wrapping of his own package. They all crowded round to look. Sharlie said, delightedly, 'See ... it's the same period as the patch-box you have. French, eighteenth-century. Wasn't it clever of Margot to have one so near a match?'

'Very clever,' said Pierre again, and added, 'In fact, I think it's exquisite,' and Margot thought none but she would sense that dry, less-than-wholehearted undertone to his voice. It chilled her to the marrow. Suddenly she felt foolish, as if she had overdone the gift to a comparative stranger. He was embarrassed by what he knew was a valuable gift. She knew a burning humiliation.

Fortunately no one noticed anything and in the rest of the present-giving and the ooohing and aaahing, it was lost sight of, but remained with Margot.

François announced that they could now bathe and they pelted off to change. It wasn't till long after the evening meal that she had a moment alone with Pierre. They had sat out on the terrace in the cool of the evening, watching the sun set behind the hills where the road to Christchurch wound its way, most of them drowsily content with the happiness of the day. Suddenly the amber and smoky rose of the translucent clouds deepened to the amethysts and purples of the dusk, and over Purple Peak, above the lights of Akaroa across the water, glowed one great silver star.

Justine said, 'And Lo, there was a Star in the East where the Infant Redeemer was laid.' She touched François on the shoulder. 'Darling, let's light up. There's a Christmas programme on TV I'd like us to see.'

Margot had been sitting on the steps, her arms clasped about her knees, dreamily watching the lovely contour of the over-harbour hills against a sky where a trace of after-glow still lingered, and finding the heavy scent of the big white trumpets of the daturas almost intoxicatingly sweet.

She heard Pierre's voice, 'Sharlie, we'll be in in a moment. I'm taking Margot for a walk.'

112

She stiffened and pulled a wry face to herself over the unconcealed eager agreement in Sharlie's voice. What an idiot Pierre was! He knew how romantic those two girls were. And she was pretty sure it wasn't pleasant dalliance in the moonlight Pierre was after. She was practically certain he was going to say he couldn't accept such an expensive present. Well, if he did, if he just did, she would jolly well hand back that *paua* necklace. That hadn't been exactly cheap.

She stood up and Pierre's hand came under her elbow to assist her down the steep terrace steps that were fragrant with rosemary and lavender, crushed with the many feet that had sped up and down them that day.

He took her, in silence, through to Madame's garden, and there, beside the chubby little stone cherub with the blob of moss on its nose, he turned her to face him.

'Where did you get it, Margot?' he asked. 'The French snuff-box?'

She blinked. 'Where did I get it? What does that matter? I thought you were going to go for me because you thought I'd—thought I'd overdone things, that it was a bit presuming for a new acquaintance to make such a present—that——'

He brushed her words aside with a gesture. 'Of course it matters where you got it from. I have strong views on this. I——'

In turn she interrupted him. 'It was only because I didn't have anything to give you. Sharlie came running down in a great state because she'd seen you tie something for me on the tree and she was sure I didn't have anything for you. She thought I'd be embarrassed and she even offered to get something out of her father's stocking. I suddenly realised that the snuff-box I had—among other things—was exactly the same period, if not the decoration, as your patch-box. I didn't mean to be ostentatious.'

His grip tightened. 'What on earth are you talking about? I didn't think it ostentatious. I thought it charming. It's something I'd love to possess ... but not at the expense of other people.'

Margot freed herself and put a hand up to her head. 'You've got me puzzled, Pierre Laveroux. What do you mean? At the expense of other people? It was only at *my* expense. And you yourself bought me a present which wasn't exactly trifling. But *I* didn't seek you out and thrust it back at you. So what——'

His expression, in the moonlight, was exceedingly grim. 'What do I mean? You know damned well what I mean. I don't approve of the antiques that belong to Akaroa being bought and sent away. You said *among other things.* How much have you sent away? How much stuff have you promised Roxanne? You're taking advantage of people who want cash and don't know how valuable their things are. And I—mutt that I am—thought Akaroa had cast such a spell on you, you wouldn't be tempted to bargain for other people's treasures. You can tell me which family you got this from and I'll buy it back from you and return it to them!'

Margot gasped. 'Buy it back? Return it? Pierre Laveroux, you must be clean mad! I bought the wretched thing in Quebec. Not off anyone—just in a shop. I paid full price for it. Because I liked it. Because it's exactly the same period and workmanship of one in my own possession that belonged—I think—to my own family. I bought it out of sheer sentiment, and was foolish enough to think you'd like it better than the tie Sharlie would have filched from her father's gifts for me to give you. I've never bargained nor bought a single antique here to send to Roxanne. In fact, when I knew Roxanne had betrayed my secret I didn't even mean to write her again, only I wanted that miniature from her for Madame. I've no intention of snapping up any family treasures here. I think every antique that is here should stay in the Southern Hemisphere.

'I've done a bit of prospecting, yes ... but only for the museum, only because people have invited me into their homes, asked my opinion on values and dates ... I've even said to some who have offered stuff for the museum to lend it, not donate it, that I'd mark it with their names on the cards and enter up addresses and particulars in the records I'm compiling. Because here, where history is so recent, I feel these things belong in their own setting. Same as I said to Mrs. Kiwaka, that we would only have the loan of that wonderful greenstone *mere* she offered for the Maori section. How dare you think I've been taking advantage of the wonderful friendship that's been shown me here by everyone except you!'

She was annoyed to hear her voice break as she uttered the last word, and because she'd rather have him put it down to

114

temper than hurt feelings, she stamped her foot furiously upon the flagging.

She got Pierre's foot and the next moment he'd said 'Ouch!' and was dancing round in a circle.

Margot's eyes had lost their pansy-softness and were blazing and she said between her teeth, 'Serves you right ... and if you dare come near me I'll do it again. How dare you think those things about me! How——'

She didn't get any further. Pierre seized her. He'd stopped groaning and was spluttering with laughter, and it made her madder still. 'Oh, Margot, Margot, stop it! I'll apologise ... I'll grovel ... I will, truly. I'd beg forgiveness on my knees but for the fact that if I did, you vixen, in your present mood you'd snatch that cherub off his pedestal and bash it down on my repentant head!' He sobered up and said, 'Margot, I'm an idiot ... I jumped to conclusions. I'm touchy on the subject. Years ago, when my grandmother was alive, but old and not very much with it, she was taken advantage of by an unscrupulous dealer and we lost a lot of our dearest heirlooms. I'm sorry, I suppose I looked for it ... the signs of deceit in you.

'I was sore when you left England without a chance for me to say goodbye to you or get an address from you. And mad clean through when I arrived and thought you'd probably skim the cream of our antiques. I'm very keen on seeing that not only the French stuff, but also the old Colonial stuff, or the German and English heirlooms, don't go overseas. So I jumped to the conclusion, because that snuff-box was French, that you'd bought it from someone here, in Akaroa. I'm sorry.'

She said, 'All right, you're sorry. But you ought to watch that tendency to judge others, to know what's best for them, to be so sure that one would do harm in a community; that——'

His hands came to her shoulders, and he wasn't listening any more. He was laughing. 'Oh, Margot, Margot, it's Christmas ... you know, peace on earth and goodwill to men. Don't let's quarrel, not in this lovely garden, built for romance. This is where Louis Rossignol first met his Elise ... what a pity to waste the setting quarrelling.'

Margot said furiously, 'You forced that quarrelling on me ... you brought me here purposely to bawl me out. Pierre! Let me go—I don't *want* to be kissed!'

He was too quick for her, the narrow eyes were dancing, his grip merciless. She could see the stars reflected in those eyes like infinitesimal points of light. Then his mouth came down on hers.

The spiciness of the gillyflowers came up to her, clove-scented and amorous, and the daturas were as cloying to the senses as an Eastern garden. She felt herself lulled into acquiescence, then suddenly she struggled and was instantly set free.

Pierre caught her hand, turned her round. 'You don't need to run, Margot. Yes, we'll go in. But don't look so mad, the family won't expect to see you looking like that, and I'd hate to risk them thinking I've done anything to upset their darling.'

She said, through her teeth, 'It will be very hard to conceal how I feel about you. But I will not spoil the accord of this Christmas day for the family here. So we will endeavour to go in looking as if we've been out for a friendly stroll.'

He laughed in the most maddening way. 'That will be easy. Your lipstick will be smudged. Sharlie and Leonie will be pleased!'

Margot uttered a sound of pure rage. 'Pierre, you're encouraging those girls, and heaven knows they don't need encouragement! Girls of that age are incurably romantic and more match-making than any mamma. It could be horribly embarrassing.'

He chuckled. 'Is that why you're treating me like this? Does it sort of goad you in the opposite direction? To put Sharlie and Leo off you pretend you don't like me.'

'Pretend! Believe me, I don't need to pretend. I could have liked you very well indeed—we have kindred tastes—but you've set yourself up in judgement upon me too often for me ever to cherish any tender feelings towards you. I hate it when you play up to Sharlie. It's only because you're a Frenchman and—and full of *amour*—and—and you can't resist it. It doesn't mean a thing.'

He said suavely, 'How nice to have one's feelings so neatly tabulated. And *you* said *I* was quick to judge! Anyway, why wouldn't Sharlie be able to analyse these things for herself? ... she's about three-quarters French. And so you ought to understand too.'

'What do you mean?' Her eyes were wary, was he going to give away what he knew about her own forebears? Oh, if

116

only he would!

'I mean it's written all over you ... you're as French as
Madame. It's in your every gesture, your every movement.
Madame said once that even the way you come into a room
is French.'

'Ah, bah!' said Margot. 'It's the result of training, not
anything inborn. We had to walk circumspectly, even ele-
gantly, in Roxanne's crowded salons. She gave us all lessons
in deportment. I found it very hard at first. I was a long,
leggy schoolgirl once, and Roxanne simply had to stop me
striding round the place. Like this!'

Pierre pulled her back. 'Not so fast, milady. Your temper,
if not your slip, is still showing.'

She said slowly, seriously, 'It isn't any wonder, is it? I
don't know my ancestors ... you wouldn't realise, since you
have a family tree you can trace back on for generations ...
how humiliating it is not to know. How could you? My aunt
and uncle who brought me up were very reserved. You'd find
that hard to understand. You people here are all so volatile,
no inhibitions. You've had a background of family life that
has made you so sure of yourself. Your ancestors are real to
you and your family history of the last century or so is
identified for you by every wall of your house, every stick of
furniture. You *belong*.'

He was serious in an instant. He caught her hands in his.
'It really doesn't matter, you know, Margot, not knowing.
You belong in the affections of the people here, not just the
Rossignols. But to the Beaudonais family, to the Dumaynes,
the Lemoines. I've been critical of you, yes, but only because
I feared you were milking the treasures of the community. In
other ways, no. I like the way you go one Sunday to St.
Peter's, the next to St. Patrick's with Madame, for instance.
Madame told me she now feels she has a member of the
family with her, instead of being tacked on to a neighbour. I
like the care you spend on each item in the museum, the way
you cope with visitors who are at times trying and incon-
siderate, your way with Sharlie and Leonie. Just let yourself
go ... I don't believe you're reserved by nature. I don't mean
just let yourself go in temper'—he grinned—'I've seen evidence of that, all right, but let yourself go in other ways.'

For the first time Margot was at a loss. This was a different Pierre altogether. Suddenly she felt the atmosphere was
charged with far too much emotion. This undermining

117

softening could be dangerous. She did not want to feel this way to anyone again. It gave a man such power to wound you.

She said quietly, 'You could be right. But we're all products of experience. We have to learn from life. And I don't want to let myself go, for all that. Let's go in, Pierre. I feel as if I don't care now what Sharlie or any of them think about our moonlight strolling. I just want to be a member of the family, I don't want any undercurrents, any strong feelings to disturb me. I like my existence exactly as it is.'

'You mean, don't you,' and his voice was harsh, 'that you really haven't got over Jonathan, even if you did say you were the one to give him up?'

Her voice was cool. 'Perhaps. But it's no business of yours. My feelings are my own.'

He uttered an impatient sound. 'Time you got over it. Akaroa is meant—apparently—to heal wounds, not to cherish and nurture a passion for another woman's husband. The man you turned down! Your career, you thought, meant more to you. And then—I suspect—in Canada you found he'd meant more than you'd realised. But by then he'd found consolation. You can't eat your cake and have it. You'd better stop hankering for the moon.' He looked sharply at her. 'You aren't listening!'

She lifted her purely oval face towards him in the moonlight and said simply, 'Another woman's *husband*? Then they're married?'

'Did you not know?'

'No. But it's just as well to know, isn't it?'

'It is. There's a finality about that—or ought to be—so it's just as well I came out with it, though I wouldn't have been so sudden had I known. My friend at London Airport said so in his last letter. Margot, *I* had to take this sort of thing. I thought I was in love with Lisette for quite a long time, then found out she was two-timing me—going out with someone else yet stringing me along in great style. Trying to make up her mind between the two of us.'

Margot said, quite gently, 'Pierre, decisions aren't always clear-cut for everyone. You're probably a yes–no person. Others find it harder to make up their minds, even to know their own hearts. She——'

'Oh, believe me, Margot, it was the other fellow she loved all right. The only thing that bothered her was that I could offer her much more security. That was what disillusioned me most. I'd idolised her.'

Margot wrinkled her brow. 'But, Pierre, she did finally choose love. Her better nature must have triumphed, though I realise——'

His laugh had no mirth in it. 'Her mind got made up for her. Austin won a fairly substantial prize in the Golden Kiwi. She thought it was providence. She said so.'

Margot was aghast. She had a vision of the young Pierre ... idealistic, uncomplicated. She said firmly, 'Then she wasn't worth bothering about.'

He said irritably, 'That's what I've been trying to tell you. I told Sharlie, didn't I, that I must have been anything but discriminating. Oh, I was sore. I'd had it in mind for years to travel because I wanted to become attached to the Tourist and Publicity Department of New Zealand. That was part of my attraction for Lisette. She wanted to travel. It did do me good to get away, to meet new people, see new places.

'Heavens, girl, I don't go round talking to everyone about my love-life! The only reason I was frank with Sharlie was because I wanted *you* to recognise that life doesn't stop because you don't get the first person you fall in love with. It carries on and sometimes you even find you're glad you had the earlier frustration. If you hadn't, you might have missed the best. It's time you stopped wearing the willow for Jonathan Worth. He's married and you've got a life of your own. You made a mistake, you think, when you gave him up. Granted. I expect you tried to make it up from Canada and found he didn't want you back, so you decided to carry on with your career ... travelling round the world. So that's that. You have a future, but it will be a happier one if you aren't always looking back over your shoulder. Any more arguments, Margot Chesterton?'

She still didn't think she'd tell him the full story. Pierre was impulsive and if he thought Jonathan had told their mutual friend Tod less than the truth he might write and tell him how it really happened. And it would sadden Betty and Jonathan that their happiness had only come about because Margot had made a sacrifice. She'd done what she had done in the best possible way for the man she loved, and she'd take no risk of spoiling it now.

So she said, 'No more arguments, Pierre. You're right. I hadn't realised it was showing so much ... my fretting for

119

Jonathan.'

His face actually softened. 'Perhaps not everyone has noticed it. They might think that wistfulness was due to the loss of your uncle and aunt not long ago, even to a longing for your home. You've done a grand job here, even if I have sneered at you for being a paragon. I was scared you'd make them all fond of you, then when you'd scooped the Banks Peninsula pool of antiques, you'd be off, leaving a gap. Now, now, Margot, no more temper. It's bad for the blood sugar. Perhaps I've misjudged you on this. I think now'—he looked at her searchingly—'you were feeling lost and lonely in Canada, and regretting a hasty decision; and you remembered your French forebears and came here.'

She stemmed the impulse to shout at him, 'Who, who are my forebears?' and merely shrugged. 'Well, now we have all that settled, let's go in and meet the knowing looks of the Rossignols. You can have an easy mind now. I promise you I shall never buy anything from anyone here, to send to Roxanne. Actually, the only contact I've had with her lately was when I sent for the miniature for Madame. Once you've left a firm your image soon fades. Roxanne has someone in my place.'

Pierre said, 'Well, now we've talked it out and I've discovered how wrong I was, may I thank you graciously—and sincerely—for that very choice snuff-box? I value it all the more now I know you bought it for yourself. I saw François Rossignol eyeing it very enviously. Justine has a jewel-box very like it.'

They came up the steps of the terrace with no enmity between them and into the lighted friendliness of the room, slipping quietly on to the big couch where Jules and Sharlie made room for them. No one spoke because the Christmas play was on, but they both saw Leonie look meaningly at Sharlie.

Pierre said in the lowest of whispers in Margot's ear, 'Ah, they've seen the smudged lipstick. I think we've made their Christmas!'

His dancing eyes met hers, brimful with mischief. And suddenly it was all fun and nothing mattered any more. Not even the fact that once she had loved Jonathan Worth more than he had ever loved her.

CHAPTER SEVEN

JANUARY was so busy nobody had time for anything but work and visitors and coping with heat that shimmered and danced on the sapphire Bay. Pierre was flat out on both farming and looking after the motels, though Sharlie and Leonie took on the job of servicing the motels after occupants left and thoroughly enjoyed being able to earn money on their own doorstep instead of having to get a holiday job in Akaroa.

The community spirit pleased Margot. Pierre and François ran the Rossignol farm and Partridge Hill almost as one property, using the same woolsheds and dipping equipment, machines and tractors. Pierre got help from Lincoln College students keen to have a vacation job, and they helped at Rossignol's too, with Justine and Mrs. Grendon coping admirably with the meals.

Margot was kept very busy in the museum, and Madame bloomed and looked much younger and insisted she showed visitors round on the days when François declared all work and no play made them dull and swept them down for a swim or to go out in one of the launches.

Pierre's time off seemed to be taken up with organising fishing parties for the folk at the motels, taking them round the faraway bays that were more accessible from the sea than the road, or running informal dances for the young fry in the old barn that served as a hall for the Bay.

Francis Beaudonais was talking of building a couple of cottages to rent to holiday-makers for next year, in the triangle between the creek and the hill. They'd have to bridge the creek during the winter, though. But Margot and Marie managed to find enough time to transplant a host of yellow and purple irises as soon as they had finished blooming, to the banks of the creek, and violets, primroses and snowdrops too. This was Pierre's idea.

'So many of our seaside resorts are ramshackle. People have put up places that are just shacks, so they lack glamour. We're getting on to it now, but I'm certain we must not only give good accommodation but beauty too. We have natural beauty all about us—the contours of the hills, the sound of fresh-water creeks tumbling down every gully, pockets of native bush, and always the rocks and the sea—but I'm sure we can improve on nature. And when you build, the surroundings look so bare for so long if you don't create a garden now.'

Margot, taking him up a huge pile of linen that Sharlie and Leonie had ironed, using her Mini for transport, said, 'Pierre, aren't you going to miss all this when your parents come back and take over the motels and you go back to the farming?'

He grinned. 'How well you know me! I would, but it's more than likely that my sister Therese and her husband will be coming down from Hawke's Bay in the North Island, to run the farm. That will leave me free to do what I like. I aim——'

Margot felt exactly as if a giant hand had squeezed her heart and let it go. She said quickly, 'You—aren't thinking of going back to England, are you?'

Her tone must have revealed her dismay, for he looked at her sharply and said, the familiar teasing glint in his eye, 'O, mine enemy, my one-time enemy . . . would you care?'

Margot said hastily, crimsoning, 'Well, I hate change . . . we've all learned to work together. Like one big family. So different from anything I've ever known. That's all.'

He pulled his mouth down. 'You're very deflating, do you know? Never boost a chap's ego. Why not admit you'd miss me?'

Margot put her hands to her hot cheeks. 'Pierre, stop it! You're embarrassing me.'

He laughed at her. 'Good to see you show a bit of emotion. That reserve of yours is crumbling fast.'

Up came her chin. 'You ask the Rossignols. They've never considered me reserved, I'm sure.'

He took the pile of pillow-cases off her, but seized her hands under them so she could not let go without tumbling them to the ground. 'That means you're only reserved with me. Why?'

She tried to wriggle her hands out gently. 'Let go, Pierre, and have done with your nonsense.'

He said softly, 'You feel you have to keep a certain distance with me? Good.'

'Good? What on earth can you mean?'

'That you're aware of me as a man. Much better than your icy aloofness when I first came home. I think it means

Jonathan is not the only star on your horizon now.'

Margot thrust the pillow-cases at him and got back into her car and pressed the starter. Nothing happened.

Pierre, with a disregard of their spotlessness, deposited the pillow-cases on the bank, wrenched open the passenger door and said sweetly, 'Margot darling, it starts better with the ignition turned on. Let me do it for you.'

He turned it on, lightly kissed her cheek, got out again, picked up the linen and disappeared into the laundry-room of the motels without a backward glance.

Margot tried not to laugh. It was almost impossible to stay mad with Pierre. Yet she must watch herself. He wanted her to show some feeling towards him. Was this sheer masculine perversity because she had cut off their association so abruptly when she went to Canada? A man who had been treated as Lisette had treated Pierre might easily have some sort of complex ... want to rouse feelings in a girl, then drop her? Well, experience made women as well as men wary, and she would never again wear her heart on her sleeve, as she had done for Jonathan.

February was the best month of all, with a tranquillity January had lacked. The visitors at Partridge Hill Motels didn't have children with them now, for the schools had resumed. They were honeymooners or older couples. Now, again, the sweet sound of the convent bell that had come out on the *Sancta Maria* with the beloved Bishop Pompallier floated across the harbour waters each day to Rossignol Bay.

Leonie went off in the school bus to Akaroa High School each day and Sharlie and Bridget were in their Christchurch flat. Pierre said the Bay would know visitors till Anzac Day, the twenty-fifth of April. April was the golden time in Akaroa, when the Normandy poplars would be torches of living gold.

Margot said, 'Pierre, am I being fanciful, or do these poplars hold their branches more perpendicularly than in England? Tighter together?'

He nodded. 'Yes, first thing I noticed over there was that they spread their branches a little more. I've no idea why, though. Ours look almost trimmed into shape, like yews. Even the ones used as hedges on the farms do it. I wonder if it's something to do with the soil. Did you notice that in England the daffodils last longer? Perhaps we get too much

123

sun and wind here. I loved the way the daffodils lingered in England.'

'I came when the daffodils were almost over, so I couldn't compare them with English ones. That reminds me ... you know that grove of oaks past the children's tree-house? The guests love wandering there. Have you ever thought of planting crocus and daffodils and bluebells there? Not hyacinths. Hyacinths are for formal gardens. Just wild bluebells. Old Mrs. Forsythe over at Akaroa is talking of rooting a lot of hers out. How about it? You and I and Jules could do it—François tells me they must go in before the end of March in New Zealand.'

Pierre looked at her, in the rose-coloured nylon overall smocked in black, that she wore when dusting the museum. He said, 'To think I was once furious to find you here!'

Margot said hastily, 'Let's not go into that again. I'm too busy these days to fight.'

His eyes were audacious. 'Not only too busy to fight, Margot Chesterton. Too busy to come to a Christchurch theatre with me. It's a lot of rot, you know. You're just chicken about it.'

'Chicken? About what?'

'About that fifty-three miles coming home in the dark with me. You're afraid I'll make love to you.'

Margot looked swiftly down. The golden-brown lashes, thick but short and straight, veiled her look. She said, 'I—I—I'm not——'

'Don't lie, Margot. I wouldn't believe you, anyway. But the fact that you're chicken about being alone with me means you're—at last—forgetting Jonathan.'

When she didn't reply he said, 'Some day soon, quite soon, I'm going to ask you to prove that to me—that Jonathan no longer matters.'

Margot walked swiftly away, pulled open the door to the stairs and went up to the attics. She heard him laugh and was glad Madame hadn't been in. She stood at the landing window and watched him put a hand on the gate-post and vault over the little picket-fence. Why ... when the gate stood open? But then Pierre had energy to burn. Justine had said once that as a child he'd been accident-prone, due to sheer exuberance of spirits. He went running along the sea-lane towards Partridge Hill, whistling. What *was* he whistling?

She didn't dare analyse her thoughts, but one thing she did know, that she was happy and that it was no longer of prime importance for her to find her father. That thought jerked her into remembering the tune he had whistled. It was Robbie Burns' 'My love is like a red, red rose...'. The words her father, in the days when he had loved her mother, had penned on a birthday card to his young wife, Laura.

Later he had been adamant at the wrong time, even if it had been the right thing for a man to do ... and Laura had died before she could tell Francis she loved him and would come to him, forsaking all others, as one was meant to do.

And somewhere her father lived, and it might just happen that all his life he had carried with him a burden of unde-served remorse ... he might always have thought, had he not been so unyielding, that Laura might not have died. It wasn't fair to anyone to bear that. So, as long as it did not disrupt his present life, with someone else, he had a right to know.

And she, their daughter, because a man had a swift, laugh-ing way with him; because he had narrow dark eyes whose glance held yours and demanded response, was in danger of feeling her quest did not matter. Not only that, but of for-getting that he alone knew of her quest and because *he* judged it ill-advised, he would not tell her where to instigate her search. Would not tell her to which family around these shores had come from Canada a kinsman of theirs, named Nightingale.

A thought struck her. Pierre had at first been doubly antagonistic towards her. Not only had he disapproved of her search for her father, but he had wrongly believed she was here to winkle family heirlooms from people. But that had disappeared. She had disarmed him. Even when he still believed it, he hadn't been able to resist liking her, completely against her will.

Why not follow that up, use him? Why not pretend to soften? Might it not be possible then, if she got him in some tender moment, to ask him where and how he had heard of Francis Nightingale? Roxanne must have told him every last detail, for he must know the name, even though she herself was legally Chesterton.

Yes, some tender moment, with his defences down. But she must not rush it. Pierre had more than a little of Madame's native shrewdness. One hint that she was using

125

him for her own ends and he'd shut up like a clam and his wrath would fall upon her.

So when the families at the Bay were discussing the Villa Maria Convent Concert in Christchurch and means of transport and there seemed to be one over without a seat, and Pierre, coming in at the tail-end of the discussion, said, 'Oh, I'll come, I love to hear the kids sing. I'll take Margot,' she assented.

Pierre was mildly surprised at this, and said to her before he left, coming out to Justine's kitchen where Margot was making the bedtime cup of tea, 'And listen, girl. No suggesting anyone else comes with us. No juggling round of passengers. I know you.'

Margot was all sweetness and light. 'I'd no intention of doing so, Pierre. It's hardly my place to say who goes in your car.'

Nevertheless, when Sharlie turned up unexpectedly for lunch next day, due to an unexpected break from College, Margot's eyes brimmed with mischief as she met Pierre's.

François said, 'Well, it's lucky for you that Pierre's got room. He's only taking Margot.'

Pierre said to Margot reproachfully on the quiet, 'You enjoyed that, you wretch. But what odds? We'll be on our own coming home.'

In which he was horribly mistaken. Margot, foiled in her purpose, was sad about it. Now she had decided to do this, she wanted to get on with it. They were so rarely alone together, and she wanted him in a melting mood. If, sandwiched in between museum visitors, motel bookings and farm chores, she said bluntly, 'Pierre, I do so want to find my father, even if only to see what he looks like ... I won't make trouble between him and his second wife and family by revealing myself if I think it better not ... but please tell me where he is and who he came to visit,' Pierre would just refuse to tell her.

No, it would have to come from him, engendered and fostered by herself, touching his sympathy by saying how alone she felt at times, how it hurt her to know that somewhere she had a father who did not know she even existed. Tonight she would shed a little of her reserve ... a few weeks of this with a susceptible Frenchman, and he might even volunteer the information himself.

Pierre said now, 'We'll drop Sharlie at the flat after the

126

concert and that will mean the other cars will go on ahead.' He looked quickly at her, expecting a protest, and was intrigued when she just cast her lashes down as any girl might. Margot dropped whipped cream on to the elderberry jelly on the pikelets and handed them to him to take through. He put them down, seized her hand. 'You're no longer wearing the willow? It is working, isn't it?'

Margot hesitated long enough to be tantalising. 'Well, let's just say I'm no longer looking backward.'

'Well, you've got some sense at last.' He picked up a pikelet, said, 'Gosh, Justine made these small, didn't she?' and popped the whole thing in his mouth. Quite the opposite of romantic, Margot thought. She lifted her chin. 'Anyway, I can't see why it should matter to *you* about Jonathan.'

Pierre gazed at her scornfully. 'Margot Chesterton! You aren't as naïve as all that. It matters very much.'

She looked mischievous. 'You take shocking risks, Pierre. Some girls would practically take that for a proposal! You ought to be more careful.'

His eye flashed. 'Margot, when I propose to a girl she'll be in no doubt whatever. But what chap wants to take out a girl who's for ever inwardly sighing for the chap in her immediate past?'

She said calmly, 'There are other girls. Why pick on me? Why not take someone who wouldn't fight with you the way I do? You could get someone who would hang on your every word adoringly.'

'Like who, for instance? Ha, you can't answer that one.'

'Can't I? What about Bridget?'

His surprise was ludicrous. 'Bridget? You must be mad. Bridget would just as soon go out with her grandfather. After all, I'm thirty, what's she? Sweet seventeen?'

Margot giggled. 'Girls of seventeen are mad about older men—didn't you know?'

'No, I didn't. That might convince you I'm not the typical Frenchman you cast me for. Full of *amour*, you said once. I say, Margot, was that why you didn't take me at all seriously in England? Why you thought it didn't matter, your clearing out like that? That you'd be just one girl among many to me?'

(So it still rankled. Margot knew an instant regret that things had gone the way they had.)

So she said lightly, 'I did think just that. It was a chance encounter, Pierre, meeting you as I did. And I had—as you know—other things on my mind, both business and personal.'

'Oh, damn!' he said, 'here we go ... back to Jonathan again!' He seized the plate of pikelets and strode off, quite forgetting Hortense had been rubbing herself against his legs, and fell flat on his face, creamed and jellied pikelets spraying out in all directions.

Margot tried to look sorry, but it was no use, she just gave way to helpless mirth. The family rushed in, and stopped staring in the doorway. Hortense, her green eyes gleaming in her jet-blackness, was improving the shining hour by licking madly at the cream. Pierre sat up, his chest covered with cream and purple jelly.

'Hell and damnation!' said Pierre. 'That thrice-damned cat! She's an absolute menace. She's so affectionate you can't walk a step without her tripping you up. And it was all Margot's fault, anyway!'

'Was it indeed?' asked Margot sweetly. 'How?'

Pierre disregarded that, got to his feet, and submitted to Justine's ministrations with the dishcloth.

François anxiously asked if that plateful was the whole issue of the pikelets, and, assured it was not, began to ladle out jelly on to what was still on the cooling tray.

Margot hadn't meant Jonathan. She'd meant discovering she had a father. Pierre was singularly obtuse in that. He could understand her distress of mind over Jonathan, but not over the knowledge that she had a father. Could he not realise how much it meant to her? Well, she'd been provocative and would continue to be so. Lead him on, then get him to reveal what he knew. Pierre deserved it for his hardness in this matter. And ... and ... Margot flinched away from the knowledge that she was enjoying flirting.

She dressed with care and Sharlie, who was an adept at such things, set her hair, piling it high and fastening in it a clasp that Madame proffered, set with brilliants.

Sharlie said, 'The kids love to see the audience dressed up a bit. Not overdone, but pepped up. Tante Elise, when we have the ball to mark the end of the tourist season—it's a fancy dress one, remember—Margot should go as Marie Antoinette ... look at her with her hair piled up. For that she could have a curl brought down over her left shoulder ... she's just the type.'

128

'Indeed she is, *chérie*, and I have had it in mind. It must be old rose brocade, with an underdress of lace, in tiers ... and with gold shoes. And of course, a black velvet mask. And we will put a patch on your cheekbone to match the one beside your mouth. I have a fan that will be ideal.'

Margot was intrigued. 'Will it be a big affair?'

'Yes, people will come from Christchurch for it. *Mignonne*, that coral frock suits you perfectly. It seems so odd, it is absolutely up-to-date with today's fashions, yet in everything you wear, you have an elegance not of this period.'

'I endorse that,' said Pierre's voice from the doorway, 'and it's a French elegance at that.'

Margot felt the hot colour in her cheeks and shrugged. 'Sure and you've all kissed the Blarney Stone, not just Justine,' she said laughingly, and picked up her coat and purse.

It was a glorious night, with a slumbrous-looking harvest moon rising in burnished gold out of the sea. 'By the time we come home,' said Pierre as they left the Bay road, 'it will be riding high and turned to silver.'

'There's a romantic thought for you,' said Sharlie admiringly, 'aren't you glad you won't have a passenger coming home?'

'I sure am,' said Pierre. 'I've never known such a place as Rossignol Bay for being cluttered up with gooseberry-playing females! A chap doesn't get a fair go at all!'

Sharlie gave a satisfied sigh. Margot did not rebuke Pierre.

The concert was in the Ngaio Marsh Theatre at the University at Ilam, a more glamorous setting than if it had been in town, for here you could see the lights of the Cashmere Hills on Banks Peninsula, sprinkled like fireflies beneath that moon.

The convent choir sang beautifully, with an exquisite purity of young voices and when at the end they sang 'Maureen' finishing with '... And may God in His heaven forgive me for loving you so.' Pierre's hand touched Margot's fleetingly. There was magic in it, a magic she'd not thought to know again. Watch it, Margot, watch it! This is a strange man, in some ways even more strange than Jonathan. More complicated, anyway, perhaps due to a very mixed heritage. With intense loyalties and volatile spirits and quick judgements. Sentimental to the core in some things, hard as nails in others. Well, in one thing.

She got separated from Pierre going out, as someone spoke

to him. They were all in a group outside, waiting for Madame and the Dumaynes, who had gone behind the stage to speak to the Dumayne girls who were boarders. Pierre came up to Margot, plucked at her sleeve, and said in a disgusted tone, 'What do you think? We've got landed with old Jasper. Jasper above anyone! Talk about glamour! He'll babble about whaling and blubber and trypots all the way home. He's been staying with his niece whose daughter is a day-girl here. We're to call at her house, when we drop off Sharlie, to pick up his bag. He's thrilled, says it will save him the price of the bus-fare.'

Margot couldn't help chuckling. Then she sobered and said, 'Pierre, he's a pensioner. It means a lot to him. You're not to make him feel unwanted. And I just love old Jasper's stories.'

Pierre said, 'Well, you can go round to Tikao Bay any time you like to hear them—oh, all right, I'll not be anything but welcoming to the old boy, but—Margot, promise me something?'

'What, Pierre?'

'That you'll come across here one night next week with me ... we'll have dinner and do a theatre and—we'll tell no one till we're ready to go.'

Margot laughed and agreed.

They took Sharlie to the door of the flat, up the dark tree-crowned drive, and saw her inside. As Sharlie opened the door she said mischievously, 'Not all gooseberries are female, are they, Pierre?' and whisked inside.

Margot and Pierre came down the drive together, the trees meeting overhead, the heavy scent of the long-flowering magnolia still on the air, and came to the little bridge over the tiny stream that sang on its way to the Avon. A faint glimpse of that silvering moon shone through the leaves. Pierre brought Margot to a stop, his grip almost hurting her.

She said, 'You're bruising my arms. You don't know your own strength.'

He laughed. 'I have to make sure of you. You're inclined to cut and run—but you can't this time.' He bent his head. His lips moved softly over her cheek, then found her mouth. In that moment Margot didn't think of this as a means to an end. She was conscious of being stirred to her very depths.

Pierre lifted his face from hers, but kept his grip. She saw

130

his well-cut mouth quirk up, the glint in his eyes as they smiled. 'Well, that's one moment even old Jasper can't spoil,' he said, and they moved on. 'But,' he added, 'I'd thought that driving home in the friendly darkness, we'd have fifty miles to get to know each other in. However, there is next week. Let's make it Tuesday.'

He said he'd take old Jasper on to Tikao first, then bring Margot back, but when they came to Rossignol Bay, Madame's light was on. 'She must not have gone up to the homestead. I don't like her being alone, Pierre. And she loves hot chocolate in bed. And it is nearly one o'clock.'

He did not demur. And they had Tuesday to look forward to.

On the Friday Margot was in Akaroa at old Mrs. Forsythe's. She dug out all the bluebell bulbs she wanted and spent the afternoon gardening for the old lady.

'I've aye liked my garden,' said Margaret Forsythe. 'I hope I'll be able to potter in it to the very end. But I'll admit my back gets a bit rheumaticky now if I spend too long in it. My daughter's boy comes over from Christchurch and does the digging, but I don't let him do more. I don't like him spending too long away from his studies. This is fine, Margot. I just felt if that much was done before the weather gets its autumn nip, it'd see me through for a bit.'

It was the very haunt of peace, this garden, running down to a gully above which rose a beautifully wooded hill. All day long here *tuis* twanged and the bell-birds Margaret called the mockies varied their chimes by mocking all the other bird-calls. Margot helped gather up what walnuts had fallen and arrange them for drying on the wire-netting frames you saw on every verandah here.

Akaroa walnuts were the best in New Zealand, falling completely free of their husks. Old Mrs. Forsythe sent hers, from six trees, to the market. 'I need the money. They help me pay the rates. When Jock was alive he made a fair bit out of his garden—we were both just on the pension and the house was always wanting something done to it, new window-frames or painting or some such. And my cylinder needs renewing.'

Yes, it could be hard going, these days of high prices, to manage, and Mrs. Forsythe was the independent type.

Margot said, 'How about if I take this stuff to the dump

now? These weeds would take ages to dry out for burning.'

Mrs. Forsythe was all for it. 'And if you've room there's a lot of old junk in the wash-house that could go.'

'Oh, plenty of room. Mr. Rossignol insisted on me bringing the truck. Did you not notice it under the beeches? He said even a couple of boxes of bulbs would fill up the boot of the Mini. But you'd better let me vet the junk. What's rubbish to you could be treasure to a museum curator!'

Margot drove home smiling. Because of that junk she had contrived to assist Mrs. Forsythe in a way that did not smack of charity. And she had Tuesday night to look forward to. Not just for the chance to find out something about her father, but for its own sake. She admitted that now. She *wanted* to go out with him.

But on Monday Pierre rang. 'Margot?—I'm sorry, but our jaunt is off. I can't make it after all. Just as well I'd not booked yet. I was going to do it by phone.'

She was disappointed, but said instantly, 'Oh, don't worry, Pierre, there are other nights.'

His answer chilled her. 'Oh, that's the last of this film. It finishes this week. It's had a long run. I should've gone before. There's nothing else on I'd like to see.'

He did not ask if there was any film *she* fancied. And she waited for him to say why he could not go Tuesday, or any other night this week. But only a silence fell. Phone conversations were maddening. You could not read an expression.

She said, keeping chagrin out of her tone, 'Well, it doesn't matter. There's nothing else I'd like to see, either, and a film has to be pretty good to warrant my travelling a hundred miles. Only mad Kiwis do that. Bye-bye.'

She stood staring at the instrument after she hung up. Blow hot, blow cold, that was Pierre Laveroux. She was very quiet all day.

Perhaps at dinnertime he might explain. But he did not come down for dinner. Justine said, bringing in a delectable salad, colourful with tomato and water-melon slices, 'Pierre won't be here tonight or tomorrow night. Seems he's busy.'

Margot hoped no one would notice her lack of spirits. But on Tuesday night, after dinner, she felt restless. She helped Jules with his stamp collection, hunted up some dates for Leonie's homework, held skeins of wool for Justine to wind, and checked some figures for François who said ruefully, 'I hate this time of year, getting things together for my accountant for the thirty-first of March. That's been a great help, Margot. I'll be finished in half an hour or so, though. Anybody want a game of Scrabble then?'

Scrabble! When she'd thought to be establishing a relationship with Pierre that might lead to a discovery!

She said, 'Mr. Rossignol, there's something I'd like to do down at the museum. Mind if I don't join in tonight? I'll come back up later for Madame and have supper, though. You can play without me, can't you?'

François glanced at her. 'Of course. You do whatever you want to do, Margot.'

She went out the back door and round to the terrace, but when she got there, François was coming out of the front door with Auguste at his heels.

He said, 'This large and lazy dog needs a bit of exercise. I'll come down with you to the museum and then back by the sea-lane.'

Margot was dismayed. She hadn't meant to go down to the museum. She'd intended to go for a good stiff walk to rid herself of what Madame would call the megrims. François walked down with her, switched on the lights. She suspected he didn't like her going into a dark, empty house alone. That warmed her heart.

He looked at her. 'You look very tired tonight. Do you really have to work, *chérie*?'

She shrugged. 'Not really, but I feel like it.'

He put his hands on her shoulders, turned her round to face him, took her dimpled chin in his hand. 'Margot, you're restless. Which is not like you. What is it, *mignonne*? We all take it so much for granted that you're entirely happy here. You've fitted into our family so well we forget you had another life before you came to us. Is something from the past bothering you? You looked strained and white when you came to dinner, and you didn't finish your dessert. I think of you just as I do of Sharlie and Leonie, you know? Is it anything you can tell me? Is it money? Because——'

Margot shook her head. 'No, not money. Uncle Noel was quite comfortable—not wealthy, but I was the only one to inherit. I get a very good rent from the house at Osterley.'

François took his pipe out of his mouth and regarded her keenly. 'You haven't sold it? Does that mean you still think you may go back? Because we've so hoped, Justine and I,

133

that you might settle here permanently.' He smiled. 'Even marry, here in the Bay. By Jove, that's it! Have you and Pierre quarrelled?'

She didn't flush. She just said listlessly, 'No, we haven't. Though you're harbouring false hopes there, Mr. Rossignol. Pierre and I are not really interested in each other. Don't pay any attention to Sharlie. She's at the romantic age—and a matchmaker.'

François Rossignol cocked an eye at her and twinkled. 'Sharlie has said nothing. But we have noticed. I won't pry, *chérie*. After all, the course of true love doesn't always run smoothly, as certainly *I* ought to know. I think I've touched a tender spot, haven't I? For assuredly you and Pierre—but I'll say no more.'

He pinched her cheek. 'Don't take it too seriously. Pierre is hot-tempered ... he'll mellow in time, just as I have. But Pierre is as quick to say he's sorry as to lose his block in the first place.' He grinned reminiscently, 'And making-up can be very sweet, too, almost worth the quarrelling. Come on, Auguste, you needn't think you can settle on that hearthrug, you hulk of laziness, you're going to walk clean round the headland. See you at suppertime, Margot,' and he bent, gave her a paternal kiss, as if she had indeed been Sharlie or Leonie, heaved Auguste to his feet, and was gone.

Margot stared after him. He'd said that very feelingly. 'As *I* ought to know.' Yet apart from the teasing give-and-take they indulged in, she had never known Justine and François quarrel. But no doubt they had when first married.

She just must walk off her lowness of spirits. She would not take the headland road, though, now. She'd take the hill track. Climbing would be good for her and the physical effort might make her sleep. Pierre wasn't worth losing sleep over.

She took the track through the oaks and beeches where on Saturday she had planted so happily, scores of bluebells on Pierre's land. He hadn't worked with them because he was out with his men clearing a block in the creek, but he'd praised Leonie and Margot for working so hard when he'd come in to dinner.

She climbed swiftly and wandered far, thinking that once she'd have been scared to be out like this, all alone. But here, in this sea-girt haven where even the winds were friends and every tree loved and known, she knew no fear.

She took the easier path down. In the moonlight it was

134

quite easy to see because it was beaten smooth and whitish with shells with the moon-stippled shadows making it look like crazy paving.

The path took her very near Partridge Hill homestead. She had forgotten how near, but now she wouldn't retrace her steps, because she needed to use the bridge.

She crossed it and looked up to Partridge Hill. The lounge curtains were not drawn and there was a light on. Sam and Griff, Pierre's men, were out, she knew, because they had called to see François on their way to Akaroa. Who could be in the house?

She gazed down towards the sea, at the lighted motels. Should she go down and ask one of the men staying there to come up with her and investigate? But what a fool she would look if it was simply that the boys had left that light on.

You didn't think of intruders in this peaceful bay. And burglars wouldn't be so blatant as to leave a light on and curtains undrawn. But she'd feel guilty if she did not investigate.

She came noiselessly across the lawn, stepped on tiptoe across the path and up on to the patio. And there, in a deep chair, in front of his fire, legs outstretched to the blaze and a book on his knee, sat Pierre Laveroux ... who had made an excuse not to take Margot out tonight. It seemed that his only reason for backing out was that he'd regretted asking her. Margot boiled over.

She flung open the doors and walked in.

Pierre jumped, as well he might, and leapt to his feet, the book crashing to the floor.

Margot said, 'So ... you hoped I'd presume you had another engagement ... you couldn't come to dinner, Justine said, because you were going out ... why weren't you truthful, Pierre? Why didn't you say you didn't want to eat with *me*? What I'm suppose to have done this time I've no idea, but let me tell you I wouldn't go out with you ever again, not if you begged me on bended knees ... you blow hot, you blow cold ... and I loathe inconsistency. Why the dickens did you ask me in the first place ... and why, having asked me, though I can't imagine why you did ... didn't you just carry out the date and then just not bother asking me again?

'Then you wouldn't have them all wondering what the devil's got into you. François Rossignol has been asking me

135

what's wrong.' She gave a mirthless snort. 'He even tried to tell me the course of true love never runs smoothly. True love! It was nothing like that ... merely an innocuous and tepid sort of date, and not of my seeking, either! What's the matter with you? Are you the sort of chap who's afraid of being trapped into marriage or something? No wonder your Lisette had doubts. She was extremely lucky! I don't like being stood up and, what's more, avoided as if I've got the plague or something. What on earth have I done *now* to offend your high-and-mightiness?'

He didn't look in the least abashed. He looked like ... like a man with a just grievance. It set her back the way he looked at her. She hadn't realised dark eyes could look so cold.

His very iciness, so foreign to Pierre, made her fury look foolish. Then when he'd stared her down to silence he said, 'Is it possible you haven't even got a conscience on it? Though I don't suppose you thought I'd ever find out. Was that it? Answer me, was that it?'

She blinked. 'Answer you? How?'

His lip curled. 'Yes, how indeed? Because even you couldn't find an excuse this time. You've disarmed me before, but you must know you can't talk your way out of this one. And of all things I hate liars. Nothing, nothing could have sounded more sincere than your promise to me that night.'

Margot continued to boggle at him. This appeared to infuriate him still more, though he still didn't shout, but forced his words out between almost shut teeth with a sort of ferocious intensity that really scared her. 'I expect you didn't think I'd ever find out, but I was at Meg Forsythe's yesterday morning. After you told me she was finding it hard to cope, I called in to see if she'd like Griff and Sam to saw some wood for her for the winter, and to fix that fence you mentioned. And she told me.'

'Told you *what*?'

He made a gesture of disgust. 'Trying to play the innocent to the last, aren't you? Or are you playing for time so you can trump up some excuse? All right, if you won't admit it, I'll tell you. Mrs. Forsythe told me you'd bought a whole lot of antiques off her for seventy-five dollars. Well, if you paid that for them, and are willing to pay freight to England, there must be a tidy bit of profit involved. I suppose they're worth ten times as much!'

Margot stood stock-still. She tried to speak and couldn't.

His face changed, from an iron control to a weary disgust. 'How could you? How could you? I could have sworn you were sincere that night, that you'd given up all idea of ferreting out bargains, that—oh, but what does it matter that you're a liar and a cheat and make promises without batting an eyelid, never meaning to keep them? But one thing I'm going to do ... you're going to give them back to me tomorrow and I'll give you seventy-five dollars! I don't know how I can return the things to Meg, but one thing I am determined on and that is that neither you nor Roxanne Gillespie will benefit by one cent! Tomorrow, do you hear? And if you don't bring them up to me—I'll do that to save your face in front of the Rossignols who think you such an angel—I'll march down to Maison Rossignol myself and get them and be hanged to the image you've built up of yourself!'

Margot was now as white and intense as he was. She said, 'You'll do this and you'll do that. You haven't got the ordering of this. I'll issue the orders. I bought the things. You'll come down and get them now. Now. This very moment. Not tomorrow. And they're not at Maison Rossignol. They're in an old shed at the back of François's garage.'

Pierre's lips were a sneering line. 'Oh, I see! You didn't dare take them to the museum. Of course not. Because Madame, even if you're the apple of her eye, would never countenance stuff like that leaving New Zealand. So you hid it! Right, I'll come.'

'Yes, I hid it. And yes, you'll come. And if you don't, I'll drag the beastly stuff all the way up the hill and throw it at you!'

'Well, there's one thing,' he taunted, 'when you lose your temper at least we come at the truth.'

'We certainly do,' she thrust back, 'and if you don't like that same truth, Pierre Laveroux, don't blame me! You asked for it.'

As he moved to the mantelpiece she added, 'You don't need a torch. It's brilliant moonlight and the shed's wired.'

They didn't speak as they moved down the hill, their tempers carrying them on at a great rate. Even when Margot tripped over a pine-root Pierre made no attempt to save her. She recovered her balance with a terrific effort and felt more furious than ever.

137

She was past caring whether or not they banged into François, but fortunately they didn't.

They came to the shed, Margot in the lead. She flung open the door, snapped on the light and marched across the floor to the far corner where some indescribable sacks lay.

'There!' she said, pointing dramatically. 'They're under there ... the Forsythe antiques!'

His eyes were thin black streaks, the lines in his cheeks deeply graven, his voice sardonic in the extreme. 'Certainly hid them well till you could ship them, didn't you?' And he yanked the sacks off, then stood staring.

There they lay, an old copper jardinière, a marble clock with the face missing, a set of rusty fire-irons, a foot-scraper, a hideous vase in deep blue and yellow, with an impossible desert scene painted on it, a wooden butter mould cracked right across, two vegetable dishes with mis-matched lids and a camp-oven.

He stood staring at her.

She stared back, defiantly.

Then he found his voice. 'You—you—paid Mrs. Forsythe seventy-five dollars for—for *this* rubbish! I don't get it. I just don't get it!'

She said grimly, 'You never did get it. You can't help yourself, Pierre Laveroux! You always *want* to believe the worst of me. So you leapt to the conclusion that I'd diddled the old lady.'

He was looking helplessly from the junk and back to her again. 'But why? Why?'

She drew in a deep breath. 'I'm going to sound smug, like a female Boy Scout, doing my good deed. You're going to hate me for putting you in the wrong. I can't help that, and I don't care if you do. It serves you right. Mrs. Forsythe is very independent. Her daughter is a widow and can't help financially—as you probably know. Evidently she always has a struggle to pay her rates and they've gone up again. And the house needs a lot doing to it.

'I was taking some stuff to the tip-face for her. She'd been having a terrific clearing-up. There *were* one or two things I felt she ought not to get rid of. They ought to go to her grandson eventually—some blue and white plates that have gone up in value and a dish she didn't know was Spode. I washed them and put them in her china cabinet. But I told her I could find a market for these, that they might find a place in some Colonial museum, that I'd see to selling them for her, and I wrote her a cheque there and then.'

She jerked her chin up. 'And not on the fund for museum acquisitions either ... but my personal cheque.' She turned fierce. 'I hope you didn't upset her ... I hope you didn't show your anger with me to her ... I hope you didn't make her think she was diddled ... when I left Mrs. Forsythe on Friday, she was delighted. She could pay her rates and have something over, without touching her walnut money!'

His face changed. He strode to her, caught hold of her arms, said, his eyes opening wide for once, 'Oh, Margot, what a heel I am! What a rotter I feel ... always jumping to the wrong conclusion about you ... but, *mignonne*, I take it all back. I'll make it up to you. Do you think she's got any more junk like this? Could *I* help? Could I buy the rest off her? Oh, you *are* sweet! Look, go on, fire that camp oven at me if you like, but don't stand there looking at me as if I was something the cat had dragged in. Look, *mignonne*, I grovel, I repeat, I grovel. Here ...' Laughing, he bent down and hoisted up the round camp oven with its heavy lid, holding it out to her.

But he didn't meet any laughing response in her. She looked at him with contempt. 'Pierre, you waste your time. Put that down. It's the only thing I can use out of all that. Some day I'm going to reconstruct a Colonial kitchen, and I'll need it. You can't get round me again. I've had enough. You've never really got over your early distrust of me. Well, it's mutual. I've no confidence left in you. I'll meet you—in front of the others—as usual, because it would destroy the atmosphere of the Rossignol homestead otherwise, if they guessed how I hate you, but I really don't want to have anything more personal than that to do with you ... with someone so prone to doubt my word,' and she walked out and left him there, still staring.

She turned at the door. 'And don't call me *mignonne*! That's reserved for Madame and Mr. Rossignol. I'm very fussy about who has the right to call me darling!'

CHAPTER EIGHT

THEY were aware that the Rossignols considered the slightly constrained atmosphere between them merely of a temporary nature and in the light of a lovers' tiff, which infuriated Margot somewhat, especially as it seemed to glance off Pierre, but it had to be endured.

For their sakes, as the days passed, she tried to make their estrangement seem less obvious. They were all more natural when Sharlie was home at weekends, as, all unconscious of tension, she was her usual sunny self, treating Margot as a sister, Pierre as a brother.

Jules had helped most of all. All unknowing he'd said the next day, 'Margot, I know you wanted to see that film. How about coming with me? And instead of coming all the way back here, we'll spend the night at the flat. I'll take my sleeping-bag and doss down in their living-room. You can have their guest-room. I'll ring up and get seats for them too.' Margot, beneath her own pain, hid a smile. Jules was looking in Bridget's direction. She had stopped being a schoolgirl and was suddenly grown-up. Margot said, 'Oh, I'd love to go, Jules!' And did. And hoped Pierre gnashed his teeth.

They were too busy for much grieving. Anyway, why lose sleep over a man like Pierre Laveroux?

It was a still, beautiful day, and even though the calendar said March, the first month of autumn, the weather said it was still summer. Margot even found herself singing as she polished the curved knives that had been used in the vineyards of France more than a century ago, to clip the grape vines, and wound up a French ormolu clock and set it back in place.

In England this would have been an early September day, because late roses were nodding in at the windows and clambering over what Madame called the *treillage* instead of the trellis, and fuchsias and hollyhocks were bright against the white woodwork. Huge white daisies nodded in the drowsy heat and the murmur of the sea through the open door was a somnolent accompaniment to the ceaseless bird-song. A thrush nodded at her from the garden path and went away, a splendidly fat fellow with a gloriously patterned breast, just like tortoiseshell. That too could have been England. Even the flash of a kingfisher in a turquoise dive into the lagoon in search of some unfortunate fingerling and the chirruping of countless sparrows could have been England, but not the faint peep of the tiny rifleman, not the harping of the *tui* or the tangy odour of the rich moist bush tucked into the gully above, sweet with fern and cool with dripping water.

She heard a car door slam. Two, no, three doors in fact, and voices, mingling and blurring on the scented air. Footsteps approached. Visitors to the museum.

Margot put her finger under a mother-of-pearl rosary to arrange it more artistically on its bed of oyster satin and black velvet and closed the glass case where it reposed.

She swung round. The next moment she was desperately trying to focus her eyes. It couldn't be, it just couldn't be! But it was. Their three heads swung and misted over in her vision ... Jonathan Worth's fair head, Betty Worth's mousey-brown head, Pierre's jet-black one. His was behind the other ones. It made a wavery triangle.

Then Margot got control of herself. Jonathan and Betty at least looked as startled as she did, so they might not have noticed she had lost her colour. How odd to actually feel your cheeks blanch!

She summoned every bit of self-possession she had and managed to say almost gaily, 'Good gracious ... maybe New Zealand isn't at the bottom of the world after all ... look who's just dropped in! Jonathan, how in the world did you get here? Though the answer is by air, obviously!'

Jonathan said, 'Margot! You *here* ... in New Zealand? I'd no idea. I thought you were in Canada. I came here purposely to see Pierre, of course, but I'd no idea *you* were here.'

Purposely to see Pierre, of course! Margot knew a black moment as before her came most vividly the memory of Pierre saying that some day he would test out how much Jonathan still meant to her. And *this* was the way he had done it. He must have known from his friend Tod that Jonathan and Betty were coming to New Zealand and brought them here deliberately. The mist was in front of her eyes again. Oddly, it was a pinkish mist. Was this what was meant by seeing red? Because she *was* seeing red. She would never, never forgive Pierre for this.

She wouldn't ask any awkward questions, give herself

141

away at all. She wouldn't even say, 'Fancy Pierre not telling you ...' Oh, no, she wouldn't let Pierre see it even mattered. He had the most peculiar look on his face.

Then, just as he was about to speak, Madame walked into the room, regal in a black frock with a diamond brooch at her throat and cameo earrings swinging.

She said smilingly, '*Chérie*, did I hear aright? These are old friends of yours from England? How truly delightful for you. We are too far away, as a rule, to have visitors dropping in unaware, which is half the happiness of friendship, and so I am very glad for her. Margot, aren't you going to introduce us?'

Margot managed to smile and said, 'I've yet to be introduced myself to Jonathan's wife. We've not met before ... Jonathan?'

He said, 'This is Betty, Margot. She has heard of you, though you'll not have heard of her.'

Not have heard of her! Margot would have recognised the little urchin face anywhere. An endearing face, a kind face, belonging to someone who must not be hurt. Oh, Pierre, how could you do this to her? To Jonathan? To me?

She managed to present them to Madame and to sound, she thought, perfectly ordinary.

'I knew Jonathan quite well in London, Madame, and he too worked at London Airport like Pierre did, though they'd never met. But Pierre and I realised this recently. He and Jonathan have a mutual friend, Tod someone. So I knew Jonathan was getting married, though I didn't dream he was spending his honeymoon here.'

Jonathan laughed and said to Madame, 'It sounds very jet-set, doesn't it, honeymooning at the other side of the world, but every few years when you're with an airline, you get a concession for longer travel, provided there are enough vacant seats on the planes. This has been marvellous. We flew to New York, had two days there, another two in Los Angeles and then across the Pacific.'

Margot wouldn't look at Pierre. She couldn't meet his eyes, she knew, and keep the blazing indignation out of her own. She felt as if with the return of blood to her cheeks, she was scorching inside, but she mustn't show it.

Her voice sounded like someone else's. She answered Jonathan's questions automatically. Yes, she had loved Canada, but, though she'd meant to move from country to country

142

buying antiques, she had so fallen in love with French-flavoured Akaroa, had anchored here.

Jonathan said, looking about him, 'This looks ideal for you. Much better than the shop atmosphere, I'd say. You always hated parting with the pieces you loved most, didn't you? Here, you wouldn't have to.'

Madame said, 'It has been a wonderful thing for us, for the Rossignols. Since Margot has come into our lives we have all been so much happier. I have been able to stay in my own home because of her. But you will want to look around. I do so hope you can stay for a meal with us.'

Margot found herself swaying, and put a steadying hand on an old sea-chest that had come out with the settlers on the *Comte de Paris*. She caught Madame's bright eyes upon her.

Madame added quickly, 'But you may have plans of your own, of course.'

Blessedly, Jonathan said, 'I'm afraid we have, though we'd love to stay. We just ran over to contact Pierre really, and to make arrangements to see him another time. A couple from Auckland have asked us to go with them to see the Maori Museum at Okain's Bay with them this afternoon. But—but we'll give you a ring tomorrow. Perhaps we could have a look round this museum now? We must be back at the hotel for lunch.'

Margot sensed that Betty wanted to be gone. She probably felt shattered, just as Margot did, wanted to sort herself out. What girl would want to run into a former rival on her honeymoon? She also had an idea that Jonathan would be as angry inwardly, with Pierre, as she was herself. So she kept it fairly brief, saying, 'As you've not a lot of time today, the attics would keep till your next visit.'

She was safe enough saying that. They'd make an excuse not to come, they would say they had other places to see. They'd want to visit Mount Cook and the Southern Lakes, not dawdle round Akaroa. Margot reeled off the history of the various pieces ... but today it was all mechanical.

Pierre was unusually quiet. Perhaps he was content now that he had done what he had deliberately set out to do ... tested her reactions at meeting Jonathan again. Though since their quarrel there was little point to it. Still, she supposed he'd arranged it earlier, and could not withdraw. He must have said to Tod to give Jonathan his address, and had craftily said nothing to either of what he planned. Well, he had certainly incensed her further against him. She looked at Pierre sideways. He looked strained. Was it possible he had suddenly realised the enormity of this thing he had done?

Margot went to the door with them as they continued to praise the setting ... the cottage roses trailing over the picket fence, the charm of having the waters of the Bay so near ... just across the road.

'It's almost,' said Betty, forgetting her embarrassment in her delight at the scene, 'as if the house itself dabbles its feet in the water. No wonder you want to stay here, Margot.'

'Well, it's no use your taking a fancy to do the same, Betty,' said Jonathan. 'My place in the world is London. This will be—in all probability—your one and only visit here, so make the most of it.'

Margot knew Pierre's glance flickered to hers. The knowledge enabled her to say, shaking hands with both of them on the verandah, 'Well, just in case you can't fit in another visit, the very best of everything to you both. You'll be very welcome, of course, if you do find time. I must go ... I hear the phone ringing. Goodbye. Goodbye, Pierre.'

She walked inside and did not see Madame standing uncertainly in a doorway. No phone was ringing, of course. Margot walked straightly, blindly through the museum cottage into the other cottage, out into the little herb-garden and ran up the rough path that led uphill into the sanctuary of trees. Madame went through into the herb-garden and watched the rose-colour of the smock flitting through the tree-trunks and knew instinctively where she was bound.

Pierre came in, calling for Margot. 'Where's she gone?' he demanded. 'Is she in her room?'

Normally Madame would have raised her eyebrows at his curtness, but not this time. Her black eyes searched his. 'Pierre, do you know something of this? Why has that man's coming upset her so?'

'I do know,' he said. 'I'm the only one who does. Where is she?'

Madame turned her hands out in a Gallic gesture, 'Where else could she be but on Puke-o-mapu?'

Pierre said, 'Puke-o-mapu ... the Hill of the Sighing. Oh, it fits, but would she know?'

Madame nodded. 'I told her once that that was where I fled, the day the telegram came in 1944 to tell me Philippe

144

too had given his life. I had an hour and a half before Louis was due home. It gave me time to agonize, then I was ready to face Louis with the news. I saw the pink of her overall through the tree-trunks as she went. Will you be kind to her, Pierre? The little one, she is so alone in the world. And I love her so dearly.'

Pierre said almost blankly, 'Kind? Oh yes, Madame, I'll be kind. I'd no idea she still felt like this. I thought she'd got over him. Don't upset yourself. I'll bring her back to you.'

Margot didn't hear him come because the carpet of pine-needles here was soft and cushiony, and the trees, as always, were sighing in harmony with the waves below. She didn't know how long or how short a time he must have stood there watching her as she lay flung down beneath the *ngaios*, sobbing, sobbing, her fingers tearing and clutching at tufts of grass as if she would draw comfort from mother earth itself, since there was no one else with whom to share this agony.

The first she knew was the sound of his voice above her dry, painful sobbing and the next moment the feel of his hand on her shoulder as he dropped down beside her.

She reared away as if he had been a wild boar come out of the bush, with one swift movement that put distance between them.

'You!' she said between her teeth. 'You!' Then, tearingly, savagely, 'Come to gloat, have you? Come to see the result of the experiment you planned? Oh, how cold-blooded can a man get? Get away from here! Get away, do you hear! Get away and leave me to get over it. How dare you bring Jonathan Worth to Akaroa!'

He moved with speed, pinioning her hands against him when in her distress she would have struck him.

His voice was quiet and toneless but convincing. 'Margot, I didn't bring him. I had no more idea than you that he was in New Zealand. It was Tod's idea of giving me a pleasant surprise ... having someone drop in from London Airport. I met him at the gate. Betty was already inside the picket fence. He was locking the car. I was coming to see Madame.

'He didn't know me, of course. But I was in farm clothes and had got out of a truck, obviously a local. He said, "Can you tell me where Pierre Laveroux lives?" And as Betty got to the door of the museum I said, "*I'm* Laveroux——" and he said, "Oh, great. Can you beat that? Betty, we don't need to ask at the museum, this is Pierre himself," and then

145

petrified me by saying, "My name's Jonathan Worth. Tod Moore asked me to call on you. I'm here on my honeymoon."

'Betty had started back towards us, and I tried desperately to stop them going in. I nearly went mad. I'm sure they thought I was daft. I absolutely pestered them to come to the farm first, but she was set on going in. The situation was right out of my control. I could only crowd in after them and hope desperately that my presence would lessen the shock for you. If only, if only they'd come to Partridge Hill first! If they had, I'd have headed them off somehow, or at least warned you.'

The wildness died out of her eyes as if it had ebbed away from underneath. Some emotion he could not recognise came into them instead. A relief, a gladness—but why?

He said, 'Margot, you were magnificent. You had such poise, such control. I think it rocked Jonathan, of course. It was a difficult situation for the two of them, but at least they had each other. You didn't even have any help from me because there wasn't one damned thing I could do. And believe me, I may have been a bit merciless on you in my efforts to stop you looking back over your shoulder at other, happier days—I wanted you to brace yourself, to forget Jonathan—but now I've seen *how* you care, I'll never interfere again. You'll get over it, I know that, because you have such strength of character, but I can see it went much deeper than my suffering over Lisette. I don't know the whole story. I only know that for some reason you gave him up, yet'—he turned and looked away out to sea, to the break in the hills where the harbour met the open sea, then looked down on her and finished it—'yet you love him rather terribly.'

At that Margot came to life. She said, flinging him away and getting her hands free—'Pierre! Still love him? ... I didn't feel a thing! You think I was crying for Jonathan—I was *not*! Don't you know why I was crying...? Because I thought *you'd* done it. Done it purposely. I just couldn't bear the thought that you could be so cruel. Jonathan's nothing to me now. I've known nothing but relief for—for ages—that I made that break. He's Betty's husband. Finish. And that part of my life is as dead as a dodo, as if I had lived it in a pre-existence. And only the present matters, the life I live with the Rossignols.'

Pierre burst out laughing. 'Oh, Margot, Margot Rose, you'll be the death of me! I thought that encounter today

146

had been the last straw, that you were up here breaking your heart over something I couldn't put right for you ... and instead of that, you were like *this* ... like *this* ... over *me*. Then——'

Margot stepped back a pace, her hands behind her back. 'Pierre, you're not to read too much into that. I'd—I'd have felt the same about anyone. Anyone here, I mean. I look on you all as—as the family I've never had. You, Jules, François Rossignol, Madame, the girls, Justine. And I don't want to be disillusioned about *any* of you.'

To her surprise he came no nearer, didn't look at all chagrined, and suddenly, to her annoyance, she didn't want this calm acceptance ... But still, perhaps he knew this moment was so charged with emotion ... it had known anguish, anger, bitterness, hot resentment and now sympathy and understanding ... perhaps he was wise to take her ruling and leave it at this.

He said gently, 'I've misunderstood you so very often, *mignonne*. But I'm going to ask you to tell me now just why you gave Jonathan up. It may not have any sting left now but it did have not so long ago, didn't it?'

She stumbled over it a little at first, then grew more coherent. 'I was all mixed up when I met you—two bereavements so close together and my uncle and aunt so sure I would marry Jonathan. Yes, I did love him. I won't deny or belittle it now. Yet under it all I knew he didn't love me as I loved him. It hurts a girl's pride to admit that, but I'm past caring now. Sometimes I felt I was up against a brick wall, other times I'd tell myself I was a romantic goose ... that the sort of caring I'd hoped to find was only moonshine and gossamer, found in glamorous films and between the pages of a book.' She spread her hands out in her inherited Gallic gesture. 'Is it, Pierre? Is it just an illusion?'

He said slowly, 'There was a time in my life when I thought so. But it was only a lack of discrimination on my part. For a time I was rather cynical, believed all women were fickle, that they didn't know what love meant. But—I remember Louis Rossignol. I was only a brash teenager when I first realised something ... that he and his Elise, after even the briefest of partings, say when she had a weekend in Christchurch without him, always met as lovers. It *does* happen outside the covers of a book, Margot.'

Suddenly the twinkle came back into his eyes. 'Margot.

you're fast becoming one of the aggravating Rossignols! You're just as bad as Leonie and Sharlie, always side-tracking. We're getting into a general discussion. Why did you give Jonathan up? I could swear it was not because you put a career first.'

'Oh no. Do you remember that letter I posted at the corner of Thornbury Road and the Great West Road the day we went to Osterley Park? Well, that letter broke it off. You see, it—it was after that lecture—the one at Chelsea—what's the matter, Pierre?'

He shook his head. 'Go on. Go on, you interest me. Don't stop. You——?'

She said, 'You saw it, you know. Only you still don't connect it. You'll believe this story because you saw it happen.'

He had a puzzled crease between his brows.

She said, 'When you met Jonathan today, didn't you think he looked familiar? Didn't you think Betty did?'

He said, 'I did ... but I put that down to working at the airport. I thought I must, after all, have seen him there some time among the thousands ... but, Margot, Jonathan had to introduce *you* to Betty. Then how could *I* recognise her?'

'Because Jonathan came for me that night. He must have got off early, I suppose. I don't know because I didn't see him again, till today. We—*you and I*—saw him from the dais. First I saw Jonathan, then suddenly I saw his face light up—in a way I'd never seen it light up for me—and the crowd sort of parted—remember?—and she came towards him. Betty. And—and you said—remember?—you said it was a delightful thing to witness. As if it were a case of journeys ending in lovers meeting. It was, of course, but at the time I couldn't understand it. But I had to find out. I saw them go into the garden. I eavesdropped, on purpose. I don't know all of it, but evidently they had loved and parted because someone had made mischief. She'd found out the truth of it, but only to discover he was all but engaged to me.

'She's sweet, Pierre. I heard her telling him she'd come to that reception to see what I was like, to find out if I would make Jonathan happy. Both he and she felt they couldn't take their happiness at my expense. Jonathan must have told her he'd asked me to marry him but I hadn't given him an answer. I knew then why I had not. Because I had sensed in him this reserve, this inability to give me as much love as I had for him. I slipped away and found you and took your offer of a lift home. They still don't know I overheard. That's why I've never told you. You were writing regularly to Tod. They were prepared to put my happiness before theirs, so I owed it to them not to have them guess I was horribly unhappy.

'I simply told Jonathan in that letter that I valued a career more than the humdrum routine of a housewife's existence. That let him out. I was so grateful to you for turning up then. Perhaps I used you meanly, I don't know. I was sort of numbed at the time, and you kept me on an even keel. That —that's about all, I think, Pierre.' Because she thought it would be enough to be going on with. She was too wrung out to go into anything else right now ... her reason for coming to Akaroa. For the first time, however, she felt she would be able, later, to discuss it quite frankly with Pierre, not worm it out of him. Perhaps Roxanne had explained it very badly to Pierre, might have made it sound as if Margot wanted to find her father for what he might be able to do for her financially. Yes, that could be it.

Pierre gave her a little shake. 'Margot, don't go into a trance now! Listen to what I'm saying.'

She tried to concentrate. He said, 'I'm not altogether sorry this has happened. Now, now, don't take umbrage again. At the time I'd have done anything to have got them away without them seeing you, or you them. But now perhaps you'll be more understanding.'

She stared and perhaps it was as well for her that she was too spent with emotion to turn on him.

He said, 'Remember the night you came up to Partridge Hill—the night you showed me Mrs. Forsythe's heirlooms? Her supposed heirlooms. You were furious with me, and rightly so, for thinking you'd taken advantage of an old lady and diddled her out of precious family possessions. You've not forgiven me for that, have you?'

She said, uncertainly, 'Pierre, if you knew how it hurt, that you could think such a thing of me. I——'

His smile grew broader. 'I was hasty, ill-considered, oh, everything I ought not to have been. We get a bit like that when we think we've been let down. But haven't you just done the same? I told you not long ago you must stop wearing the willow for Jonathan. Was I likely then, thinking you

149

still cared, to have been cruel enough to have confronted you with him—and his wife—on their honeymoon? Yet you did think just that of me!'

Margot's eyes fell before the look in his. She kept her eyes on the ground for some time, then heard his voice, gentle, understanding, 'Margot, *you* misjudged *me* this time. Doesn't that make us quits? Doesn't it give us a basis for—starting again? Look up at me! I don't like staring down at the crown of your head. Doesn't it?'

She drew in a deep breath that went into a hiccupping sob, aftermath of the storm.

He added, 'Hurry up and tell me, *mignonne*, because I can see Madame coming, and if she thinks I haven't made my peace with you, I'm more than sure she'll be after my scalp, and the thought of having Madame on the warpath would strike terror even into the heart of a volatile Frenchman, *full of amour*! Besides, I'm only about a quarter French, and a quarter English ... the rest is all Irish, and they're more known for fighting!'

She looked up instantly, their eyes locked, and she burst out laughing at him, and with him. He put out his hand and took hers and turned her round towards the path.

They both hurried then towards Madame. Pierre reached her first, put out both his hands. 'Madame, you ought not to have done it. This is a very steep hill. I promised you I would be kind to her.'

She looked at him sharply, then at Margot, and began to smile, but shook her head over them. 'I had to make sure. The young are so clumsy, so full of pride. I so well remember what it was like to be young, and not even for all its renewed vitality and eagerness would I go through it again. Can you tell me, *chérie*, or is it something solely between you and Pierre and—strangely enough—those other two who came here today?'

Pierre said quickly, 'It may be painful for Margot. Perhaps I could come and see you tonight, Madame, and tell you.'

Margot said, with a lilt in her voice, 'It won't be painful at all—now. Madame deserves not to be eaten up with curiosity. It's just that—as Sharlie and Leonie know very well but have kept to themselves—Pierre and I met in London just before I left England. Jonathan Worth, who was here today, and myself had kept company for a year. I couldn't

150

make up my mind to marry him. I sensed something wrong. What was wrong was that Betty was his true love and some-one had made mischief between them. I found out, and faded out of the picture—they never knew I'd found out—and I got away. That's all. But it was a shock today.'

Madame regarded her shrewdly. 'I think it is not quite all, *ma petite*, but perhaps the rest is between you and Pierre, yes?'

Pierre said, 'It isn't quite all by any means, Madame. She has been gallant and gay and I've grossly misunderstood her at times. She made a great sacrifice. She acted very con-vincingly her story about wanting a career and went to Canada, then came here.'

Madame's eyes were as bright as a thrush's. She put her head on one side and regarded them with great interest. 'She came here? Because it was *your* home, Pierre?'

Margot caught her breath. Would he say now, in this softened mood, why she had come?

But he hesitated, then said easily, 'Not exactly. Though I would like to think so. I'd talked of Akaroa as a haven of peace . . . so she found herself here.'

Madame said, 'But something I do not understand yet. When you fled up the hill, *mignonne*, you looked stricken. You do not look like that any longer. Why? I was terrified because it looked to me as if you loved this man Jonathan—and I sent Pierre after you.' She smiled, 'That is not quite right, he was flying after you even then, calling for you, demanding to be told where you had gone. But now—you look almost happy.'

Almost happy would about describe it. Because there was one more thing she must clear up with Pierre, but now she had confidence that perhaps that too could be explained. He must have a very good reason for being unsympathetic towards that quest.

Meanwhile she did not know how to answer Madame, because it involved Pierre. He took it out of her hands. 'Madame, it's a long story, and I promise you that you'll know it all soon . . . when I know it all myself. But I will tell you this. Margot did not come flying up here because it was too painful meeting Jonathan again. It was because she had thought I'd brought him here purposely to test her reactions. I hadn't. I met him—them—at the gate. We—we've just sorted that out.'

151

Madame's old eyes were wise and kind. She had noticed their linked hands as she had gained the crest. She twinkled, 'Perhaps I need not have climbed the hill, my children. You may have needed longer to yourselves.' She broke off as the sound of the dinner-gong, banged by Justine no doubt, reverberated.

She laughed and shrugged. 'This is life. Banality in the midst of dreams. You will, no doubt, find it an anti-climax to have to come down from the heights and eat, but Justine was making a very delectable veal-and-ham pie.' She looked at them with love in her eyes. 'Pierre, you want solitude, I know. It has been so busy ... the tourist season, the motel guests, the museum visitors, even old Jasper! All here at the wrong moment. Do you know the best place to be alone? I make you a present of the suggestion.... Beyond Bossu, on the saddle, where you can look a hundred miles north to the Kaikouras, and a hundred south to Timaru, and no one can come near you.' Her mouth twitched. 'I am quite capable of attending to visitors this afternoon.' Then she added, 'But if you do take her up the cliff road, Pierre, no discussion till you stop on the saddle.'

Margot had a feeling of being unable to refuse. Pierre could get himself out of it if he wanted to. But he didn't. So the three of them, Madame in the middle, went down the hillside to Justine's veal-and-ham pie.

CHAPTER NINE

THE fact that the others knew nothing of this morning's doings helped. The usual small talk restored Margot's pulses to normal, though now and then she was possessed by a feeling of unreality.

Pierre drew her out on the patio immediately after lunch. 'Margot, let's forget Bossu today. I'd rather take you up the mountain after the Worths have left the Peninsula. But I have a yen to tie up some ends.'

Margot looked alarmed. 'Pierre, not here within sight and sound of the Rossignols. They could come out. Interruptions are so——'

He smiled, shaking his head. 'Oh, I'm not embarking on

what I feel should be left to Bossu ... I want to tidy up this situation between you and the Worths.'

Margot looked even more alarmed. She clutched his arm. 'There's no need. They know nothing about this. It must stay that way. I want them to be happy.'

He possessed himself of her hands. He looked down on them. 'Margot, your hands are icy. And in this weather! You must warm up. I don't mean to tell them anything. It was just that you looked so distrait, so shocked, when they came in. You hadn't a vestige of colour. Oh, damn Tod for sending them here—though of course it was quite natural. He knows nothing of this. I know now that it was only because you thought I'd played a dastardly trick on you that you looked upset. But I think Jonathan and Betty must have wondered. Certainly Madame noticed it. That was why she practically withdrew her invitation to lunch, gave them an excuse not to accept.

'I admire you terrifically for the way you reacted when you saw Jonathan and Betty meet at that reception. I kept thinking back to it all through the veal-and-ham pie.' He grinned at her, willing her to smile back, to lighten the situation and was rewarded by seeing her lips twitch. 'That's it, there's always a funny side. But I'd not be a bit surprised if Betty is thinking right now—even if she isn't saying it to her husband—that Margot isn't as indifferent to Jonathan as she had hoped. And Jonathan must have noticed it too, even if he's probably wise enough to say nothing to her.'

Margot looked completely dismayed now. Her hands gripped his. 'Pierre, this is doing nothing for my peace of mind. Until now I hadn't thought of that. I was only furious with you—and hurt. I——'

The warmth of his hands was putting life back into hers.

'Idiot!' he said. 'I'd not have said a word if I thought we could do nothing about it, but we can. We can put on an act. That's why we won't call on old Bossu today. After you excused yourself and fled, I went out to their rental car. Jonathan, naturally, seeing Tod had asked them to look me up, asked was it possible for me to go with them, and this other couple, around the Eastern Bays this afternoon. I pleaded urgent work, because I had to find out first how you felt. I was going to wring the truth out of you, but I didn't have to. But now I've a plan.

'Let's ring them, say I've managed to wangle an afternoon

off and I'll come, but that *of course* you'll be coming with me. We'll be very, very affectionate towards each other, and in the next day or two I'll drop a few hints. They know you met me at that lecture. They can think you fell in love with me at first sight'—his eyes danced—'and that you knew immediately I was your true love, so, to sort out your feelings, when Roxanne asked you to go to Canada, you cut and ran. Then, after exchanging many letters, I asked you to come to Akaroa to see where I lived. That way neither of them will ever dimly suspect you saw them at that lecture.'

Margot's pansy-dark eyes widened, assessed the possibilities, then she started to laugh. 'Oh, Pierre, what cunning! I think you've got something. But are you sure, quite sure you want to be involved to this extent? It could be embarrassing.'

'Imbecile! What amorous Frenchman could find anything but delight in such a situation?' He sobered. 'Besides, I owe you something. Twice I've condemned you outright—quite mistakenly—questioned your motives, credited you with all sorts of unethical behaviour, sneered at the way you settled in here, wormed your way in was how I described it once—— Oh, Margot, how could I? But we can't go into all this now. Because we'll want a longish afternoon and I'll have to ring right away. But we have all the time in the world ahead of us.'

She clutched him again. 'Pierre, do you think I can do it? Convincingly? Do you think *you* can? It would be dreadful if they suspected it was a put-up job.'

He came back to her, his dark eyes glinting. 'How little you know me. I shall be outrageously full of *amour*. Like this!'

He seized her, his grip like iron, and kissed her.

Margot had no time to dodge.

As he freed her, she heard François's voice, rueful, yet with a hint of laughter, 'Oh, my apologies ... I'd no idea you two were even out here.'

Pierre burst out laughing. 'Serves us right! There are less public places than this patio, in full view of all Rossignol Bay, Frank, but who cares? Margot, I'll go and phone them.'

Justine was washing the dishes and Madame drying, and they were fairly sure Madame had said something was going on. Pierre simply announced, 'Justine, you'd be able to assist Madame if she gets a lot of visitors this afternoon, wouldn't you? By the oddest coincidence Margot knows this couple

154

my friend Tod sent here. I'm skipping work, and taking them and an Auckland couple to the Eastern Bays this afternoon. They'll have a much better time with two locals along.'

Two. At long last Pierre Laveroux no longer regarded her as an outsider. Margot knew a glow at her heart unequalled ever before and was afraid to face what it meant. She pushed the thought away from her.

Pierre said, 'Put on that new pink suit, Margot ... it's just right for today. And a string of pearls. I always think you look just right in pearls.'

There was a note in his voice that made Justine look at him and look away again. And François was wearing a very benign look.

Oh dear, Margot realised the whole family cherished match-making plans. This could be a complication. Unless Pierre—she snapped down the thought.

She said to Pierre they could be creating a complicated situation. He only chuckled. 'Let's take each complication as it comes. Having got you very neatly out of any awkward aftermath of this morning's shock, I'm sure I can cope with anything.'

'Did anyone ever tell you how egotistical you are, Pierre Laveroux?'

'I don't remember that particular adjective. The only person who has been devastatingly candid with me in sitting beside me at the moment, and I'm practically sure she has never used that one before.'

In their shared laughter, it became glorious, mischievous fun.

Pierre said, 'Tell me, are they going to like the things we like ... the old, old things? Crumbling gravestones with moss almost obscuring the names, Maori artifacts that are really Stone Age relics ... are they going to get a thrill out of the hole in a greenstone *mere* that took months of patient work to drill, because they had no metal tools? Will they be able to see the Peninsula as it was, with timber down to the water's edge, almost impenetrable?'

Margot hesitated, then said, 'Will I sound smug if I say I don't know if Jonathan will—quite? He'll enjoy the novelty, but he may not be able to people these hills as we do, with our imagination. May not be able to project himself back into the past.'

She was surprised to hear Pierre say, 'Good!' rather

roughly.

'Why good?'

'I don't know—particularly. Never thought of myself as a jealous sort of chap before, but——' He hesitated, and it was something to see Pierre at a loss for words. He looked down on her. 'Forget it. Some things are better not analysed.'

He saw the dimple in her chin deepen. She said, 'You are really getting right into the part, aren't you?'

'If you like. I said, don't let's analyse. Not today, anyway.'

They passed Barry's Bay and came into Duvauchelle and Margot looked at the harbour, lying as vividly as a giant *paua* shell, with Onawe Peninsula lying on its bosom like a jasper pendant.

She said softly, 'Te Pa Nui O Hau ... The Chief Home Of Wind.' She said it with love. Then added, 'You asked, in effect, Pierre, if Jonathan was a kindred spirit. The answer is, not quite. Perhaps kindred spirits are few and far between, but occasionally I was conscious of a gulf. Perhaps I was too high-falutin' by far, yet it is so nice to be able to share the little thoughts one has. I felt we had big things in common, but the little things that so delighted me, he thought were just a bit silly.

'Do you remember the day you told me that the Peninsula meant The Chief Home Of Wind, that among the huge boulders of rock that crown the hill, dwells the Spirit of the Wind? And I said to you that perhaps there was a trypot on the top, but instead of trying blubber, the colours of the wind were tried out ... azure blue for a summer day, turquoise for one like this, a green wind for spring, a soft baby-pink one for the dawn, a coral and amber wind for sunset ... do you remember?'

He glanced at her swiftly again. No hint of strain in the oval face now. 'I certainly do! I even added a few of my own ... ice-blue and diamond-white with a cutting edge in winter, gun-metal for a wind presaging storm, scarlet for the early morning red sky that is the shepherd's warning, lavender for the wind that springs up at dusk. Why? Why are you asking me?'

'Because once I asked Jonathan, on a day in Wales, when we stopped for a picnic on the Brecon Beacons, if he thought winds had colour, because if they had, the wind was golden and roystering that day, blowing in the tussock, just as it does on these Peninsula Hills. And he thought I was silly.'

156

She saw the lines in his cheeks deepen. 'And you took this lack of kinship for a signpost, telling you this was less than ideal?'

She nodded. 'I was never never quite sure. I told myself I was stupid, that most people approaching an engagement have *some* doubts. But, most of all, Jonathan wasn't a reader. He liked to be doing things. I always wondered if, when we were married, he might think I spent too much time reading, too much money in buying books. And I could never cut down on reading.'

Pierre said, 'I think that's a vital thing. I know, of course, that there's a certain attraction in opposites. It can make for variety. But I regard reading as fundamental and I think in fundamentals you must be one. Like Justine and François. Once when all the kids were away on holiday—ages ago—I came over with a message from Dad. I went to open the glass door off the patio. I had my hand raised—when I saw them. They were each sitting reading by the fire, absolutely absorbed. I felt their silence had a bond that speech couldn't better. Dad thought I was clean mad when I came back without delivering the message. But I felt I couldn't break that up.'

He was silent a moment, then asked curiously, 'You weren't afraid, then, after the rebuff you suffered from Jonathan, to try it on me—your whimsical fancy about the colour of winds?' When she didn't reply he said sharply, 'You were testing me, weren't you?'

Her eyes came up to his and fell. 'Yes,' she said, then because she didn't want him to probe further, 'There's my favourite *ngaio* tree ... see, all twisted and gnarled. It has such character.'

'Red herring,' said Pierre. 'Yes, it's a lovely tree, I've known it all my life. And further on I like the stunted olives ... you can see them silhouetted against the blue of the Harbour. Right, Margot, I'll leave it. The next two days we'll give to Jonathan and Betty and they can go away perfectly satisfied. Not feel guilty about their own happiness. We're nearly into Akaroa, better slip into your part now ... shed your prickles, girl, be all loving and dewy-eyed and radiant over me ... hope you don't find it too hard.'

Martin Resborough and his wife Lois were completely fascinated by Akaroa. Lois said, 'I read of this, long ago, at school, but you have to come here, to realise how French it is. The first glimpse of the notices in two languages at that garage made me aware of it right away ... to see an A-grade mechanic listed as *mécanicien première classe.*'

Her husband looked mischievous. 'To say nothing of the following notice ... *Cabinets propres* for clean toilets!' Lois aimed a blow at him.

Even Jonathan waxed enthusiastic about the beauty of the Peninsula, even if he wasn't as responsive as Pierre to fanciful flights of imagination.

They were all spellbound over the beauty of the bitten-in Eastern Bays. Betty said, 'They're so unspoiled, so tranquil ... the roads from the crests just wander down to them and finish in a solitary beach ... no souvenir shops, no merry-go-rounds, just peace and solitude.'

They wandered along the sands, listened to tales of old wrecks from Pierre, took off their shoes and splashed through little creeks that ran down to the sea, watched the tide swirling up a tidal bore, picked up strange shells and specimens of volcanic rocks and pebbles, pitted by an eruption of long ago, ruby-red ones, deep lavender, green, blue and all the lesser shades.

Pierre offered to treat them in his stone-polisher, so they might have permanent reminders of this halcyon day ... he would mail them to their Auckland home and their Christchurch hotel ... they explored caves, hunted for relics of long ago occupation, and saw a small plane land on one beach and take off with fertiliser for top-dressing these steep hills and gullies. They did more than justice to the afternoon tea Justine had so hurriedly packed.

Lois egged Pierre on to tell all he knew. 'You see, they're not fiords proper,' he said, 'because they were not gouged out by glacier action. Banks Peninsula is due to two extinct volcanoes that were active less than half a million years ago.'

'Practically modern,' said Lois, laughing.

'The craters got eroded by the streams running down from the watersheds of the hills—took thousands of years—then they were invaded by the sea during the post-glacial world rise in sea-level about fifteen thousand years ago, and so formed the harbours of Lyttelton and Akaroa. Akaroa means Long Harbour. Akaroa, of course, was much earlier in use by whalers of many nations than Lyttelton—called Port Cooper in those days—was. But its difficulty of access in those days kept it a backwater.

'From Lyttelton, the pioneers had to climb just one hill to be over the top on to the fertile Canterbury Plains with its great spread of unforested land for building and pasture. So we remained less developed.'

'But it has been a blessing, it has retained its old world charm this way,' said Lois. 'I'm going back to spread its fame in Auckland. I'm sure many North Islanders have never visited here. And Akaroa itself is just like the French villages I saw when I was overseas two years ago. How wonderful that we met up with you and Margot, who know so much about it all ... especially its history. I find it fascinating that Madame, whom you talk about, can actually remember one of the first pioneers, her grandfather.'

Margot's eyes were shining. 'That's because in Akaroa the past is only yesterday.'

Lois said softly, 'You love it, don't you? Even though you were born in England. You love it as much as if your roots were here.'

Pierre said swiftly, glinting laughter in his eyes, 'Her roots *are* here.'

Margot caught her breath in and bit her bottom lip to still its trembling. He was admitting that her forebears were here. Then he no longer knew antagonism to her quest.

But no ... it was part of the game they were playing, because he added: 'Even a transplanted tree's roots go deeply, in time, and Margot transplanted very easily. And her future, *of course*, is here.'

Lois played into his hands. 'Margot, Pierre said you first met when he gave a lecture and showed slides in London, on Akaroa. Did you fall in love with the place from thirteen thousand miles away?'

Pierre got in before Margot could say yes. The audacious light was in his eyes, but his tone natural. 'Let's say rather ... to boost my ego ... that she fell in love with me! It was mutual, even if I insisted she came here first to find out how she would like living at the other end of the world. If she hadn't, I would have stayed in London.'

This was a declaration with a vengeance! Margot had thought he was only going to give the impression they were starting to fall in love, but this—he was going too fast. She gave him an imploring look which he read aright, because he added, 'It's not being announced yet, so keep it to yourselves,

159

would you? We're having a ball in April, just a couple of weeks away, to mark the end of the tourist season. It's going to be an especially important function for me ... at it, they're going to make official announcement of my new position ... publicity officer for the Peninsula. Our property joins the Maison Rossignol garden at the sea verge. I'm going to build my own motels there, and an office for tourism.

'It's too bad you four won't be here for that ball ... it's going to be really something. It's to be in costume, French Period stuff. We were going to hire costumes for the girls, but Madame had insisted on ordering gowns of their own for Margot, Charlotte and Leonie. Can't you imagine Margot in rose brocade ... just like Marie Antoinette? Oh, my stars, it was to be a surprise! Tante Elise countermanded the order for hiring. But, Margot, I'm sure you can pretend surprise when Tante Elise gives it to you. But the ball will be the ideal setting for the announcement, we think.'

He was outrageous! They took Margot's confusion for merely delighted shyness. Well, he'd made his point, even if not as subtly as Margot had supposed he would.

It was a day made to order, with gulls shining like beaten silver against the cobalt of the sky, little puffs of cloud clinging lovingly to the crags on the peaks. They found small pockets of native bush sweet with fern and cascade, heard the *riroriro* singing its small, sweet song, watched fantails in curving, flirting flight against the clay cliffs of Okain's Bay.

They were charmed with the private museum of Maori relics at Okains, fingering *taiahas*, *meres* and *patu paraoas*. They heard that the owner had brought back several pieces from England after more than a century away from New Zealand. A treasure-box, for instance, the *waka huia* where the prized *huia* feathers were kept. Other pieces were non-Maori, a French Charleville military flintlock musket for instance, still capable of firing a ball with accuracy, and a French flintlock pistol, dated 1822. There was a bullock wagon, a buggy with a dickey seat, a governess cart, a sulky and a spring dray.

They went on to Little Akaloa, a corruption of a Maori name, since the Maori alphabet contains no 'L'. It ran back in a green triangle into hills that were the very epitome of pastoral felicity with sleek black-and-white cattle and snowy flocks, and with gabled homesteads tucked into colourful gardens.

They visited St. Luke's church, admiring the stone cutting and the use of *paua* shell in the exquisite Maori carving. It stood serene on its headland, dreaming of its past. Margot traced with a loving finger the words: 'In the morning sow thy seed and in the evening withhold not thine hand.' She said, 'They didn't. They sowed it broadcast and left a heritage of beauty for us.'

As they came out into the hillside graveyard she said, without thinking, 'Not so many graves bearing the name of Francis here...'

Pierre took her up. 'As where?'

'As in the cemetery at Akaroa.' She saw him frown and said easily to Betty, 'It seems to be the most common name among the men. Just as Rose, particularly as a second name, seemed to be the most frequent among the women.' She looked at Pierre, but his face gave nothing away. As if he didn't know why she said it!

Jonathan said, 'Like yours ... Margot Rose.' He paused, said, 'Actually, that could be French. Isn't Margot a French name?'

Pierre looked at him amazedly. 'Of course it's French. Margot *is* French.'

Jonathan said, 'I hadn't realised. Have you really got some French blood in you? You never said.'

Margot said firmly, 'I only found out the day I first met Pierre, from the family solicitor. It was on my father's side, the father I never knew. And I expect that as Aunt Ruth detested my father—quite unfairly—she never mentioned it.'

Lois said, 'That makes Akaroa doubly the right place for you, Margot.'

Again Pierre's expression gave nothing away.

By the time they had visited Pigeon Bay and Port Levy, it was time to come back to the hotel for dinner. Later they wandered round the foreshore in the twilight and Pierre made arrangements for them to go out in one of the fishing boats the next day so they could see the more inaccessible bays from the sea and he promised them a visit to Nikau Palm Gully if they didn't mind a fairly arduous walk. Lois was all for this, saying seeing was believing and she'd no idea *nikaus* grew so far south.

So that would take care of tomorrow morning and afternoon ... and Pierre had asked them all to the homestead at

161

Rossignols' for dinner the next night. It seemed it was going to be hard to get Pierre to herself to ask him straight out where her father was, which family had he visited here. Then she thought of the drive home, when they would leave the others at the hotel. She was confident now that he would tell her. She thought she would wait till they came into the dark serenity and solitude of Rossignol Bay tonight.

But they were only as far out of Akaroa as Takamatua Bay, once called German Bay, when the car packed up. They had to walk back to Akaroa and knock up that A-grade mechanic.

So Margot held her tongue. This wasn't to be introduced when a man's thoughts, even anxiety and irritation, were centred on his car. It proved more serious than Pierre had anticipated and it was fortunate it hadn't happened on the hills. The oil sump had sprung a leak. They went back with the mechanic towing it, and rang François Rossignol.

François arrived with his trousers pulled over his pyjamas, and a turtle-necked sweater on. He laughed, 'The course of true love never runs smoothly, Pierre. Even in the old days, coaches could lose a wheel or a horse a shoe. Pile in. The girl goes in the middle like the filling in a sandwich. Leonie is sleeping at Maison Rossignol tonight. You can turn into her bed, *mignonne*. Justine switched it on and is so sure you'll be cold, she's heating up some soup.'

Soup! How romantic. It should have been nectar and ambrosia. Nevertheless, it had been a most successful day. Jonathan and Betty couldn't possibly have a doubt left, due to Pierre's outrageous behaviour.

When they got to the Bay, François said, 'Coming in for some of that hot soup, Peter?' These two men often anglicised each other's names.

Pierre said, 'No, but one thing I'd like.'

'What? You have only to name it.'

'Five minutes alone with Margot.'

François burst out laughing. 'I must be pretty dim when you have to ask me. Take all the time you want. I'll tell Justine to put the soup in a flask for her.'

Margot said firmly, 'You'll do nothing of the kind. I'll be in in less than five minutes so the family can settle down again. I mean it, Pierre.'

She said, as soon as they were alone, 'Pierre, there's no need to carry this to extremes. It's mighty late and you did get Mr. Rossignol out of bed. He's very good-natured, but there are limits. And no need, since Jonathan and Betty are not here, to carry on with——'

'Oho, you think I want to carry on a little pleasant dalliance? I don't. I merely wanted to say that when you and the others went back round St. Luke's to see if they could get a better view for photos, Jonathan said something to me. Remember he went with me for petrol?

'He asked me about our meeting this morning. He said he was well aware in his own life how situations could get out of hand; could get gummed up. That he was very upset about how shocked you looked when he and Betty walked in without warning. He put it down to the fact that you just might not have told *me* that you had once kept company with *him*. He said that obviously it had been love at first sight with us both, and had probably been a deciding factor in your refusal of him. He felt it was a pity if his coming might make us quarrel later. I had to admire him. He said I ought to know that all along you had been very half-hearted about saying yes to him, and he hoped this would not spoil anything.

'I think I can pride myself I handled it pretty well. I told him that you had been completely frank with me. Well, so you have been—now—I said that once you met me, you knew you must say no to him. I said I hoped he'd not find this too deflating, that these things just happened. But I didn't think he would, as he and his wife were so obviously happy and well matched. I said it had given you a bit of a shock—that you'd thought it better we should not meet, but that as I hadn't minded, you were reassured now.

'He rose to this, said that in actual fact, Betty had been his first love, and that, although he had felt you and he could make a go of life together, it was better the way things had turned out. And he was very happy to think we were about to announce our engagement.'

Margot gave him a wide, happy smile. 'For plot and counterplot, Pierre Laveroux, you have no equal.'

She turned to go and said a quick goodnight over her shoulder.

He reached her as she put her hand to the knob. 'There's gratitude for you! Not even a thank you.'

She pulled a face at him, said mock-seriously, 'Then thank you, your high-and-mightiness. Now can I go in, having said my piece?'

'You can in a moment,' he said, kissed her quickly but thoroughly, and ran down the terrace steps to the lane.

The next day was as idyllic as the one before, yet Margot found herself longing for it to pass. The other four were delighted with the evening they spent at Rossignol Homestead, and fascinated with Madame's tales that she had learned at her grandfather's knee. Pierre was outrageously attentive to Margot, and paid no attention whatever to her reproachful or imploring looks when she thought no one was looking. Leonie sat and gazed at them with a beatific expression and Margot had no doubts at all that she would retire to bed to write Sharlie at length.

François and Justine tried unsuccessfully to hide their delight and only Madame remained herself, chatting to their guests and taking it as if it had been a foregone conclusion and an established fact. Jules wore a broad grin and spent ages on the study phone talking to Christchurch. Bridget for a certainty, so possibly Leonie's letter-planning would be unnecessary.

Finally the guests were sped. Pierre did not linger but went off to his own house as the guests got into their car. He said, 'I won't see you till tomorrow afternoon, Margot, about one-thirty. I've a chap from Dalgety's coming. Mrs. Grendon is cooking dinner for us. Justine will take over the museum, I'm taking you up Bossu.' Just like that.

Margot went to bed conscious of a singing happiness pervading her whole being. Bossu. There would be nobody on the mountain save themselves. They ought to have all the time they wanted to sort out their differences. Though only one remained ... Pierre's strange reluctance to help her find her father.

There must be some good reason for it. Knowing him as she did now, she credited him with that. Especially as he had been so unsure of her for so long. Margot knew now why she had never quite brought herself to say yes to Jonathan. It was so simple. It wasn't just that she'd felt Jonathan lacking in real feeling. She herself had lacked it, but you had to meet up with the real thing to know.

The *real* thing.

How odd ... a year ago and Jonathan had seemed to be her whole world. Yet tonight when she had said goodbye to him for ever, she had said it so casually, saying to Leonie,

'Let's get in out of this wind, for goodness' sake. There's a real edge to it.'

Now all she could think of was Pierre and if, once more, they might quarrel over her father.

CHAPTER TEN

He rang next morning to say it would be two before he picked her up, and added, 'Wear that pink outfit.'

So it was important. She wasn't just indulging in wishful thinking. She dressed carefully, made up her face three times before it satisfied her, and came out to where Justine sat, ready for the museum visitors. 'You may not be very busy today, Justine, the tourists are getting thinned out now. Oh, here are some, after all.'

Pierre's station wagon that Margot called an estate car, was drawn up beside the gate. The visitors manoeuvred their car on to a patch of turf on the shore side of the road.

Justine said, 'It's funny and all ... we've got "Car Park" marked in letters on that board, two feet high, yet still they run their cars there. I've come to the conclusion the public just do not read notices. It's so much safer off the road verge, though at least they're getting out on the side away from traffic.'

Pierre was standing by his car, evidently waiting till the visitors should cross the road before he came for Margot.

Margot said to Justine, 'I'll go and speak to them ... seems to be a whole family.'

Pierre saw her coming and turned to her. His eyes met hers and there was no reserve in them. She thought they challenged her to smile unreservedly back, so she did. 'That's my girl,' he said softly. The sound of a car approaching made him turn his head.

At that moment, a toddler from the car freed her hand from her mother's restraining one and dashed out from the far side of their car, across the road.

Margot had never known anyone's reactions so fast. There was a light grey streak as Pierre hurled himself almost horizontally across the road, scooped up the little girl and continued hurtling to the verge with her.

The top part of him cleared the wing of the car, but his legs trailed out behind him. The mudguard caught one leg, twisted him over in his headlong flight; by some superhuman effort he dropped the child on to the grass and somersaulted in the air, past the child, flying right over the edge and down on to the rocky beach five feet below.

The car made a magnificent stop, though it slewed all over the road and finished up against the pickets. Margot was across the road before she realised it and down on to the rough, shell-encrusted boulders of the beach. Sea-birds, at the edge of the tide which was far, far out, rose squawking.

Pierre lay spreadeagled and still.

Justine reached him just one moment after Margot. Madame had disappeared inside—to ring François, they found later.

The driver of the car left the apparently unhurt child and was with them. Gently they turned Pierre's face a little. Already a livid bruise was spreading, but his eyes were closed and he hardly seemed to be breathing.

Justine said quickly, hopefully, 'I think he's just knocked out ... and possibly winded. Careful ... look, get——'

But Margot had stripped off her soft pink woollen jacket and was already packing it with infinite care beneath his head on the inhospitable rocks. Justine took his hands and began to chafe them, saying his name over and over.

Margot turned her attentions to his arms, feeling them gently, then said to the man, who was in great distress, 'I think they're all right. We mustn't move him till we get a doctor, I know, but help me to feel his legs. Please don't be too upset ... it wasn't your fault—— Oh!'

On the rock below Pierre's left leg was spreading a thick red stain. Margot didn't hesitate a moment. The cuff of his trousers was already ripped. She tore it further with a sort of desperate intensity that was nevertheless aimed at not doing any damage by movement. It was between knee and hip, an ugly spread-out wound, like a cross, with the edges turned back, enough to turn anyone sick. Yet she knew, somehow, that it was not a terribly serious wound, that it would heal, that no artery was cut.

The next moment Madame was there, no longer frail, and ten years younger in her actions. She had blankets caught up from one of the beds and a pile of freshly ironed table-linen. Margot hoped Pierre would stay unconscious for the next few moments, even though another part of her desperately hoped he'd give some sign soon that this was only temporary concussion and not severe damage to his head.

She said to Justine, 'Hold the edges of the flesh together, will you, as much as possible?' then she pressed down a table-napkin on the wound, shook out two others into long folded strips, laid them across, with Justine and the man holding them tightly in position, then, tearing a tablecloth into longer lengths, bound them firmly into place.

She looked up to see François and Jules. Jules said, 'I got the doctor just as he was leaving the hospital. He'll be here very soon. But the ambulance is away over to Pigeon Bay. I said okay, there are trucks here and station wagons. Oh God!'

Jules knelt down at Pierre's head. At that moment Pierre opened his eyes, looked puzzled, turned his head, winced, turned it again and stared curiously at—of all things—a large mussel-encrusted boulder. Then realisation dawned and he said, his lips moving with difficulty, 'Is she all right? The child?'

Margot managed to keep the tears from falling at that, but only just. She said crisply, 'Yes, she's only scratched, I'd say. She landed on the grass, but you went all the way and crashed on the beach. But you'll be okay soon. No, no, don't move. Not yet, Pierre.'

She saw his eyes cloud over and momentarily he lapsed into semi-consciousness again, then with great determination he lifted his lids and kept them open. 'What about the chap in the car? Did he run off the road? Is he hurt? No? Tell him it wasn't his fault at all. Nothing he could have done. Who's crying?'

Margot said, 'The child's mother. Reaction, I suppose. Relief that the little one is unhurt, thanks to you, and upset that you took the brunt of it. Pierre, shut up talking and tell us—in case you black out again—if you're hurt anywhere else. Your leg is gashed—as you're probably aware—but no artery was cut. The doctor will be here soon, but if you could tell us before he arrives if you're hurt badly anywhere else, it would help.'

Pierre began moving himself cautiously. He tried to manage a grin, very unsuccessfully. 'Hard to find a spot that isn't sore, darn it, but I'm pretty sure nothing's broken. Unless I've got cracked ribs. I feel bruised all over.' He drew in a

167

deep breath. 'Well, that's okay. If any ribs are gone, must be outward, not inward. Safer that way.'

'Don't move too much,' cautioned Margot, 'wait till the doctor arrives.'

Madame and Justine were packing the blankets round him to ease the hardness and chill of the boulders and Mrs. Grendon appeared with two hotwater bottles. 'And I've some hot sweet coffee here too.'

'Don't like it sweet,' muttered Pierre.

For some reason his pettishness cheered Margot. Too much compliance would have worried her. She said severely, 'You'll take it just as sweet as we give it to you and like it, what's more.'

'Bosscat!' said Pierre. 'I'm at your mercy, you fiend. Okay.'

By the time he'd sipped half of it, rather awkwardly, with them supporting his head, and Margot holding the cup to his lips, the doctor was there.

He grinned at Pierre. 'Well, Peter Partridge, I've had over two years of a very pleasant existence while you've been away. I see you've been bashing yourself up again. What's the damage?'

He examined him thoroughly, found no bones broken, then turned his attention to the leg wound, bleeding less now. He strapped it more expertly and said, 'I see you've got things ready for the trip. Good for you, Jules. You can drive and I'll go with him. Frank, you can drive my car to the hospital.'

Margot said calmly, 'I'm coming too. I'll sit with Jules.'

The doctor knew her well enough. He called regularly on Madame.

'You can sit on the floor with Peter if you like. My bones are older than yours.'

Jules and François had arranged a low camp stretcher with a rubber mattress and blankets. They lifted Pierre very carefully on to it and the bank was low enough to be negotiated without too much trouble in one particular spot.

The little girl who'd caused all the trouble was still wailing over her scratched knee. She was much too young to comprehend her share in it, only that she'd been caught up and thrown down by someone. Pierre said to the stretcher carriers, one of them the driver of the car, one the father, 'Stop a moment, would you?'

168

He put out a hand. 'Don't cry, poppet. It'll soon be better. I've got a sore leg too, but I can't walk on mine. But keep hold of Mum's hand next time.'

Pierre, on the way in, was determined to make light of it. 'How often is this you've stitched me, doc?'

The doctor sounded mock grim. 'The record sheets aren't big enough for the tally!' He turned to Margot. 'You want to thank your lucky stars you didn't know him in his green and salad days. He kept me busy. He and that madcap sister of his, Thérèse, I stitched them both up in one day once. Peter, when did you eat and how big a meal?'

Pierre, startled, said, 'I say, doc, you aren't going to put me out for it, are you? I thought a local.'

The doctor snorted. 'It's not just a straight stitching job. It's a repair, more than a split skin this time. You didn't think you'd be going home after it, did you? I'll want an X-ray of your head too. Merely precautionary.'

Pierre groaned, 'And I'm running that ball in a fortnight's time. I've a thousand and one things to do.'

The doctor was singularly unimpressed by this. 'I've never known illness come conveniently for anyone. You may be able to attend that ball, my lad, but you'll certainly not be tripping the light fantastic.'

He swung round in his seat and gazed in amazement at Pierre. 'Great Scott, I can remember when you had to be practically shanghaied to these affairs. You *must* be keen on the tourist trade to run a masquerade ball. There's patriotism for you, or is there a girl in this?'

'Yes,' said Pierre simply, 'Margot here.'

He was a gorgeous doctor, just like a big growly Teddy-bear. He actually hurrumphed. He inspected Margot over his spectacles. 'Well,' he said at last, 'sitting out with a pretty girl's as good as dancing with her. Better sometimes. I'll patch you up so you can hobble around.'

Margot said, 'Oh, for goodness' sake, Pierre, what's a ball matter? If you knew what we went through when you were hurtling through the air ... and all you can do is grizzle about a dance!'

He grinned. 'I really didn't enjoy it myself, but it could have been worse. Though to be cooped up in hospital just now is particularly galling, when I wanted to——' He caught her eye and shut up, the old twinkle faintly in them. Then suddenly the sedative the doctor had administered took

169

effect. Just as he was sinking into the billows of sleep that threatened to engulf him he caught her hand and said, 'Don't let Mum and Dad know, will you? They'd worry like hell and perhaps come home.' Then no more.

Fortunately he'd had a light lunch, meaning to have dinner at Rossignols' at night, but even so they had to wait some time. Pierre slept most of it. Jules and François and Margot waited. They rang the Bay and said they would stay till the repair job was over and Pierre had regained consciousness.

Then at last he was out of the theatre. François said to Jules, 'It will be some time before he comes out of it. I think you'd better get back for the milking, son. You'd better see if they need any help at Partridge Hill too. And come back for us later. We'll ring.'

François sensed that Margot was feeling the reaction. He set himself out to take her mind off it. It was significant that he talked mainly of Pierre and the Laveroux family, as if he were catching her up on its history. Margot just accepted this. Pierre had played his part so well to assure Jonathan and Betty that all was well, that the outcome was this and she and Pierre must go along with it meanwhile. How serious Pierre was, she did not know. And even when he was out of hospital, the business about her father must be cleared up first.

At last Pierre was conscious and they were called in to him. He was very white and lying very still and seemed to have trouble focussing his eyes. But he essayed a faint grin. 'You couldn't call me a volatile Frenchman now, full of *amour* and what-have-you, could you, *mignonne*?'

She said, wishing she had the right to hold his hand and ask if she might stay through the night, 'You mustn't talk, Pierre, you need quiet now, and sleep.'

He closed his eyes, opened them again with a great effort, 'It's been a very upsetting day for you all. Must go home now.' Then as they said goodnight to him, he said, his words slurred, 'My apologies to Bossu. But tell him I'll see him ... another day. He ... won't mind. He's a kindly hunchback, isn't he, Margot?'

François looked considerably startled. Margot said, patting Pierre's shoulder, 'Yes, Bossu will understand ... and wait. Goodnight, Pierre, we'll be back tomorrow.'

Pierre was disgusted to find himself quite a hero and the centre of much publicity. It seemed as if all Akaroa came to cheer the hours of recovery and he and Margot were never alone together.

Margot told herself it would teach her patience, that she had borne with fortitude all the setbacks about finding her father for months. Why then find this postponement—not longer than a week, probably—so irksome?

In honest moments she admitted it was more because when that was explained, the last barrier between herself and Pierre would be down. But the time dragged.

Then came an afternoon when she was quite alone. The Rossignols had received word that Australian friends were on board a cruise ship that was putting into Lyttelton Harbour, and had gone over the hill by way of Purau and would be spending hours showing them round Christchurch.

Mrs. Grendon was on duty at the motels and Margot was printing details about the latest acquisitions for the museum on some white cards when she heard the car stop. She went to the door.

Here was Pierre, getting out of what must be a rental car. He had a stick and was saving his left leg all he could and was rather thinner and paler, but he was here, he was here, and that was all that mattered.

She flew towards him, then stopped a little short. He sighed. 'You never quite forget yourself, do you, Margot Rose? I think when a chap comes home from hospital he deserves a spontaneous welcome.'

Margot said a little breathlessly, 'It's so public ... right on the road.'

He turned and surveyed the deserted road quizzically, then looked down at the shore. 'One little blue penguin, a kingfisher, three gulls and an oystercatcher. And none of them interested in anything else but food, Margot!'

She laughed, suddenly feeling deliciously lighthearted, and lifted her face. He steadied himself on the stick and bent his head. When he lifted it, he had an odd light in his eyes, as if he had proved something. She said, flushing, 'You must come in and get your weight off your leg. Oh, Pierre, why didn't you ring and I'd have come for you? You ought not to be driving.'

'The doctor had no objection. François rang me and said you'd be home alone, if by any chance I was coming home

171

today. He said to ask Mrs. Grendon to come down here—she'd see anyone coming to the motels. We are going to keep our appointment with Bossu.'

Margot said, 'Oh no, Pierre. Not on your first day out.'

'Don't cross me. Invalids should be humoured. And damned if I'll have interruptions this time. Margot, from now on the arrangements for the Ball are going to crowd in on us, even if I've done a lot from the hospital by phone. I know what's ahead, it's now or never. We owe ourselves this one afternoon to get all our wires uncrossed. My leg is marvellous—not for walking—but when driving.'

As she hurriedly slipped a brown parka over her brown tweed skirt and coral jersey she knew a regret for her pink suit, but they were still struggling with it at the cleaners, trying to remove seaweed stains and blood. What did it matter? Her heart was singing. Pierre was home, urgent to get up Mount Bossu, his favourite place...

As they drove round the shore road towards the Heads, he said, 'I kept to this small car, it's easier for passing on so narrow a road, though during weekdays there's hardly any. Most people take the Wainui road up. But I love the view from the cliff road. Anyway François told me the Wainui road is closed today. Margot, we'll do what Madame suggested and not talk—seriously, I mean—till we're on the summit. On the saddle where we can see south and north and the most glorious view in all the world ... if I'm allowed to be so prejudiced!'

The road climbed the hill on the very outer edge of the cliffs, it seemed. Margot was glad they were in a car smaller than the estate car. She said so. Pierre smiled, 'I know every inch of the road. Nobody speeds on this, *mignonne*. And we approach every corner with care ... like this...' He sounded his horn well before the corner and every succeeding corner.

'Nothing between us and the Chatham Islands five hundred miles east,' he said, waving, 'or the South Pole, just over three thousand miles south. Ever thought you'd like to visit the South Pole, Margot?'

She said hurriedly, 'Pierre, keep both hands on the wheel, *please*! No, not the South Pole for me, thanks. I didn't realize this road was so steep or so near the edge ... I expect you're used to it, but from here, I can only see sea and sky ahead.'

He laughed, but not scoffingly. 'Well, as long as you see

172

them in that order, it's okay, Margot. When you see them reversed ... sky and sea, then is the time to get alarmed!'

His very nonchalance was reassuring. He said, 'But we won't come back this way, we'll go right along the summit and drop down to Little River.' He blew the horn again and rounded a corner, said sharply, 'Watch it!' and threw on his brakes, coming to a shuddering stop only feet from a gaping, washed-out hole in the road where just a crust remained of what had been a well-shingled and solid hill road.

But for their safety belts they'd have injured themselves on the windscreen. Pierre lost no time in going into reverse against the hill and letting one back wheel slide into the groove of the water-table.

Margot was appalled. Pierre said, 'It's okay, we ourselves are all right—it won't undermine any further here—but we must inspect it and see what we can do ... that far edge is much nearer the upper corner than this one is, and if anyone comes round there, downhill, it would be much harder to pull up in time.'

He got out with surprising agility, but took his stick. They crept a little nearer, because if the crust this side was as thin as the overlapping crust they could see at the other, it could crumble any moment.

They were aghast when they realised the extent of it. It dropped right into an enormous hole, and not only the surface had caved in, but the most huge boulders had been torn from their embedding and lay far below at the bottom of the hollow, that did not extend, fortunately, to the edge of the cliff.

Pierre said, 'I don't get it. This has never been prone to subsidence here and we've had no excessive rain. If it was right at the gully, I'd think the creek had suddenly worn it all away, but it's not.' He peered over. 'But that is water below. I'm inclined to think this is due to some geological fault of long ago suddenly caving in—in fact, has fallen into an unsuspected cave below it. The Peninsula is full of them. Back in the early days the railway tunnel contractors gained time and money because of huge caves beneath. It's taken out the whole width of the road, so we can't edge past. But we've got to do something—and pronto—about that far corner. I can put the car across this corner—anyone coming up would then see it—oh, if only someone else would come up, then they could return to the shore road to a telephone. And

I could climb over the bank and across the gully and take up a warning stand in the middle of the road.'

Margot said, staring, 'With that leg? Don't be ridiculous. The stitches are only just out. One slip and the wound would open and how much help would you be to anyone then? If anyone gets to the other side, it will be *me*.'

They got into an intense, low-toned argument, fast and furious, because they knew that whatever they decided must be done quickly. Even as they fought, they were looking and listening fearfully to each side, dreading the sound of a car coming.

Pierre dropped his stick and thumped one clenched fist into the palm of his other hand. 'How do you think I'm going to feel,' he demanded, 'watching the girl I love climbing up that clay bank, all eroded, knowing it may crumble and crash below, any moment and——'

She broke in hotly, 'How do you think *I'd* feel, watching the man I love, *injured and lame*, attempting it? How would I ever get you off that bank if anything happened to you? Oh, what *did* I say? . . . what did *you* say——?'

For one startled moment they gazed at each other, then Pierre said savagely, 'If ever the stars in their courses fought against anyone, they've fought against us. There's a hoodoo on us. Imagine declaring myself at a time like this! Oh, blast Madame and her old Bossu . . . Margot, it'll have to wait, but come what may, at least we know!'

Pierre added irritably, 'We've got to decide what's best to do. All right, Margot. I'll turn the car and go for help. I may meet someone coming up and they can go. If not I'll reach the first telephone. But I'll see you up and over first. Oh, God, be careful.'

Margot felt strength from an unknown source flow into her. She was suddenly shining-eyed. 'We'll make it, Pierre. I could face anything now.' Suddenly her face changed. It blanched. 'T—turn the car—on—this road? Oh, no, Pierre. But you couldn't walk that far. Oh, what are we to do?'

He said quietly, 'Margot, I've turned on roads as narrow as this before. You do it a few inches at a time. I've got to get it across . . . I mean in any case, to act as a barrier. You know I have to do this, don't you?'

She swallowed, painfully, because her mouth was dry. 'Yes, I know, but you must do it before I go across that gully. I—couldn't watch you from there. Just don't ask me.

174

It would be no use.'

He recognised implacability. He got in the car. Margot was bathed in perspiration as she watched him yet she knew he would make it. He was infinitely patient. Her hands were clenched, her ears straining for traffic coming either way, prepared to act as needed.

She knew an exquisite relief when she saw the wheels make their final turn and the car face downhill right on the bend, where it could be seen from below. Pierre chocked the wheels with big rocks.

He came to her, limping, leaning heavily on the stick. He took her hand with his free one. His eyes held misery. 'I've got to let you do it, but God go with you. We'll waste no time because lives may depend upon it. When you get over there, go right out on the bend where any car coming will be bound to see you. The car that comes—if one comes—will take you straight to the first homestead.' He told her roughly where that would be. 'The people there will know who to contact, but I'd better tell you in case they're out ... if they are, break in if the place is locked. But the driver must not go down to the house with you. He must stay on the road to stop any oncoming traffic.

'Don't worry about me. The road coming up was very solid. Now listen, Margot. You must climb high, away from that fault. When you get well up past it you'll still have the gully to negotiate and you will be out of my sight. The little stream that drains that gully will be very low, but there is just a chance that the fault may go under it, unseen. The further you go up, the firmer the ground will be, but watch the terrain as you go. Don't worry about the road till you're safely over. I'll keep a good lookout and if I hear a car coming I'll yell like blazes hoping he'll have his window open. On your way!'

They had not time to kiss. She clambered up on to the powdery clay bank, clutching at tussock, and once she was up shouted to him, 'Oh, it looks very firm in the gully, even fairly near the edge.'

'You keep away from that edge,' he roared. 'Take no chances, no shortcuts. Right, on you go ... I'll stand out in view as much as possible.'

To each of them, but possibly most to Pierre who had to stand and wait, it seemed an age, though in actual fact it was only twenty minutes. It wasn't particularly hard going ...

175

except for one bit where Margot thought there had been some subsidence and she had to fight her way upwards in the small stream, where the bush met overhead, and struggle through supplejack and wild blackberry.

Then she gained the shoulder of the hill, tussocky and slippery, but gloriously firm beneath that tussock. Now Pierre would see her again, so it would lessen his dread. She waved to him as she disappeared down the back past the corner, slithered ungracefully down a six-foot bank and landed on her hands and knees in sharp shingle. She scrambled up and rounded the corner cautiously.

She heard Pierre shout, 'Margo—o—o! Keep back. Not too near that edge!' And she cupped her hands about her mouth and called, 'It's okay, perhaps I look nearer to it, than I am. Now go, Pierre, and be careful. I've got a good view here of any car that might come.'

She saw him remove the chocks, and inch slowly forward downhill. Her straining ears followed the sound of his retreat till it was lost in silence. Foolish to be so fearful. He knew this road so well.

He would be back with help before long. And here she was, with half the South Island East Coast spread before her ... here was the solitude they had sought ... how ironical, when now all she longed for was proof in human form that someone else beside her and the sea-birds and that uncaring lark singing so madly and happily in the blue inhabited this lofty, dangerous world.

She looked up at Bossu, with his shoulders hunched up against the sou'west where the cold weather came from, and, to give herself courage, said, 'But *you* are here, Bossu. And Pierre did declare himself in your shadow, after all. Oh, God of all the hills and of kindly old Bossu, be with Pierre. Keep him safe, and all people who travel on this road today. Send help soon, for all our sakes.'

She kept an anxious eye on the subsidence ... it might even have been a minor earthquake, unfelt by themselves because they had been in a moving vehicle. A verse of Isaac Watt's great hymn sprang into her mind,

> '*Let mountains from their seats be hurled*
> *Down to the deeps and buried there,*
> *Convulsions shake the solid world ...*
> *My faith shall never yield to fear,*'

176

and she felt immeasurably comforted.

Five minutes later she heard a car coming. She walked towards it, arms outstretched. It was a lovely sight.

The motorist pulled up, surprise on every feature. He stuck his head out of the window. 'Well, that's the most definite way of thumbing a ride I've ever seen! How come you——'

She interrupted, explained quickly and forcibly, and he came to see the gap. He whistled.

She said, 'So Pierre said to go to the first homestead. Let's get cracking.'

'I happen to own the first homestead. In you get. And when I take the driveway, you can stay out on the road.'

He seemed to take an age, but when he reappeared he was in a truck and accompanied by his wife, and in the tray they had some hurdles to act as temporary barriers till Ministry of Works men could get to them from Little River.

His efficiency and the help his wife gave him were marvellous to watch. He had stakes in the car and some huge pieces of red cloth, roughly torn up. They both laughed. 'Our little girl wanted a red frock! What she'll say we don't know.'

They tacked the red cloth to the stakes to act as preliminary warning flags, then drove them into the road verge. Across the road they placed the hurdles, well back from the corner.

Twenty minutes later they heard trucks coming up the far side and went to the edge of the gap but far enough back for safety. The trucks would not come round the corner, they thought, but one did, very slowly. The driver got down, assisted his passenger to alight from the high step. Pierre. He looked overwhelmingly relieved to see Margot had company.

Doug Brixton shouted across, telling them what had been done, to the approval of the Ministry of Works men.

Margot called out, 'I'll start across now, same way as I came over.'

There was immediate dissent from the other side. The foreman and Pierre shouted across that a lot of loose stuff must have come down since she climbed across, and that on no account was she to risk it.

Doug Brixton said to Margot, 'It will be late before we can leave here ... it will take time for the gang to get from Little River and get flashing lights up and so on. You must spend the night with us. It's just too far for me to take you into Little River and get back again in time for milking.'

Margot felt a terrific sense of anti-climax wash over her. Wouldn't it! ... just when there was practically nothing to keep her and Pierre apart, they were separated by a landslip!

But she had to accept it. There had been danger enough. She cupped her hands about her mouth and shouted to Pierre that he must go home now and rest his leg and it might be as well to get the doctor round. And he was to spend the night at the Rossignols' where Justine could keep an eye on him.

She hoped desperately that Pierre would suffer no lasting harm to his leg. The doctor was going to be furious and justly so. Though at least their foolishness may have saved a tragedy. The thought of any car coming downhill into that didn't bear thinking about.

CHAPTER ELEVEN

IT had been worse than she thought. When she got home at midday the following day, she found Pierre was back in hospital. As soon as Justine had seen the wound, she had taken him straight to Akaroa.

What was worse was that Justine would not take Margot in to see him. She said severely, 'If you could be seeing yourself as others are seeing you, you'd know there was but one place for you, and that: bed! And not just for this afternoon and tonight, either, but for tomorrow besides. It will do the two of you all the good in the world to be lying quietly in your beds, having a rest from each other. The next week is going to be really hectic ... with the Ball so close. I've had a talk with the doctor.'

François openly chuckled. 'Margot, when my wife gets into a mood like this, it's so rare, we just give in. And there's sense to it. It *has* been a very trying time. You're thinner and paler than I like to see you. We would like you and Pierre fit enough to enjoy yourselves. Neither of you is going to do a thing to getting the woolshed ready. Charlotte and Leonie and Bridget and Jules are in charge. They're planning some marvellous decorations. Leonie—suppose I do praise my own

178

daughter—is doing some wonderful murals and her class at the High School is coming over the day before to go up into Beaudonais's Bush to get ferns and vines and orchids and *toe-toe* fronds for decorating.'

Sharlie arrived with some boxes that must contain the frocks Leonie and Margot were supposed to know nothing about. 'Those,' she said to Margot, 'are not to be opened till tonight when the museum is closed. Gosh, I wish Pierre were here, but Dad said the doctor said he might be well enough to come home tomorrow.'

'And he will stay here,' said Justine, pushing her red hair out of her eyes, 'where I can keep an eye on him. I don't know what his mother would say, the way he's been going on. Oh, it wasn't your fault, Margot. I know Pierre. He's hard to turn from a set purpose, that one. Men are like that, especially the tough ones. It makes them very bad patients. They feel it an insult to their manhood to be ill. So they have no sense and abuse their convalescence and all.'

Margot was amused to see how often Madame cast an eye on the boxes and smiled to herself. Finally they were ready to settle for the evening. The dishes were washed, the fire glowing red to its heart, and the murals Leonie had been busy on, stacked against the bookshelves, face in.

'And now,' said Madame, 'the time has come. Sharlie, dear child, I can contain myself no longer. Open them.' Her black eyes swept round the room. 'Sharlie acted for me in this. She smuggled garments belonging to Leonie and Bridget and Margot to my dressmaker in Christchurch. Possibly they may need altering, but—go ahead, Charlotte.'

Sharlie cut the strings of the first one and shook out a frock. 'Oh, that's mine. I meant to leave it till the last ... look, an Alice-blue gown, like the girl's in the picture ... isn't it sweet? And this is Bridget's. She's going to drop sophistication for the ball and be *une jeune fille*.'

Margot saw Jules look quickly from Bridget to the gown and back again. Bridget caught his eye and smiled back. They would not have a stormy courtship, those two. Already they were one. Bridget would look enchanting in this ... it was Empire style, with knots of roses under the high waist, and a pleated bodice of white ninon, and golden satin ribbons fell to the hemline.

Leonie's eyes were like stars as a green taffeta came into view. 'Mine?' she gasped. She held it up against her, her

179

bright hair like a newly-minted copper coin above the green. It had silver lace panels and clusters of silver ribbons at each corner of the square neck. Madame had spared no expense.

Then Madame said softly, 'And now my protégée's. Margot's!'

It was exquisite, pure eighteenth-century. Rose-coloured brocade and gauze, elegant panels opening over the lace flounces of the underdress, with a high, fitting bodice, cut low, but with an off-the-shoulder fichu caught across the breast.

There was a rush for the bedrooms to try them on. Although Sharlie wouldn't allow Margot to emerge till she had altered her hair style. 'Your hair lends itself to almost any style, but particularly this, without much setting. Please let me. It will enhance it for Madame.' So Margot submitted.

Sharlie was a born hairdresser, and Margot's hair curled naturally at the ends. Sharlie backcombed very quickly, piling up the golden-brown locks. She twisted and pulled at the long hair Margot usually tied back so carelessly with her nylon bows, and succeeded in coaxing two curls to fall forward on to her white shoulder. 'It will be better on the big night, of course. Madame has coaxed the girl from Céleste's to come here for the day and style everyone's hair. Margot, you're to sit still while I fasten this around your throat.'

It was a black velvet ribbon, with a very old enamelled pin, with a design of wreathed roses on the enamel, and a brilliant clasp at the back to fasten it with. It was a Rossignol heirloom that usually reposed in Madame's jewel-case.

Sharlie fastened in the matching earrings, that had fragile gold chains swinging from them. Margot, looking at her reflection, knew a quickening of the pulses at the thought that Pierre would see her in this, on the night of the Ball. There was just something about a masked ball.

Margot felt overwhelmed as she went forward into the living-room to meet Madame's critical but loving eye. Suddenly Margot felt overwhelmed with love for them all. She came forward, sparkling, said, 'I believe I could even curtsey in this wonderful gown,' and suited the action to the word, sinking down to the accompaniment of a *frou-frou* of silk, and a froth of petticoat lace.

Bridget and Leonie and Sharlie ranged themselves with her and sank down too. François Rossignol was almost bursting with pride ... he couldn't hide it for once.

Margot said, 'Justine, what about you? And Madame?'

Justine laughed, 'Oh, Madame and I have ours too, but they're not quite ready. We've been able to have fittings. So has Sharlie. But we wanted these first in case they needed altering. Oh, is that someone at the door? Jules, open it, please.'

They came in from the patio ... the doctor—and Pierre.

The doctor spread his hands out. 'I brought him myself. Thought I'd see him safely delivered this time. And he's not to get about outside for two whole days. But what's this? A dress rehearsal?'

'Just that,' said Sharlie happily, and her eyes irresistibly went to Pierre to see what he thought of Margot in her rose brocade gown. Margot caught his gaze, burningly admiring, and looked hastily away.

The doctor said, 'Surely it represents Marie Antoinette?'

Madame spoke very clearly. 'Yes, that period. But I had it copied from a dress of one of the Rossignol ancestors. From a picture I had.'

François Rossignol snapped his fingers. 'That's it! You mean the one that crashed off its hook months ago? I meant to ask you the other day had you never got it back. Goodness, I suppose it's just the dress, but Margot is extraordinarily like that picture. I've always thought she reminded me of someone.'

Madame nodded, well pleased. 'I have been waiting for someone to comment on it. I thought if I said so, you might think it was merely wishful thinking. Well, my little ones, this gives me the greatest pleasure. There will be no Ball like this one.'

The doctor said, 'I'm bidden by my own daughter not to come home without seeing Leonie's murals. Show them to me, Leo.'

They all turned to them. Leonie was pink with pleasure at the doctor's praise, for he was known as a very fair artist himself. She had used some of Charles Meryon's sketches of old Akaroa as a basis for them. Here, she had portrayed the French landing, the block-house, the first few dwellings. It was fascinating to see the bush crowding down to the water's edge, the settlers working at mending their *seines*.

There was a sketch of Madame Rossignol in the gown she had worn for the opening of the Museum, and one of

Maison Rossignol, and a huge reproduction, very faithfully done, of the county map of Banks Peninsula.

The doctor's eyes narrowed as he saw it. He said, quietly, to François, 'You will, of course, be sending her to Art School?'

François nodded. 'Yes, we've already made arrangements.'

It was beautifully conceived and was to be the background to the stage. The bays were marked in detail, because it was so large, with small sketches of the trees and the historic associations they were noted for. Paua Bay had a *paua* shell of course, Pigeon Bay a native pigeon in its glorious colouring, bronzy green and iridescent. Le Bons had whalebones, arched against each other, Peraki had a trypot, Pompey's Pillar had Pompey, the beloved dolphin of long ago, leaping out of the water, Robin Hood had a couple of Merry Men.

They all crowded round, pointing out features, all talking at once. Margot said, putting a finger on Laverick's Bay, 'What's that bird? Is it meant to be a lark? It's much too bog for a lark, though. But I suppose Laverick is Scots for lark.'

Pierre's voice behind her said, 'No, if it were Scots for lark, it would be spelled with an o, not an i. Laverock. You've forgotten—that Bay was called for Charlie Laveroux, who was always known as Peter Partridge, though why, we don't know. But it's persisted. I'm Peter Partridge, remember? So that's a partridge. Almost every Bay has fitted in to Leonie's scheme of things. Note how she has cleverly anglicised our Bay with its motif. The English branch of the Rossignols is called Nightingale, of course. See ... Leonie has put a row of English nightingales here to indicate that Rossignol Bay is really the Bay of the Nightingales. Margot, what on earth is the matter? What's so odd about——'

She had whirled around, cheeks paling, then flushing, her lips parted, her eyes wide ... she said, with a curious blank, unbelieving look in her eyes, as if the words were jerked out of her, 'Nightingale ... *nightingale*? Does Rossignol mean nightingale?'

Pierre said, 'Of course it does. Didn't you know? Did——'

She flung away from him and rushed straight at François, taking him by the lapels. 'Mr. Rossignol, tell me, tell me, tell me where my father is? Did he—did Francis Nightingale come here twenty years ago looking for his French relations? Did he? Did he? Please tell me! Even if I can never make myself known to him, I must know. Tell me, did he come?

And where is he today?'

They all stood as if transfixed in tableau. Nobody even seemed to breathe.

François Rossignol's very nostrils were white. He was staring at her, two deep lines between his brows. He swallowed, then said, 'Your *father*? Francis Nightingale? Margot, *I'm* Francis Nightingale—or was for the first thirty years of my life. I changed it so the property would never go out of the family. Changed it back to its original form. So there should always be a Rossignol at Rossignol Bay.'

He closed his eyes for a moment, then opened them and said, 'But—but I—we—my first wife and I never had a daughter. At least...' His eyes searched hers. 'Margot, *who* was your mother? But it couldn't be. Your name is Chesterton—how? Margot, *who* was your mother?'

At that very moment Pierre caught Margot and steadied her. She put out a hand to him, he caught it in his, kept his other arm about her. Francis Nightingale was still staring, his eyes searching Margot's face.

Margot put a hand to her mouth to still its trembling. She got control, said, 'I'm sorry. I'm sorry. I—never dreamed, you see.' She turned to Pierre, said piteously, 'Oh, Pierre, it would have been kinder to have told me, then I'd never have given myself away. No wonder you did all you could to stop me finding out.' She turned back to her father, so did not see the expression on Pierre's face.

At that moment Justine came to life. She came forward to Margot, tears streaming down her face. 'I've got it,' she said softly, 'I think I have it now. You said once, I remember, that your mother's name was Laura. That your father and mother were separated, that your father never even knew he had a daughter!'

She added, taking Margot's ice-cold hand, 'François, wake up! You have a daughter, already beloved for her own sake ... already belonging to us. Children, you have an elder sister, Jules ... Sharlie ... Leonie!'

They rushed forward, but François swept them back. He opened his arms to Margot and she went into them with a little run. François swung her round so that his back was to the room, because no man likes other men to see him fighting tears.

Then he lifted his head from her hair and said, and nobody else even existed for him, '*Margot* ... she called you

Margot Rose. My grandmother's name. I'd said once that if ever we had a daughter I would like her named Margot Rose. But when Charlotte was born I didn't mention it to Justine because I didn't want her to feel I was blotting out the image of her own little Margot. But—but if Laura did that, she must have forgiven me for being so hard, so unyielding.'

Margot said softly, 'When she found out I was coming, she came to believe the fault was hers. You were in the right of it, you know ... *Father*. Her place *was* at your side. I'll tell you it all in detail some time. But for now, it will be enough for you to know that she wasn't allowed to travel before I came, and Aunt Ruth filled her up with the non-sense that you'd think she'd only gone back to you because a baby was on the way. So she waited, then when I was born she wrote you, asking you to come for us both ... and gave the letter to Aunt Ruth to post. You can guess the rest. Aunt Ruth destroyed the letter. And Mother had a return of the blood-poisoning. Aunt Ruth never wanted you to know you had a daughter.

'She married and changed my name to her husband's name, in case you ever returned to England. But when she was dying she confessed to Uncle Noel. He died soon after and left our solicitor a letter. *That's* why I came to Akaroa. I wanted to find you. The solicitor found a bill for freight for some things you once sent for.'

Justine nodded. 'His books. And, among other things, my jewel-case, *mignonne*.'

'So I left London. I came here hoping to find you, Father. But if you'd married someone who wouldn't like the idea of another woman's child turning up, I was just going to go away again. But tonight I was betrayed into it by sheer surprise.'

Then they made a rush at her, her brother and sisters. 'You absolute idiot!' said Sharlie affectionately. 'As if any-one wouldn't be glad to have *you*!'

'That's a pretty sensible remark for you, Charlotte,' said Jules, and hugged Margot. Suddenly she felt completely one of a family for the first time ever. She looked over their heads at Justine. 'But since *you* are my father's second wife, I have no doubts left whatever. Justine, don't cry.'

Justine said, 'But you are knowing they are tears of happi-ness, you are. I have a Margot.'

Margot kissed her, then came to Madame. 'And I have a

Tante Elise,' she said, and put her arms about her.

Madame said, 'I was beginning to have my suspicions ... oh, not that you could be a daughter of François, oh no, so wild a surmise never crossed my mind, but that you might have Rossignol connections, so very far back that you did not know. When I got that picture back from the framers. You see the subject was a twin sister to the girl in blue ... the one who is so like Charlotte. Only one sister had brown eyes and one blue. Oh, how we could not see it passes my comprehension. We even noticed Margot was like Angela.'

Margot blinked. 'But that must be just a coincidence.'

'No, my child. Marie's mother is related to the Rossignols. And we have always said that the likeness has persisted ... don't you realise Angela is very like François, even to the cleft in his chin ... and yours, *mignonne*?'

It was true. Angela's grandmother and Francis Nightingale had come from widely separated branches of the family, but the likeness was there.

Things were becoming clear to Margot. She said to Madame, to Tante Elise, 'I was rather puzzled once when you told me you had been an only child. Especially because you said Jules was like your Louis, and I knew Louis had come from France. There again you meant a family likeness, not because they were closely related. But I wondered how François Rossignol could be called your nephew—then put it down to the fact that he must be a cousin's child. Oh, if only I'd asked! What a lot of heartburning I would have been saved. But——'

At that moment Pierre's voice broke in, strongly, and with an injured note. 'I've been very patient, but I can stand it no longer. What's all this about me knowing? I just don't get it. You could have knocked me down with a feather when Margot suddenly mentioned the name of Nightingale. What on earth did you mean?'

Margot felt that surprise was piled upon surprise. She said flatly, 'But ... but you said Roxanne had told you the *truth*. That you would stop me in my quest ... you thought I was here for what I could get out of my father. You said——'

Pierre's look stopped her. 'I knew nothing of the kind. What ambiguous sort of remarks I've been unfortunate enough to make to give you that idea, I just can't remember. Yes, I said Roxanne told me the truth. What I *thought* was truth. She didn't betray your confidence at all. She said you

185

were coming here to dig out antiques ... a buying expedition ... and we've had all that out before. I had no idea you had a father alive!'

The doctor said, pathetically, that he for one hadn't the foggiest idea what anyone was talking about. 'It—it's like one of those Georgette Heyer romances I like so much ... everyone in a muddle about everyone else's motives ... you're even in the right sort of costume for it, Margot. But you all seem to be at cross-purposes. It beats me.'

Madame said, 'You are wrong, Georges. I think for the first time these two, Pierre and Margot, are *not* any longer at cross-purposes.'

Margot said, with shining eyes, 'Pierre, I thought all along that you knew and that you were trying to prevent me from finding out.'

There might have been no one there but themselves.

Pierre said, 'But that would have been despicable ... would have meant I was callous.' He stopped. '*Did* you think I was all those things?'

Margot said helplessly, 'Oh, Pierre, don't get mad with me. I *did* think those things, but——'

But he didn't look mad. He said with a note of triumph, 'And even though you thought that of me, you still said what you said to me ... before you climbed the gully? That——'

He became aware of his audience and stopped dead.

'Oh, Pierre,' implored Sharlie, 'what *did* she say?'

Pierre swung round and looked at her, the audacious glint back in his eyes. 'That you will never know, Sharlie,' he said, and laughed.

The doctor rubbed his hands together. 'This is capital, capital! I've always said a doctor shares the big moments in the lives of his patients ... he's present when they come into the world and when they leave it and if he's lucky they occasionally invite him to their weddings, but I'm damned if I ever thought I'd be present at a proposal! Damned if I did.'

Margot thought of something else. 'Dad,' she said, smiling, because it was so wonderful to be saying it, 'no wonder I never connected you with Francis Nightingale. The letter that was left for me said you'd married a French-Canadian. And Justine is Irish.'

Justine smiled. 'My parents, a couple of years after I lost

my husband and baby, sent me off to some French-Canadian cousins for a year. That was when I met François. And he had heard that French connections of his lived here. It's as simple as that.' She turned and looked at her husband, took his hand. 'François, we must have her name changed to Rossignol. She's not a Chesterton.'

'That won't be possible,' said Pierre, his eyes dancing. 'It can't be done speedily enough. By the time it came through her name would be Laveroux. I meant marriage, Margot, only that darned road caved in before I could ask you. François, may I marry your daughter?'

'As long as you live in Nightingale Bay you may. I couldn't bear to lose her, not so soon after finding her,' said Francis Nightingale.

Pierre turned to Madame. 'You know I've got that post with the Tourist Department, and that I'm building my motels right next door?'

'Yes, Pierre ... you interest me. Continue.'

He said, smiling, 'If we lived at Maison Rossignol with you, we would be right on the spot. And you wouldn't be parted from Margot.'

Madame looked swiftly down so no one would see how moved she was. Then she looked up at him and smiled. 'Thank you, Pierre. Although I wished so much for you and Margot to resolve your differences, I did dread the thought that I might have to leave here. For I could not now live alone. I appreciate, Pierre, your taking time to assure me of this, when you must be longing to get Margot to yourself for a while. And by the way, I think you have called me Madame for long enough ... I think Margot's betrothed should call me Tante Elise.'

Pierre looked at Margot, a question in his eyes. She laughed and blushed. 'Yes, I think perhaps we need a little while alone. You once told me that when you proposed to a girl, she would be in no doubt whatsoever. I can believe that now. Yet, despite all this signing and sealing, with my father and Tante Elise, I haven't been asked.'

The doctor said firmly, 'No further than the patio, Peter.'

'I should say not,' said Margot, laughing, 'not in this precious frock!' As she gathered her skirts up, Madame rose and divested herself of a black woollen stole she wore, spangled with silver. Imperiously she called them back, and draped it about Margot's shoulders. Margot turned an enquiring face to her. 'We're only going on to the patio, Tante.'

Madame looked scornful. 'So Doctor Dumayne said,' she said scornfully, and turned to the grinning doctor. 'Georges, you have no soul.' She turned back to Pierre and Margot. 'Lift your skirts well, *mignonne*, because there may be a little dew. *My* garden is a much more romantic one ... it will be something for you to remember always ... and Louis would have been so pleased.'

They understood immediately, all of them. Madame was stepping back into yesterday.

Pierre said, 'I don't need that stick,' and opened the door for Margot. As she went outside she turned and smiled lovingly at her father and her stepmother.

Below them the lights of the coast road girdled the Bay of the Nightingales like a golden bracelet, and stars looked down at their own reflections in the waters of the harbour. They did not speak till they came through the picket gate into Madame's garden of memories.

Pierre said, 'No wonder you were interested in seeing how many graves bore the name of François, that day at St. Luke's. How could I have been so blind? But I'll make it all up to you, Margot. Not that we'll waste time with explanations out here ... just watch your skirts as you brush past the pink bignonia. Ah, here we are at last ... with our kindly ghosts.'

A few late Bourbon roses still scented the air, and honeysuckle, and in the centre bed, the gillyflowers, the mignonette ...

The little cherub with the blob of green moss on his nose had seen it all before of course ... a girl in rose brocade, with stars in her eyes and a tall, dark Frenchman.

He knew it all, yesterday, today and tomorrow.

Below him, round his pedestal, a little wind stirred the clove-pinks, and in the aspen poplars he heard them laughing ... the kindly ghosts.

And two figures became one.

188

BARBARA DELINSKY
Fingerprints

Carly Quinn is a
woman with a past.
Born Robyn Hart, she
was forced to don a new
identity when her intensive
investigation of an arson-ring
resulted in a photographer's death
and threats against her life.

Ryan Cornell's entrance into her life
was a gradual one. The handsome
lawyer's interest was piqued, and then
captivated, by the mysterious Carly — a
woman of soaring passions and a
secret past.

RIDE A PAINTED PONY

by **BEVERLY SOMMERS**
The third
**HARLEQUIN AMERICAN ROMANCE
PREMIER EDITION**

A prestigious New York City publishing
company decides to launch a new historical
romance line, led by a woman who must first
define what love means.

Volumes #7 through #12

Once again, Harlequin is pleased to present a specially designed collection of 12 exciting love stories by one of the world's leading romance authors. Each edition contains two of Janet Dailey's most requested titles.

Vol. #7—The Ivory Cane
Low Country Liar

Vol. #8—Reilly's Woman
To Tell the Truth

Vol. #9—Strange Bedfellow
Wild and Wonderful

Vol. #10—Sweet Promise
Tidewater Lover

Vol. #11—For Mike's Sake
With a Little Luck

Vol. #12—Sentimental Journey
A Tradition of Pride

Available now wherever paperback books are sold, or available through Harlequin Reader Service. Simply complete and mail the coupon below.

- -

Harlequin Reader Service

In the U.S.
P.O. Box 52040
Phoenix, AZ 85072-2040

In Canada
5170 Yonge Street, P.O. Box 2800,
Postal Station Q, Willowdale, Ont. M2N 5T5

Please send me the following editions of the Harlequin Janet Dailey Collector's Edition 2. I am enclosing my check or money order for $2.95 for each copy ordered, plus 75¢ to cover postage and handling.

☐ 7   ☐ 8   ☐ 9   ☐ 10   ☐ 11   ☐ 12

Number of books checked _____ @ $2.95 each = $ _____

N.Y. state and Ariz. residents add appropriate sales tax $ _____

Postage and handling $ _____.75_____

I enclose _____   TOTAL $ _____

(Please send check or money order. We cannot be responsible for cash sent through the mail.) Price subject to change without notice.

NAME _____
(Please Print)

ADDRESS _____ APT. NO. _____

CITY _____

STATE/PROV. _____ ZIP/POSTAL CODE _____

JD-N

Harlequin reaches into the hearts and minds of women across America to bring you

Harlequin American Romance ^{T.M.}

Get this book FREE!

Mail to:

Harlequin Reader Service

In the U.S.
2504 West Southern Ave.
Tempe, AZ 85282

In Canada
P.O. Box 2800, Postal Station A
5170 Yonge St., Willowdale, Ont. M2N 5T5

YES! I want to be one of the first to discover **Harlequin American Romance.** Send me FREE and without obligation *Twice in a Lifetime*. If you do not hear from me after I have examined my FREE book, please send me the 4 new **Harlequin American Romances** each month as soon as they come off the presses. I understand that I will be billed only $2.25 for each book (total $9.00). There are no shipping or handling charges. There is no minimum number of books that I have to purchase. In fact, I may cancel this arrangement at any time. *Twice in a Lifetime* is mine to keep as a FREE gift, even if I do not buy any additional books.   154 BPA NAXG

Name _____ (please print)

Address _____ Apt. no. _____

City _____ State/Prov. _____ Zip/Postal Code _____

Signature (If under 18, parent or guardian must sign.)